TO SPEAK THE TRUTH

And Other Stories 2011-2019

Martin S. Cohen

D1521606

ISBN-13: 9798646934346
ISBN-10: 1477123456

Cover design by: Art Painter
Library of Congress Control Number: 2018675309
Printed in the United States of America

CONTENTS

INTRODUCTION

The stories in this collection were written between 2011 and 2019. Because I like best to write of what I know best, all are related in some way to Jewish life. Nonetheless, it is my hope that the truths they suggest about the world and the underlying assumptions about life, and particularly family life, that animate the personalities described in these fifteen stories will resonate with people of all ethnicities and faiths. I would like to stress that the stories presented in this book are all works of fiction. One or two are loosely based on the real-life experiences of actual people, but even those stories should be taken as fully fictional. There is no such place, for example, as the Vincent R. Impellitteri Archive. Nor does any of the synagogues or synagogue communities mentioned in any of the stories actually exist. Here and there, readers will find references to individuals of who they have previously heard, people like Martin Van Buren or Yo Yo Ma. But even in those cases two simple rules can be applied. If the personality in question is depicted as an actor in the story being told, as is the case with Mr. Ma in "Under the Wheel," then the reader should assume the details to be entirely fictitious. If the personality is merely mentioned in passing but without being brought into the narrative as an active player, like President Van Buren in "To Speak the Truth," then the details mentioned in that person's regard may be presumed to be accurate. More or less.

I would also like formally to note that the original versions of most of the stories included in this collection were distributed to members of the Shelter Rock Jewish Center in a series of private editions funded by Dr. Marius Pessah as a memorial to his late wife, Dr. Victoria J. Pessah, for which act of philanthropy all Shelter Rockers, and myself surely among them, remain truly grateful.

M.S.C.
Roslyn, New York
June 1, 2020

TO SPEAK THE TRUTH

I had no idea what to expect. How could I have? The whole *concept* of a man like my father being in jail was itself so crazy as to be wholly unimaginable! And yet in jail—or, more precisely, in the jail attached to the Lumpkin County Courthouse in Dahlonega—was exactly where he was. Or at least that's what his lawyer, one Curtis L. Summers, had said in his letter.

It was a while ago: I was just nineteen years old—one third of my current age—when I left Savannah that June morning in 1839 to find out what exactly had happened to my father. Now that we all know what horrors were in store for our country at mid-century, we tend to recall the parts of our history that preceded them as a kind of golden age. But in its own way, the fourth decade of the current century was an extremely complicated time for our nation. We were into the second year of the Van Buren administration. In some ways, our eighth president was a novelty. He was the first American President actually to have been born in the independent United States. He was the first New Yorker to live in the White House. He was, at least so far, our only President raised speaking a language other than English. But Martin Van Buren was also a complicated man riddled with inconsistencies. Not a decade after leaving office—he lost the election of 1840 to William Henry Harrison, who was in office for about twelve minutes before dying of pneumonia (or something)—he re-emerged into public life as the leader of the strongly anti-slavery Free Soil Party. But that came later and, while in office, Van Buren had no trouble continuing the horrific policies of his predecessor towards the Indians in the Southeast, the specific program that my father opposed so vociferously and fully publicly that I was sure even before I got anywhere near Lumpkin County that it was that very vocal opposition to the President's plan that had landed him in hot water. The only real question, I think I knew even before I arrived, was just how hot that water actually was and what it was going to take to cool it down sufficiently for my father not to end up permanently scalded.

It all really does feel like ancient history now. After suffering losses during the War Between the States that would once have been considered unimaginable (more than 600,000 dead, almost all young men), the number of natives who died on the death marches west during the Jackson and Van Buren administrations—something close to 17,000—seems almost inconsequential. But the horror of being stripped both of one's possessions and one's dignity, having one's land seized, and then being rounded up and sent off either to walk on foot to Oklahoma or to drop dead *en route*—that nightmare cannot be passed lightly by, even now, by people who like to think of themselves as moral human beings. At least the soldiers on both sides in the War were fighting *for* their governments! The Choctaws, on the other hand, were the victims *of* their alleged government. As were also all the others tribes uprooted and sent west to survive or not to survive: the Cherokees, the Seminole, the Chickasaw, and the Muskogee.

My father, Rabbi Aaron Caleb Klass, was born in London in 1789 and came to this country with his parents as a boy in 1803. His parents taught him at home until age ten, at which age they enrolled him in the yeshivah of Rabbi Asher Levitas, housed in those days in a clapboard house on what was then called Baxter Street in the Five Points neighborhood of lower Manhattan. It wasn't a brief stay either—he remained under Rabbi Levitas's tutelage for years, finally receiving rabbinic ordination in 1813 at age twenty-four. He got married to my mother that year as well and together they moved to Philadelphia, where my father took his first pulpit. He apparently liked the congregation and the city far more than his minuscule salary and so, when the opportunity presented itself five years later to move to Savannah to serve the United Sons of Israel Congregation and be paid more than twice as much as he had been earning in Philly, he took it. They settled in easily. I was born two years after that. Life was good. But, as is true of all life's journeys that begin with single steps (which is all of them), no one could have imagined where this one was going to take him.

It all started, I suppose, with the passage of the Indian Removal Act of 1830. In and of itself, the law needn't have been the herald of any misery at all because it merely gave the President the right to negotiate land exchanges with native tribes and to use federal funds to cover their transportation expenses if they agreed to move west. The key element, though, was that the President was specifically *not* empowered to force anyone at all to move west in the absence of a formally negotiated treaty between that individual's tribe and the United States government. A lot of people supported the idea. Even my own father didn't think that it was such a bad idea. But, of course, he didn't know at the time what was yet to come.

The story of the Indian Removal Act is long and complex, but the specific part that features my father getting himself arrested took place in 1838. The Treaty of New Echota, negotiated during the Andrew Jackson administration with some renegade Cherokees who specifically did not represent the legitimate tribal leadership, was neither ratified by the Cherokee National Council nor signed by their then-chief John Ross. To the U.S. government, however, these were mere details…and far more important was the discovery of gold in Dahlonega and the ensuing Georgia Gold Rush. By 1838, they had somehow managed to talk about two thousand Cherokees into abandoning their land and voluntarily moving to Oklahoma. But that was nowhere near good enough for President Van Buren, who sent in one of his best generals forcibly to uproot the remaining Cherokees from their homes and send them west as well. And that is when my father stopped being just a rabbi and also became a kind of a prophet. And a radical. And, yes, a bit of a crazy person.

The jail turned out not to be a freestanding building, just a wing of the courthouse—albeit one with bars on the windows and doorknobs only on the outside of the cell doors. My father was wearing tan slacks and a white shirt when I was ushered into his cell. There was no place to sit down—just a bed, a toilet discreetly positioned behind a paper screen, and a shelf hanging down from the wall. On the shelf I could see my dad's familiar prayerbook and a Bible. He looked healthy enough, but thin and tired.

"Where are your *t'fillin*," I asked idiotically. *That* was the first question I had for my father?

"Not allowed."

"What about freedom of religion?"

"This apparently doesn't extend to things you can hang yourself with."

"Are you thinking of hanging yourself?"

"No, Daniel, not yet." He actually chuckled. "But they have no way to know that."

I chuckled too, but with less enthusiasm. And then I moved onto more weighty matters. "What are you charged with?"

My dad focused his gaze directly at me. "With speaking the word of God aloud and in public."

"That's not allowed?"

"Apparently not if you are standing in the road in front of a general's horse and preventing him from taking the general to whence he would go."

"And were you doing that? Standing in the road to keep the general's horse from moving forward?"

"Yes, I was."

"And how did you know the horse wouldn't move forward anyway and knock you over before trampling you?"

"I didn't know that."

"I thought you were a prophet speaking the word of God. Shouldn't a prophet know stuff like that?"

"You'd think." Another wry chuckle.

"And when are they going to let you out?"

"You'd need a real prophet to answer that one, Daniel. I am neither a prophet nor the son of a prophet."

I knew the quote and I got the point. "Amos said that of himself, Dad. But he's remembered as one of the great prophets nevertheless. But let's talk about more important things."

"More important than Amos?"

I ignored his question. "So you have no idea when they'll let you go home?"

"No," he said. And then he fell silent as we both considered the possible implications of that thought.

Eventually, I got the whole story out of him. I myself had been in Charleston that week visiting with friends, but he had been home on Shabbat afternoon two weeks ago and had had a few hours free to read between waking up from his nap and the Afternoon Service at Sons of Israel. And the specific thing he chose to read was the letter Ralph Waldo Emerson had written to President Van Buren just three months earlier and then published for all to read. As he never did, Emerson didn't mince words. That a treaty about to affect eighteen thousand people had been formally and unequivocally repudiated as illegitimate by more than fifteen thousand of them, he wrote, was not irrelevant and could not be thought so by decent people. And then he asks the three questions at the heart of the matter. Will the American government steal? Will it lie? Will it kill? And then he asked, plainly and simply, whether it can possibly be so that "the millions of virtuous citizens, whose agents the government are, have no place to interpose, and must shut their eyes until the last howl and wailing of these tormented villages and tribes shall afflict the ear of the world." Emerson himself was foremost among those millions of citizens. But among them too was my father, Rabbi Aaron Caleb Klass, one of Emerson's greatest admirers and a man who did not take the suffering of innocents lightly.

And then we finally got down to it.

"So what exactly *did* you do, Dad?"

"I responded to Emerson and decided no longer to shut my eyes and make deaf my ears."

"And how exactly did you do that?"

"Well," my father replied slowly, "probably not in the very best way possible. I read in several places that the President was sending Brigadier General Winfield Scott to 'relocate' the remaining Cherokees to Oklahoma. The fact that relocating them without a treaty signed by their legitimate leadership was 100% illegal seemed to trouble no one. But it troubled me. And you know what I get like when I have a fire in my belly."

I knew all too well. "And what exactly did you do?" I asked again.

"Well," my father hesitated for a long moment, "well, I closed my eyes and looked into the future. I saw people dropping from exhaustion on forced marches. I saw barefoot men and women falling aside when they simply could walk forward no longer. I saw children fainting from hunger and dying of disease. And I decided not to turn away."

"Go on," I said, only partially wanting to hear the rest.

"I went to Dahlonega because I had heard that that was where General Scott was going to begin the forced removal of the natives. It was a long journey, too—about three hundred miles if you travel through Swainsboro and Athens. But of course you know that now yourself."

"How did you know the general's plans?"

My father closed his eyes and waited a long moment before responding. "I didn't know the specifics, but it was no secret that he was to be the agent of the President's pernicious policy. That much was in all the papers. So he seemed the man to confront."

"Why didn't you go to Washington and address yourself directly to the Commander-in-Chief?"

"I didn't think they'd let me anywhere near him."

"Moses seems to have gotten in to see Pharaoh easily enough."

"True enough. But that was then. And, besides, Washington is six hundred miles from Savannah, not three hundred."

"So what happened?"

"I don't know what I thought I was going to do—I just went and figured that the spirit would move me to act wisely. And decisively."

"And did it?"

My father hesitated again. "Maybe."

"What did you do exactly?"

"I got to Dahlonega easily enough. And once I arrived it was simple enough to find out where the general was lodging. There aren't *that* many hotels here to choose from, after all, and he was surely going to stay at the nicest one. Which is precisely where I found him. Not in the hotel, I mean, but right in front of it."

"And what was he doing?"

"He was getting ready to leave, already mounted and surrounded by an honor guard of very well-armed military men."

"And you confronted him."

"You make it sound like I accosted him."

"You did accost him."

"But in a good way, Daniel. I simply stood in front of his horse and forbade him to rip innocents from their homes or to uproot legal landowners from their legally-owned land."

"That's all you said?" I knew my dad better than that.

"Well," he allowed, "I may have said something about God having sent me to prevent him from sinning grievously. About the price men pay when they turn their backs on the Almighty."

I could actually feel the color draining from my face. "Anything else?"

My father looked away for a moment, but then answered. "I think I may also have quoted from that story in Daniel about the king who behaved like a beast and so was driven from the company of men and forced to live among the beasts of the field."

"Really, Dad? You threatened old Fuss and Feathers with the punishment God meted out to Nebuchadnezzar of Babylon? Did you mention the part about the king having to eat his grass naked in the field like an ox while his finger-and toenails grew as long as a bird's talons?"

Dad smiled. "I'm impressed you know your Bible that well, son. How many people read Daniel or remember anything from it?"

Now it was my turn to smile. "He was my namesake, after all."

"Yes, he was." Dad was clearly pleased.

"And that's it? They arrested you because you quoted the Book of Daniel to General Winfield Scott?"

Dad looked surprised by my question. "I may also have had a gun in my hand," he said just a bit sheepishly.

"A gun?" I couldn't believe my own ears.

"Well, not that *big* a one. Just a little one, the kind you shoot rabbits with."

"I think people use shotguns to go rabbit hunting."

"Whatever. I got his attention!"

"I'll bet you did."

"And now I'm in jail."

"I can see that. And what happens now?"

"I was hoping you could help me work that part out, Daniel. My lawyer seems able and he's eager to meet with you. His office is just across the street in that white building next to the bank. It must be very convenient when he has clients in jail."

"I'm sure that's the case."

"So you'll go see him?"

"I can hardly wait."

Curtis L. Summers could not have looked the part more precisely if he were playing a southern lawyer in some music hall production. As gaunt as General Scott was stout and as tall a man as I have ever known, my father's lawyer would have cut an imposing figure in any context at all. But dressed as he was when I walked into his office—in an off-white three piece suit and pale yellow silk necktie that matched both the shade of his moustache wax *and* the color of his silk socks, he really could not have looked more the part of the Southern lawyer and gentleman.

He was more than cordial and didn't appear to be at all worried about my father's fate. At first, we talked around the topic. He asked me about our life in Savannah and I answered his questions honestly. He hadn't known that my dad was born in London—Dad doesn't sound like a son of Georgia when he speaks, but he also doesn't sound at all English—and was interested, slightly to my surprise, in genealogical details that I would have imagined to be wholly irrelevant to the situation at hand. But, hardly being in a position to second-guess the specific individual I was counting on to spring my dad from the hoosegow and restore him to his congregation and his family, I just answered all the questions he had about my paternal grandparents as best I could.

Finally, done with the preliminaries, he asked me if I myself had any questions. As it happened, I only really had one.

"What happens next?" I asked.

"You mean to your father?"

"Yes, of course. Can you get him out of jail?"

"He was denied bail," Summers said.

"I'm well aware. But where does that leave him?"

"It leaves him in jail. But they'll want to clear this up quickly. I expect we can expect your father to appear in court within a few days."

"Do you know the specific charges against him?"

"The usual. What you'd expect. Disturbing the peace. Aggravated menacing. Vagrancy. Threatening a government official. It's impressive they didn't charge him with Attempted Murder, but I suppose the fact that the gun wasn't loaded steered them off that course."

I could hardly believe my ears. I had expected him to be charged with something *like* disturbing the peace, but this sounded way more serious than I had anticipated. I said as much to the lawyer, then asked the obvious question. "Can you get him off?"

Summers smiled slightly. "The last person I defended who was charged with a similar litany of crimes had waved a *loaded* pistol at President Adams two days before the latter left office back in '29 and I got him off."

"That's very impressive."

"Mind you, he's going to have to spend the rest of his days in an asylum for the criminally insane. But the point is that he was not convicted of any crime at all."

"That couldn't happen to my Dad, could it?"

"Not in a month of Sundays, son," my father's lawyer answered, leaning back in this chair and smiling broadly.

The lawyer was right about them wanting to deal with this quickly and Dad's trial was set for the following Monday. It made sense to me too: why *wouldn't* the government want to avoid granting an articulate, forceful preacher a public soapbox to stand on while denouncing illegal, unjust, and morally reprehensible government policies while they were actually being carried out? They were probably sorry no one had just shot him on the spot, which could then easily have been justified after-the-fact with reference to fact that there had been no way at the time to know that the weapon in my father's hand had not been loaded. But that option no longer being viable, a speedy trial started and concluded before the General's work got underway was clearly their second best chance to tamp down public opposition to the government's plan before some crazy rabble-rouser got the locals all riled up.

I had nothing to do until Monday. I was permitted an hour each morning and afternoon with my father, which privilege I accepted gratefully. I had brought two volumes of Gemara with me, so that's what we did for those few days—learn Talmud—and try to ignore the fact that we were doing it behind bars. The rest of the time, I wandered around Dahlonega and tried to amuse myself. I sat in a public park and read. I went to a local lake and swam. I had no way to cook for myself, so I basically lived on cucumbers, tomatoes, bread, and beer. (I had brought a few of my mother's sausages with me, but I gave them to Dad since he was obviously not going to eat the meat they served in the jail and I figured he needed that kind of fatty nourishment more than I myself did.) I *davened* each morning in my hotel room, trying to find some solace in saying prayers that I knew my father was reciting daily in his cell as well. Shabbat was as dull a Sabbath as anyone ever spent: no public worship, no Torah reading, no invitations for meals, no one to talk to, and, in fact, no company at all. And then, somehow, it was Monday morning. The trial was set to begin at ten o'clock. Wanting to be sure of getting a seat in the visitors' gallery, I was in place a single minute after the courthouse opened its doors at eight o'clock. I remained the sole person present for almost a full hour. Eventually, though, people started to trickle in. By half past nine, the room was full. I recognized no one at all other than the assistant who had ushered me into the lawyer's office when we had had that initial meeting and then, a moment later, Curtis Summers himself, dressed in what I now understood to be his customary off-white suit and yellow cravat. From my seat, I could not see the color of his socks, but I presumed them to be pale yellow as well.

And then, at ten o'clock sharp, the door behind the judge's chair opened and the assembled rose to their feet as Judge Isaac L. Garfield took his place. A moment later, a different door opened and my father, dressed in his own clothing, was ushered into the court. He was rumpled looking, but neither handcuffed nor restrained in any visible way. He made his way to his lawyer's table and there they both stood, side by side, until the judge sat down and the bailiff (or whoever he was) invited everybody else also to be seated. The public prosecutor, one Lemuel Shaw, was seated at an adjacent table.

Some officer of the court read out the charges. It all seemed very cut and dried; even the judge looked a bit bored. But then things suddenly started to happen. The judge asked my father to rise and to state his name, his home address, and his occupation for the court. My father did so in his customarily clarion voice. The judge appeared to be listening carefully, then asked my father how wished to plead. A quick huddle between my father and the lawyer, after which the lawyer, not my father, spoke.

"Your Honor," Curtis Summers began, "my client has a proposal he would like to make."

The judge looked surprised, but not hostile. "Go on," he said.

"My client will plead guilty to all the charges except for the charge of vagrancy—because the very last thing Rabbi Klass is, or even could imagine himself being, is a vagrant—but he will plead guilty to all the *other* charges in exchange for the right to explain this incident at length to the court before sentencing."

My mouth actually hung open at hearing this, but the judge looked as though he could hardly believe his good luck. "Does the defendant own a home in the State of Georgia?" he asked, clearly trying to sound genuinely curious.

"Yes, Your Honor," Summers said, "he does."

The judge, smiling broadly, turned to the Public Prosecutor. "In light of that fact, Mr. Shaw, do the people agree that the charge of vagrancy be dismissed?"

Mr. Shaw did not seem at all surprised. "Yes, Your Honor," he said.

Judge Garfield turned to face my father directly. "Rabbi Klass, the charge of vagrancy is dismissed, but it was the least serious of the charges you are facing. Do you understand the implications of pleading guilty to the others? They are not without weight."

Now it was apparently my father's turn to smile. "Yes, Your Honor," he said. "I have an excellent lawyer and he has made me fully aware of their gravity."

"And all you are asking is the right to address the court in advance of sentencing?"

"Yes, Your Honor."

"Well, then, your plea of guilty is accepted by this court. Go right ahead and give your speech!"

My father stood up. His posture, always erect, was ramrod

straight. His white hair was neatly combed. His black *yarmulke* was firmly in place. He looked like he had lost some weight in jail, but he radiated, not the sallow pallor of the temporarily incarcerated, but the robust demeanor of a prophet barely able to keep the word of God from issuing forth on its own from between his lips. He looked, in short, a bit crazy. I suppose people thought the same of Amos in his day.

Taking the invitation to address the court to imply permission to speak to the entire courtroom, my father stepped to the side of the room so he could address the judge and the visitors' gallery at the same time. For a long moment, he said nothing. And then, as though responding to some signal that only he could perceive, he spoke.

"Your Honor and welcome friends," he began as though he were welcoming guests to the sanctuary of his own congregation, "I am here today to explain my actions of just a few days ago. On the twenty-ninth of April, I stood up in a public thoroughfare —a place in which I, as a member of the public, had every right to be—and saw before me a mighty sorrel steed bearing on its broad back Brigadier General Winfield Scott, the officer whom I knew to have been charged by President Van Buren with undertaking the fully unlawful task of removing the local Cherokee from lands they had possessed since time immemorial and forcing them into exile, an illegal act specifically and unambiguously *not* permitted according to the terms of the Indian Removal Act."

When my father paused to catch his breath, the judge asked a pertinent question. "But, Rabbi Klass, is there not a treaty in place that makes the removal of the Cherokee legal?"

My father looked at the judge as though he could hardly believe his ears. "There is not," he said simply. "Nor is there a living soul in this state," he said, stepping onto even thinner ice, "who doesn't know that that the Treaty of New Echota, the treaty to which I presume you are referring, was a sham that was neither ratified by the elected tribal leadership of the Cherokee Nation nor accepted by any but the tiniest minority of its members. And the Indian Removal Act solely grants the President the authority to use federal funds to assist Indians in abandoning their ancestral lands if and when the government successfully negotiates such a removal to the so-called Indian Territory beyond Louisiana with the legitimate leaders of the tribe in question."

The judge seemed slowly to be realizing what a huge error of judgment he had made in permitting my father to speak at all, let alone "at length." But he could hardly go back on his word: the reporters seated in the two rows behind me were visibly taking notes, as, of course, was the court reporter who was busy taking down every word spoken in the courtroom in some sort of shorthand script.

And now, having moved himself into position, my father opened up with both barrels. "Your Honor," he began, "I am neither a prophet nor the son of a prophet. But...."

My father glanced upwards as though corroborating with the Almighty what he was planning to say next.

"...I am a man who knows right from wrong. I am a man who knows what it means to be held in contempt by people whom I have never met and who have no basis for judging me positively *or* negatively. And I am a man who understands that the Commander-in-Chief of our great American nation has ordered his army to betray the very principles upon which this Republic was founded sixty-three years ago. He has ordered soldiers to ignore the law of the land, to turn their backs both on mercy and on justice, and to rip people from properties that they have farmed not for centuries or even for millennia...but, as far as anyone knows, for the full length of human history in this place. And he has done so by relying on a treaty that a man of his great perspicacity and intelligence certainly knows is not worth the paper it is written on. Indeed, it would be a mark of disrespect unworthy of *any* citizen of our great land to suppose, even for a reckless moment, that our President could possibly be sufficiently dull-witted not to understand the evil he is perpetrating in this place.

"I stand here today, therefore, not to preach or to scold, but to attempt the simplest and most difficult of all tasks: to speak the truth. But because the psalmist wrote that truth and justice are the twin works of God's hands, I have come here today not solely to speak the truth but also to demand justice for the downtrodden and the powerless in our midst. But I will not lie to do so." My father raised his voice slightly as he closed his eyes. "I will never lie. Certainly not to the court, which sin the Ten Commandments could not more clearly forbid, but also not to myself. I am an honest man. And I that is why I have pled guilty to all the charges leveled against me except the one of which I was in truth not guilty. What I have done, I have done. I hurt no one. I threatened no one in any consequential way. The court is surely aware that there were no bullets in the gun, which I carried solely to get the attention of the man I wished to address. But every single word I spoke to General Scott was true. He surely knows that. As, I am certain, does also every single person present here today. I pled guilty because I did the things of which I am accused. I stand before you, therefore, in the expectation that the punishment meted out will fit the crimes to which I have admitted. That, I will accept as my due. And so I conclude today by observing that the real challenge to be met today is not mine, but this court's." Here, my father pivoted to look directly at the judge. "I have the voice of a single man," he said. "I doubt I could raise my voice loud enough for it to be heard beyond the four walls of this courtroom. But you, Your Honor, you have the ability to speak loudly enough for the President of the United States to hear what you have to say. I bless you with courage. And I pray that you too will stand up today for justice...and for truth." And, with that, he sat down.

The courtroom was completely, utterly silent. For a long moment, all I could hear was the sound of birds twittering around in the trees outside the courtroom's windows. My father whispered something in his lawyer's ear, who smiled and then handed my dad his handkerchief to wipe the sweat off his fore-head. I felt a bit lightheaded, but fully focused on my father as I wondered how I could ever live up to the example of graceful-ness, eloquence, and courage he had just set.

Things wrapped up quickly after that. Since the accused had pled guilty, there was no need to prolong the proceedings. The judge asked my father to rise in his place. He and his lawyer both stood up. It was so completely still in that room at that mo-ment that you really could have heard a pin fall to the floor. I felt somehow like I too should stand up, something in the way my mother and I do at home when my father is called to the Torah. But no one else was standing, so I remained in my seat. Honestly, I'm not sure I would have been able to stand up at that moment even if I had wanted to.

For a long moment, the judge seemed lost in thought. But then he looked at my father and spoke. "I've already accepted your plea, Rabbi Klass," he said quietly. "And now I sentence you to time served. You are free to go." And it was at that very moment, while the word "go" was still hanging on the air, that the entire courtroom, with the sole exception of the judge himself, rose to its feet and applauded. I felt overcome with so many conflict-ing emotions that I can't even begin to separate them. Relief, of course, that Dad would be coming home with me to Savannah. Love for my father too, also of course, but the specific kind rooted in respect so genuine and intense that for a long moment I found myself wondering if just possibly my father wasn't *actu-ally* a prophet of God sent to this specific place to say the words he had spoken. And intermingled with all those positive emo-tions, of course, was also a deep sense of foreboding tinged with outrage rooted in the fact that we all knew that, whatever else might happen in the distant future, the near future was going to include the exile of the Cherokees—and the other tribes caught up in the net Van Buren had willingly inherited from Andrew Jackson—without regard for the law and without regard for even the most elementary canons of justice.

MARTIN S. COHEN

This was all a very long time ago. I was nineteen in 1837. Now, thirty-eight years later, I can already see sixty on the horizon. My father is long gone, as is also my mother. I haven't lived in Georgia since I was in my twenties, but the recollection of those few days in Dahlonega stays with me still, days in the course of which I learned what it means to speak the truth....and what it means to earn the right to bear the image of God in which we are all made.

MY MOTHER'S SON

I have a nice office at home, but when Gwen has to work late I generally like to work in my office in the synagogue instead. And so there I was on the night on which my story begins—it was a Tuesday, if I remember correctly, in the third week in October—and so there I was all alone in our huge building enjoying the solitude and trying to finish a book review that was already four months late. Even the custodian on duty that night had gone home.

I was fifty-nine years old in 2005, plenty old enough to remember when going through the mail was the first thing I attended to each day, not the last. But that was then and these days the mail tended just to sit there until I got to it, which was usually late in the day. I myself was in a good place. Gwen was happy at work. Our kids were out of college, done with grad school, gainfully (more or less) employed, well on their way into reasonable futures. Each had an acceptable—or acceptable enough—mate, although no one seemed to be making any discernible progress towards the *chuppah*. Life was good.

And so it was late at night in my office in Southern Sons of Israel, the sole synagogue serving our section of Savannah, and I was *finally* looking at the mail Fran had stacked up on my desk about ten hours earlier. It had been a busy day, too. In the digital age, almost nothing too important ever actually came in what my children thought it was hilarious that I still called the "real" mail, but occasionally there were exceptions to the general rule. And this, it turned out, was one of those days.

Towards the bottom of the pile was a long, undistinguished-looking white envelope. It had my name written on it and the *shul's* address, but it also had the words "confidential and personal" in large capital letters in the lower left-hand corner. It was unopened; Fran knew not to open anything that even possibly seemed private and she never did. There was no return address. The handwriting was not neat, but also not childish. I had no idea what it was or from whom it might have come. Nor did I know anyone in Baton Rouge, where the postmark said the letter had been mailed two days earlier. I slit the envelope open and took out its contents, a single piece of lined loose-leaf paper with its three holes torn on the side as though it had been ripped out of its binder by someone too pre-occupied (or possibly just too lazy) to open the rings first.

I have spent my entire professional career in Georgia—and could pass, especially after a few drinks, for something like a *bone fide* Southern gentleman (albeit one with a *yarmulke* on his head)—but for all I am *of* here now, I am not actually *from* here. Instead, I grew up in Queens, one of New York State's original twelve counties and since 1898 the largest of New York City's boroughs, but even that thought comes with an asterisk because, although our overheated, cramped apartment was indeed in Queens, we spent the summers of my youth in the Berkshires where my parents owned a cottage on Pontoosuc Lake in Lanesborough, Massachusetts.

And until they ended rather abruptly, those summers really were magical. We went to hear the Boston Symphony at Tanglewood. My parents always purchased a season's subscription to the Williamstown Playhouse, where years passed without us missing a single production. We occasionally went to Becket to see a performance at Jacob's Pillow, sometimes to Lenox to see something (usually not Shakespeare) at Shakespeare & Company. More often than you'd think, we went to Arrowhead—where Melville wrote *Moby Dick*—and Dad and I would attempt to commune with the great man's ghost merely by wandering aimless around his property. Those were side dishes, however, and the main course each and every summer consisted of the more ordinary things people do at gorgeous lakes in the country. We swam. We fished (although more often in the Hoosic River than in "our" lake). We eventually acquired a motorboat and learned how to water ski.

I knew nothing of my parents' marriage. What child does? When I think back on the last memories I have of those halcyon days, I suppose it does seem odd how much more relaxed both my parents were relating to me than to each other. I remember them fighting too. They would eventually make up (or it appeared to me that they did) and we'd all go out on the lake and take turns water-skiing, but I don't remember having the insight even to wonder optimistically about the future of their marriage itself. That's not how things work when you're too young to know much of the world and you just take the givens of your life as immutable facts, as unalterable features of How Things Are. At fourteen, I wasn't an idiot. I knew that marriages *could* end. But it was entirely theoretical knowledge, something along the lines of the way people know that there are such things are cyclones and tsunamis, but don't *really* expect ever to experience anything like that themselves.

And then everything changed one evening in the summer of 1960 when my mother mentioned over dinner one night that she was going to have a baby. My father had obviously been pre-informed, but I myself wouldn't have been much more surprised if she had announced that we were moving to Mars. Still, something wasn't quite right and I somehow had the insight to know that...or at least to sense it. For one thing, on television announcements like my mother's were generally met with great joy and excitement. But in our cottage on Lake Pontoosuc, my parents did not seem particularly happy, let alone over-joyed. This, even the fourteen-year-old me understood, did not bode well. My mother asked if I had any questions. I couldn't think of any, so I said nothing. And then Dad proposed an evening excursion to Pittsfield to see Kirk Douglas in *Spartacus*, which had just opened, and that, at least for the moment, was that.

My mother lost the baby two weeks later. That story—traumatic in its own right—I won't tell in detail. (I've probably repressed most of it anyway.) But what I will tell is that my mother was gone less than two months after that and that I never saw her again.

The letter was brief and to the point. "Dear Jonathan," it read, "I have to tell you something. Come and see me." It was signed, simply yet bizarrely, "Mom." And then, just beneath "Mom," whoever wrote the letter had printed the name Alice Sommerville in block letters. I read the letter through several times before I set it down on my desk and sat back in my desk chair to consider my options.

My mother disappeared in the fall of 1960, a full forty-five years earlier than the day I was reading this letter that *purported* to be from her. For years, my father claimed to have no idea where she had "gone off to" (I can still hear my father saying those exact words as part of his stock answer to that specific question) and eventually was granted a divorce by a judge who agreed that enough time had passed for her disappearance to be considered an act of spousal desertion. Dad never remarried. Instead, he went through a series of lady friends that began to come into his life just a year or so after my mother's disappearance and never really ended. He died in 1999 at age eighty-nine, still the inveterate lady's man, still the charmer, *still* almost physically incapable of not leaping forward to open a door for a woman in his company.

And then my thoughts turned to my mother. She, I knew, was born in 1915, so would have been ninety in 2005, and her name was indeed Alice. The name "Sommerville," on the other hand, was unknown to me. Had she remarried? I suppose she could have, that she probably did. And could her married name then have become Sommerville? Why couldn't it have been? How she could possibly have ended up in Baton Rouge, I had no idea. But neither could I think of any reason why she shouldn't have made her life in Louisiana. Maybe that was where Mr. Sommerville was from! And it would have been a good place for her to hide too—my father had no family in Louisiana, so the likelihood of me or my dad somehow running into her accidentally must have seemed remote as well. Could it have been her? I supposed it could have been.

It was one of those things that happens by you becoming aware that it's already happened.

I was in eighth grade. I came home one day from school and my dad was sitting in the living room. He wasn't *ever* home in the middle of the day, so I knew something was up.

"Jonathan," he began, "your mother...." His voice trailed off.

"Mom what?"

"She's gone."

"Gone? You mean she's dead? Mom is dead?" I could hear my voice rising in panic. Could miscarriages eventually be fatal? They certainly hadn't told us *that* in Boys' Hygiene class!

"No, not dead. Just gone...from here. From us. From this place."

"Where did she go?" Even though he had spoken clearly enough, I was still missing his point.

"I have no idea."

"When is she coming back?"

"My guess would be never."

"But where *is* she?"

"Somewhere...." My dad's voice trailed off. My mother was somewhere. *Everybody* is somewhere, I remember thinking. But where was she *exactly*, that was the question I wanted answered.

Then, I suddenly realized my dad was speaking in code. "Are you getting a divorce?" I asked, proud that I had finally seized where things stood.

"I don't know." He didn't know? How could not know if he was getting a divorce or not?

I decided on a new tack. "Is she coming home?"

"I don't know."

"Can I call her?"

"You'd need to know where she's gone off to."

"And where is that?"

"I don't know."

Later on, the refrain changed as my dad's shock wore off and was replaced first with anger, then with resignation, then finally with a kind of acceptance tinged with bitterness. This conversation, we had a million times in the course of the next few years.

"Have you heard from Mom?"

"Dead to me."

"If she wanted, could she come back?"

"Dead to me."

"Do you still love her?"

"Dead to me."

And so it went. Dead to him, dead to me, dead to the world. For years I expected her to reappear, possibly in as magical a way as she had disappeared in the first place. I did all the things you'd expect. I never got on a bus without scanning the passengers to see if she was there. I checked the obituaries in the Times every single day of my entire adolescence to see if she was listed among the dead. I never heard of anyone at all named Alice without investigating further. I don't recall it ever dawning on me that she might have changed her name—to me she was always Alice Friedman, my only mother and my father's only wife.

Years passed. Eventually I met Gwen—she was a year behind me at Yale, but then I spent the year after graduation working for Habitat America and she ended up at Columbia Law School during the first three years I was at the Seminary. When she finished, she got a job working for a big midtown law firm, which she hated almost from day one. When I was finally ordained and took my first pulpit, an assistantship in Atlanta, she gave her notice enthusiastically and hasn't ever looked back.

When we first began to date, Gwen obviously asked me about my mother. I told her the truth—why wouldn't I have?—but never felt called upon to follow up in any significant way and she mostly just let it be. Now that I am forcing myself to say all of this out loud, however, I have to admit that the story has some huge holes in it. When we came to Atlanta, Gwen went to work for a much smaller firm—the kind generally featured in John Grisham novels—and became a very accomplished criminal defense attorney. And when we left Atlanta for Savannah, she stuck with criminal defense work and became very successful all on her own. So the bottom line is that she knew and knows a million cops. And she knows another million private detectives. She *could* have found her. Or, at the very least, I could have gotten her to try. People vanish into thin air on television all the time, but things are a bit more complicated in the real world. People apply for passports and pay their income tax. People's names appear on voters' rolls where they live and vote. People belong to different kinds of organizations, at least some of which keep public membership rosters. It's not that easy simply to drop off the face of the earth. Even dying doesn't really do the job because death certificates are public records in every one of the fifty states. And prisoners' names appear on rosters maintained by the fifty states' fifty Departments of Corrections that any may consult. Gwen could have found her. Or she could have tried. I could have too, obviously. But I never did, preferring to tell our children that their grandmother had run off, never to be heard from again…and preferring not to notice how little sense that made if I had really and truly wished to know where she had run off *to* and what had finally become of her. None of the kids ever pressed the point, thinking of my mother's disappearance as something that once happened to me but not to them.

I suppose my lack of interest in locating her was an expression of the degree to which I felt angry. She hadn't *just* abandoned my father, after all—she had run away from me as well. My father occasionally noted that she was running away from marriage, not from motherhood. But, of course, that wasn't even remotely true: she may have been *primarily* motivated to run away from him, but she was *also* running away from me and she can't possibly not have understood that.

And so the years passed. I stayed in Atlanta for three years, then came to Savannah in 1980. Gwen opened her office and became successful almost overnight. The kids grew up. (We have three sons and a daughter.) Eventually, we bought the manse from the *shul* and meant to signal by that purchase that we hoped to stay permanently in that place. Which we have, actually, for what next year will be a full quarter-century. I thought about my mother rarely as the years passed, occasionally wondering what became of her but never doing anything actually to find out. I skipped the "For a Mother" paragraph during Yizkor, telling myself that I'd say it if I ever found out that she was dead. And then, one day, my secretary left a white envelope marked "Personal and Confidential" on my desk and, when I was too tired to do anything *but* read through the day's mail, I opened it and read it.

Now, after all those years of finding it beyond me to do any real research into my mother's disappearance, I swung into action. The letter was written on the stationery of a nursing home in Baton Rouge and I googled it and learned that it operated by the local Catholic parish. I googled my mother's name too—or, rather, the name of the woman claiming to be my mother—and found the usual detritus of a reasonably well-documented life. She, whoever she was, was a registered Democrat. Her name was on the roster of a gardening club in Merrydale, a town just outside the Baton Rouge city limits. She hadn't ever been arrested, much less spent time in the custody of the Louisiana Department of Corrections. There was indeed a woman with her name residing in the facility on whose letterhead the letter was written. So she was there. But was she my mother? I could only think of one way of finding out.

I had accrued months of untaken vacation time by then and hardly even needed to ask formally for a few days away. The cost of the trip was something we could handle easily. For a couple of days, I did nothing. A few evenings later, Gwen and I went out for a long late-evening walk. As we walked, I told her in as off-hand a way as I could manage that I had received a letter from a woman who claimed she was my mother. You could say she was surprised. But Gwen was also supportive and kind…and she told me that if I didn't go to Baton Rouge, she herself would go and let me know what she found out. I considered that plan briefly, then realized how ridiculous it was. Either I went or no one did. We spent an edgy Shabbos at home. For only the second or third time in my career, I repackaged a sermon I had given a few years earlier because I was just too distracted to write something new. (No one appeared to notice or care, which both pleased and annoyed me.) And the following Monday, I was on my way to Louisiana. When my flight touched down in Dallas for a two-hour stopover, I seriously considered turning around and just going home. But then they announced the continuation of the flight and I boarded the plane almost without thinking about the potential consequences of my decision to see this sorry story through to its end.

The city looked more or less as I expected it would. (I'd been once or twice to New Orleans, but never anywhere else in Louisiana.) I checked into a nice hotel on North Street just six blocks from the nursing home. It was already seven o'clock in the evening, too late to drop in unannounced. I was extremely ill at ease, but there was no turning back. The hotel had a pool, so I went for a swim. Then I went out and had a strange meal in a vegan restaurant just a few hundred yards down the road from where I was staying. Then I went for a walk. Then I went to bed and eventually fell asleep. Having decided not to phone first to announce my arrival, I walked to the home and was there at nine thirty the next morning.

I walked through the front entrance and approached the front desk. Slightly overcome with emotion, I dispensed with the small talk that comes naturally in situations like this.

"Alice Sommerville, please," I said

The woman, whose name tag gave her name as Jan, smiled and said, "Room two hundred."

I suppose I looked confused. "Second floor," she added helpfully. "Last door to the right."

Did I know? In retrospect, I suppose I did. The place was run by a church. My mother's second husband had been a Mr. Sommerville. It hadn't ever seemed that important to me that I knew nothing of my maternal grandparents, that when I asked about them my dad used to say he hadn't ever met them either, that they had died when my mother was still a little girl. But now that story, more or less believable when first told, sounded unlikely and outlandish. Why hadn't I ever insisted on knowing more? I realized, somewhat to my chagrin, that I wasn't even sure what their names had been...and we're speaking about my own grandparents. As I walked down that carpeted hallway and took in the early-morning smells of a nursing home, I felt assaulted by questions I hadn't ever thought to ask. It made sense that my dad wouldn't have displayed his and my mother's *ketubbah* after they were no longer married. But where was it? I hadn't found it among his papers after he died in 1999, nor did I find evidence of a *get*. I was used to suppressing any questions related to my mother or her disappearance, but now these details surged forward in my consciousness and asserted themselves, mocking me and forcing me to consider their implications.

And then I was there, standing in front of room 200. I knocked, but heard nothing in response. I walked in anyway and there, sitting in a chair by the window, was my mother. I knew her immediately. And I also know the secret my father had kept from me all these years.

We talked briefly. This was clearly not going to be a Hollywood-style reunion. We weren't going to fall weeping into each other's arms. We certainly weren't going to move forward to share her last years as mother and son. Within a few moments of opening that door, I knew—and knew perfectly well and without the slightest doubt—that I would never see her again. Ever.

She didn't try to excuse herself, nor did she make any effort to solicit some sort of after-the-fact forgiveness from me. She did tell me that I was her only child. She had no wealth at all, having signed her money over to the home as a precondition of admission, so the fact I was her sole heir meant more or less nothing. She had lived with Mr. Sommerville for forty years, then came to Magnolia Manor when he died in 2000. She used his name, but they hadn't ever formally married. When I told her Dad had been granted a divorce, she seemed surprised. She had had, she said, a good life.

The script clearly called for me standing up to protest. She had had a good life? What about me? What about the child she abandoned to his fate, to whatever life might bring him without her being present to watch over him, to care for him, to *be* his mother in the years that boys need their mothers on the ground and present if they're to grow up well-adjusted and well-looked-after? But I said nothing, focusing on the sole detail that was shaking me to the core and which I knew I needed to resolve either now or never.

"What was your maiden name?" I asked, attacking from the side.

She seemed surprised by the question. "Doyle," she said.

"Doyle," I repeated idiotically.

"Doyle, she said again. "My parents were Joseph and Ellen Doyle. They died when I was still a child. They're buried in Brooklyn, in Green-Wood. Near Prospect Park."

So my dad *was* telling the truth about never having met them. "I know where it is," I said. I had come all the way to Louisiana to have the conversation we were now about to have. But now that we had come to the crux of the matter, I felt nauseous and slightly dizzy. "They were Irish?" I asked.

My mother smiled. "Clearly."

"Catholics too, I suppose."

"Yes, Catholics too."

"Like yourself?"

"Yes, Jonathan, like myself."

I felt my throat constricting almost to the point of being painful, but I had to press forward. "You converted to marry Dad?"

"No."

"No?"

"No. I didn't want to. And he said it would be enough just to tell people I had. It worked for me. I had no parents and no siblings whose approval I needed. So we just told people I was Jewish, that I had converted years earlier when I was engaged briefly to a different Jewish fellow."

"And everybody believed you?"

"Why wouldn't they have?"

"Because you knew nothing of Jewish life?"

"I knew as much as your father, which wasn't much. And it really was no skin off my teeth to live that particular lie as a favor to your father, so I granted it. I never went to church anyway, so what did it matter? We had a nice wedding. And a nice life. Until....."

"Until?"

"Until it stopped being nice. Is your father alive?"

"No."

"Then I'll pay him the respect of not saying more. But I couldn't stay. I just couldn't. My dignity wouldn't permit it. And that's all I'll say."

"You mean he was unfaithful."

"I won't say more."

"But you left me too, not just him."

"I won't say more."

"And you never looked back, not even to worry if I was okay?"

Her face darkened for a moment, but then her color returned. "I won't say more."

And she didn't. I thanked her for her time. To that, she only smiled. If she wished for more from me, she didn't have the courage to ask for it. Or the nerve.

I was back in the hotel before ten-thirty and on a flight home, again through Dallas, that afternoon. I had no *concept* of what to do. Nor did I have any idea whom I could or should ask for counsel. Gwen, I supposed. But being honest with her ran the risk of fundamentally altering our life together as husband and wife. Nor was I prepared to go to a colleague for counsel. For a few minutes in the car I thought of turning to Victor Jackson, the pastor of the Abyssinian Baptist Church on Montgomery Street and my occasional squash partner. He was a decent man, a good guy...and someone I thought I could trust. But then I decided against involving him as well and chose instead to keep my own counsel.

I drove into town just before ten. I drove past our house, thinking I would drive on to Tybee Island and try to find some counsel from the sounds of the sea before facing Gwen and having to tell her *something*. But then, almost unexpectedly, I found myself driving into the parking lot of the *shul* instead. The parking lot was deserted. The building was dark. There wasn't a soul present. I let myself in.

I wasn't sure about anything, and that's really saying the very least. I wasn't who I was. I wasn't *what* I was. My life was a sham. My position in the community I served was a palace built not *even* on sand, but rather on nothing at all. My marriage itself was a fantasy, a dream. What my children would think, I couldn't imagine. What I *myself* thought, however, I also couldn't say. I felt unchanged. But that, I told myself bitterly, was only because nothing *had* changed. Things didn't feel different because they *weren't* different. I just knew how things were now, that's all. But what I was going to do about it...that, of course, was another question entirely.

I walked into the sanctuary. It was utterly still. The only light in the room was the dim flicking of the Eternal Light that hung over the Holy Ark, but the first few row of pews were also almost completely in the dark. In the dimness, I could see my own seat on the *bimah* just behind the lectern from which I had given twenty-five years' worth of sermons. For a moment, I wondered how many sermons that actually constituted, then gave up trying to do the arithmetic in my head. I didn't want to know. Each of them—hundreds upon hundreds of them—had been a lie, each one preached by a rabbi who wasn't even a Jew to a room full of people trusting him to guide them forward on their own spiritual paths. But it was all bogus, all smoke, all phony. I felt truly sick to my stomach. My head was suddenly pounding. My eyes filled with tears. I sat down in the front row, wiping my face dry with the sleeve of my jacket.

Like any observant Jew, I try to *daven* three times a day. Mostly, I succeed. I know the prayer service more or less by heart, could *easily* recite my prayers without a prayerbook without getting lost or making any too serious mistakes. Maybe I wouldn't make any at all! But that was all behind me now, all of my synagogue skills the accouterments of the man I thought I was but not the one I now knew myself to be. I felt my heart contracting in my chest as, for the very first time, I understood what prayer was... or at least what it was meant to be. I could hardly breathe. I felt hot under my clothes, as though I had a fever of some sort. But I didn't feel ill at all...just nauseated and hot. I could feel the sweat soaking through my undershirt. A strange shiver worked its way down my spine. I somehow understood that I was transcending the moment, that I was somehow stepping over a line I hadn't even known existed.

And then I began to pray. I must have said a million times from the *bimah* that prayer can never be *just* reading words from a book, that to be real prayer has to be as emotionally disorienting as it is potentially transformational. But who knew such a thing really existed? And yet there I was, weirdly shivering not from the cold but from some inner source of heat that was making me queasy almost to the point of faintness *and* energizing me in a way that even now I can't really characterize clearly in words.

I heard thunder in the distance, but when I looked out the window behind the *aron kodesh,* the Holy Ark, all I saw was a starry, cloudless night. I felt a kind of buzzing in my ears, almost like some sort of distant murmuring in language I couldn't quite make out. And then I saw some glimmer of light shine forth for a split second from between the doors of the *aron kodesh.* Did someone leave the light on in there? But then why hadn't I noticed it before? And why was it gone almost before I could register its presence? And then I felt my mouth opening and a rush of air that somehow was exiting and entering my throat simultaneously.

When I looked at my watch, I could hardly believe that only a minute or two had passed. I waited for a second surge of...of whatever it was that had just surged through me. But whatever had just happened was over now...and I knew what I had to do.

I did it too. I told Gwen everything and insisted she sign on to my plan before I put any of it into effect. I confided in Rabbi Albert Sheinwort, an older colleague in Atlanta who was able discreetly to put together a *beit din* of colleagues he felt certain he could trust. In their fully discreet presence, I immersed myself in the *mikveh* owned and operated by one of their congregations (and opened that morning solely for my personal use), then sheepishly allowed them all to congratulate me. Rabbi Sheinwort re-ushered me (or, rather, ushered me) into the covenant. It was more weird, that last part, than humiliating, but as I emerged fully dressed from the changing room and each stepped forward wordlessly to embrace me without ruining the moment by saying anything at all, I knew they would keep my secret. But what of my ordination? Surely that was a sham, a phony *semikhah* earned under false pretenses by someone who only now could truly claim membership in the House of Israel.

But even that part I got past. I flew to New York to see a senior colleague with whom I had studied at the seminary and whom I have revered as my spiritual master for as long as I could remember. He listened quietly, asking the odd question along the way but mostly just trying to fathom what I was telling him. He was well past ninety at that point, but still possessed of every one of his marbles. And when I finally got to the point, he nodded without saying a word. I understood that he would do it, but that I was going to have to agree to keep his secret just as absolutely as I was asking him to keep mine. And so he granted me his private ordination—something he was almost famous for saying he would never do under any circumstances for anybody at all—and, with that, I was whole again. Gwen was a good sport about going through another wedding ceremony, an intimate affair held in our backyard and attended solely by ourselves, Rabbi Scheinwort, and the two ultra-discreet witnesses he brought along from Atlanta to sign our *ketubbah.* And then we drove to Hilton Head and spent our wedding night at the Sonesta.

Months later I drove out to Tybee Island to listen to the waves, this time actually getting there. It was dusk. The sun was a giant red ball sunk almost to the horizon. There were a few stray tourists still around, but mostly I had the beach to myself. I felt calm and peaceful. I had actually been rethinking the possibility of attempting to have some sort of relationship with my mother, but earlier that same day someone from the nursing home phoned me to tell me that she had died. I did feel a pang of regret when I heard the news, but regret isn't grief and I felt nothing approaching the kind of sadness a child should experience upon the loss of a parent. I didn't fly to Louisiana for the funeral. I have no idea who paid for it or with what funds, or even if it ever actually took place. No one asked me to do anything. Eventually some lawyer I hadn't ever heard of wrote me to confirm that I was my mother's sole heir, but also to note that her estate consisted solely of her physical possessions because whatever funds had accrued to her from the sale of Mr. Sommerville's home had long since been turned over to the nursing home. I called the home, introduced myself as the owner of my mother's effects, and asked that they be given to the thrift shop of their choosing. They asked if I wanted her Bible. I said no. They asked if I wanted her photo album and, slightly to my own surprise, I said no to that as well.

The sky was becoming darker by the moment. The waves were loud. I felt at peace, relaxed in that favorite place now that the day was almost over and I had the space almost to myself. The sea was dark red, almost black. For a while, I just stood there and watched the sun sink beneath the horizon. For a moment,

I thought I heard my father's voice calling to me from within the waves and asking me to forgive him. That stopped me in my tracks and I actually stood still for a few minutes and listened carefully to see if I would hear him again. But then I felt ridiculous and, finally at peace with my dad *and* my mother, I chose to end this whole adventure the only rational, healthy way I could think of: by getting back into the car and driving home to Gwen.

UNDER THE WHEEL

I didn't really know that I was going to do it until I did it. If anything, I thought I wouldn't. I actually had a whole speech written out, one I had let my mother see and which she had pronounced "generous" and "kind." What she *meant* was that she knew the whole thing was a complete crock but nevertheless thought highly of me for being willing to deliver it in public without laughing out loud. I got that. But what she didn't know was that I *also* had a different speech ready, one I hadn't shown anyone, one that wasn't written down anywhere at all. And *that* was the one I was going to find out if I was brave enough to deliver to a room full of people whom even at the tender age of sixteen I knew perfectly well were going to be mad as hell at me if I did. I am not by nature such a brave person. I tend to avoid confrontation. (I am an only child, after all.) And yet, mild-mannered West Village junior hipster that I was—this all happened back in eleventh grade when I was rarely without a copy either of *A Coney Island of the Mind* or *Leaves of Grass* in my backpack— I found myself in those couple of days before my father's funeral uncharacteristically unwilling to behave as expected.

On the big day, I woke up early. My mother walked uninvited into the bathroom while I was brushing my teeth and still deciding whether or not to shave to tell me that "my" people— my two aunts and one of their daughters—were already in the living room and that, because they had come to support me, I was to be grateful and polite. My dad's people, presumably, were gathering elsewhere. Probably, they were nearby...but I had no idea where or, for that matter, who they might actually be given that my dad had no true friends. That, he had told me many times. And he had no family either, he used to say, except for me. I was blood. I was bone. I was his flesh. My mother was none of the above, of course. That, in and of itself, can hardly come as a surprise—they never married, never lived together, never even really dated and were so little part of each other's lives that my mom managed to be pregnant for nine months and then produce a child without him even noticing her swollen belly or, eventually at least, its absence. So it's not like he and my mom were an item or anything. The truth is that they barely knew each other.

Interestingly, though, Lizi was apparently *also* not any of the above. And her, he actually did live with and actually was sort-of married to—in the eyes of God, he once told me, if not quite in the eyes of New York State. (How he could imagine himself married in the eyes of God without actually believing in God, he didn't explain. Nor will he now, obviously.) I can't remember what I exactly thought of the whole bone and blood thing when I was ten or eleven, but later on, when he would put his hands on my shoulders and tell me that I was his "entire family" and that there was no one else who was "of his flesh" alive in the world, I always wondered if Lizi knew that my dad had an entire family and she wasn't it or part of it. I don't believe it ever dawned on me to wonder if he was telling her the same thing, let alone any of her kids.

Mom finally left me alone to get dressed, but the rest of that part of the morning is a blur to me now. I didn't shave—I remember that clearly—and I must have eaten something…and then, suddenly, there we were at Levenstein's. For a long time, we were in some sort of fancy sitting room. My dad's people, mostly musicians and assorted hangers-on of various sorts, huddled on the side of the room with the casket and kept asking when the lid would be raised. This question they repeatedly put to the guy from Levenstein's who was serving as whatever they call maître d's in funeral homes, but he punted to Alan Benson, my dad's lawyer, who punted to me. As my dad's sole living relative, it was, he said, my call. (Later, when I actually read my dad's will I learned that he had specifically excluded Lizi from any decision-making role "should I die." I didn't know what to make of that then and I still don't. Not really!)

At any rate, I accepted my role graciously, asking only for a few minutes to consult with Mr. Dukakis, my English teacher and spiritual advisor (it was Mr. Dukakis who first introduced me both to Ferlinghetti and Whitman), and the sole person from school actually to show up at the funeral. Taking me aside into a kind of office down the hall a few feet, he told me to keep the box—that's actually what he called it, the "box"—to keep the lid down and the box closed. So that is what I told Mr. Benson we'd do and that, semi-amazingly, is what we actually did. I was relieved and, although some of my dad's people seemed to feel that they were being unduly penalized by not being granted a peek, I stuck to my guns and declined to revisit my decision. Mr. Dukakis had specifically predicted that I'd be bullied—or that some people would attempt to bully me—on the matter, but told me just to hold firm. No raised lid. No peeks. Jews, Mr. Dukakis said—he later surprised me with the news that only his father was Greek but that his mother was a Jew from East New York—Mr. Dukakis said that Jews commune with the dead through the medium of memory, not by looking at them. I liked that idea…and eventually people just stopped asking.

We were in the room for a while when things began to pick up. The rent-a-rabbi showed up. He seemed nice enough, but he really perked up when I told him that I myself was going to deliver the eulogy and that he therefore wasn't going to have to cobble something together at the last minute. (For what it's worth, he appeared to have no idea who my dad was or why there were reporters from the Times and CNN in the lobby.) And he really didn't need to speak—I was going to give either my written or my unwritten eulogy, but Alan Duchênes, the head of Lincoln Center, and Brian Dirk, the New Yorker music critic guy, were going to speak first. Then it was going to be my turn. And then—this part no one knew yet—then, if he showed up and was able to slip into the building without starting a riot, Yo Yo Ma was going to speak and, possibly, play something from one of the Bach cello suites in my dad's memory. To wrap up, two of my father's students were going to say something, probably the exact same thing, about studying under him and that was going to be that!

Where Mr. Ma was, I had no idea. But the others were in place. The students—two of them, both in their twenties, both Julliard types—looked dazed. Dirk looked stressed and unhappy; Duchênes looked ridiculous (in my opinion, at least) in his dark purple velvet blazer, white shirt (no tie), and grey slacks. Only I myself seemed fully to be bearing the weight of my father's death; even my mother looked confused, something like an actor who somehow wandered onto the stage in the wrong theater and was trying to improvise lines without knowing the actual plot of the play unfolding around her. Lizi, to her credit, did look sad...or at least sad-ish. (She also had the most to lose by my father's death, and by far.) Her kids, three girls I hadn't ever actually met, looked angry about something. Needless to say, the place was packed.

The service unfolded along the pre-organized lines. The rabbi read some very long prayer in Hebrew and English, then introduced the various speakers. Duchênes spoke first. Then, while he was stepping down off the podium and Dirk was coming forward, one of the guys from Levenstein's came up to me and whispered in my ear that Mr. Ma had arrived and that he had his cello with him. I was, I guess, pleased. But then Dirk finished—he basically said exactly what Duchênes had said, only with even less emotion—and it was my turn.

Suddenly, I felt a little queasy. I had an easy turn-off from my chosen route: the pre-approved eulogy was in my jacket pocket just waiting to be read. Even as I walked to the podium, I wasn't sure what I was going to do. I felt queasy, but also emboldened by…by something. Maybe it was the actual presence of my father's casket, or maybe it was the unbelievable number of TV trucks and other sorts of media vans I had seen in the street through the greasy window in the men's room that I had visited eighteen times before the funeral actually began. But whatever it was, I felt myself outside the action in a way I think I had read about somewhere but hadn't ever experienced: I could almost see myself walking down the center aisle, purposefully unshaven and looking, I hoped, suitably somber in my black corduroy jacket, black t-shirt, and black jeans. I was even wearing black boxers…but, of course, no one but myself could have known that.

I took my place at the podium. The room, as noted, was packed to overflowing. For show, I took the printed-out eulogy from my inside jacket pocket and dramatically, I thought, unfolded it and smoothed it with the heel of my right hand. And then I looked up, just as Mr. Dukakis had suggested, at the crowd. Then I looked down at the casket. Then up again, this time at my mother. Then down again at the "box," imagining (Mr. Dukakis hadn't suggested this part) my father's lifeless body just a few inches beneath the mahogany lid. In my mind's crazy eye, I think I imagined him winking at me, urging me forward, telling me to be a man, to speak the truth.

I looked up at the crowd one final time, then pretended to look down at my text. "My father," I began, I hoped, forthrightly, "was one of the world's greatest cellists, but he was also a drug addict." That certainly got the room's attention. You could have heard a pin drop. I felt encouraged as I waded further into even deeper water.

"So far both our speakers have dismissed his death as an accident because Dad wasn't specifically planning to kill himself last Thursday," I said. "But that's not exactly the whole story. What he did last Thursday *before* he died is part of it too: his regular guy being temporarily incarcerated on Riker's Island

and therefore unable to conduct business as usual, my dad chose to improvise, scoring some low-grade dope from a guy on Avenue C he didn't really know and had no real reason to trust. And then he went home to inject it into his veins anyway. Did he know he was about to die? I'm sure not. But my dad wasn't a fool…and he certainly wasn't crazy. He made a decision, and if you all want to honor him today then you have also to honor that decision…his decision that being here for me, for any of you, for Lizi or her kids, for my mom, for his students, for his handlers at Sony…for any of us…being here *at all* was less important than getting high. And so he rolled the dice…not accidentally as Mr. Duchênes politely said but fully aware of what could easily happen. What was likely to happen. What, in fact, actually did happen. He shot poison into himself and, as poison does, it killed him."

Someone in the back of the room coughed, but it was otherwise totally still. I felt a sudden chill creeping over me. I still could have turned off and somehow segued into my prepared text, but now I really couldn't see the exit ramp at all clearly so I just kept on driving straight ahead. As I was speaking, it suddenly struck me to wonder how exactly I knew that Nick, my dad's dopebuddy, had been telling me the truth when he told me the whole story of my dad's death, a story he also told me that he was specifically *not* planning to share with the police. For a moment, I felt a wave of serious doubt wash over me. But then I recalled how kind Nick had been to me—he had actually hugged me and told me he would always be my friend, just as he had been my dad's—and I willed myself to dismiss even the possibility that he had been anything but fully honest with me as he told me details I could only ever have heard from him personally.

"So we have two options, basically," I continued. "We can say that he was a wonderful dad who always put his kid first and who accidentally killed himself. Or we can say that he was a dad who put his kid—and the rest of the world—second, right after his love of getting high. Oh, I know you're not supposed to think that. It's a disease! That's the ticket! He wasn't just some-one who paid with his life for making a really stupid, bad de-cision, for taking a chance that he was plenty smart enough to know could lead directly to where it actually did lead. He was sick! Drug addiction isn't a choice, after all…it's a *condition*. He couldn't have helped himself even if he had wanted to. He didn't really kill himself anyway, did he? The heroin, or whatever crap was in that syringe, that's what killed him. He wasn't a suicide, therefore—he was a victim, a poor little guy who was gunned down in cold blood by…by whom exactly? By the guy who sold him? By the people in rehab who failed to wean him off his drug of choice? Or maybe by the cops who haven't yet managed to make Manhattan a poison-drug-free zone! But if not any of the above…then who? Or maybe "what" would be better than "who." The syringe killed him! The needle killed him! The uni-verse killed him! Something killed him!"

I was about to vomit, but I kept on speaking…propelled by some demon that I knew wasn't going to let me go until I was done. I could almost feel Mr. Dukakis putting his hand on my shoulder and telling me to finish what I had begun. Like a man.

"But none of that is true, is it?" I actually looked up to see if anyone was going to answer, which it would have been insane if anyone did. And then I looked down again and continued, after making believe I had found my place. "If my dad had put a gun to his head and pulled the trigger, no one would call it an accident just because guns sometimes misfire so he could conceivably also not have died. And that's exactly what happened here. He put a gun to his head, figured it probably wouldn't kill him even though he knew perfectly well what happens to addicts who shoot garbage they buy from strangers into their veins. And so he died. Not willingly or intentionally, perhaps. But at his own hand and only because he cared for all of us too little to worry about the possible consequences of his actions."

And now for my big finish. "I won't be saying Kaddish for my dad. And I won't be attending his burial either. After I'm done here, I'm going back to school. I suppose I'll eventually need some therapist to help me figure this all out. But for the moment, all I have is a broken heart and a dad who was too self-absorbed to put anyone else's needs above his own need to get high. And now, it is my pleasure to introduce you all to one of Dad's best friends and most highly esteemed colleagues, Mr. Yo Yo Ma, who is going to play a little something in my dad's memory."

There was a collective gasp in the room, but I couldn't tell if it was in response to my eulogy or to the surprise visit of a first-tier celebrity like Mr. Ma. I had met him a few times over the years, but even I was surprised when he actually appeared in the doorway, cello and bow in hand, and came forward. He was supposed to say a few words about my dad, but instead he just sat down on the chair that had been provided for him and began to play the Sarabande from Bach's Suite in C minor for unaccompanied cello. It was gorgeous, actually. I was entranced. Everybody was entranced. Years later when he played the same piece on the first anniversary of 9/11 as they read out all the names of the people who died, I felt like it was some sort of memorial to my dad as well. But that thought, of course, was years in the future when I was first listening to Mr. Ma play at my dad's funeral in the chapel at Levenstein's.

The students were up next. They spoke briefly, but I wasn't listening and don't have any clear recollection of what they said. Then the rabbi chanted something and it was all over. I suppose I probably should have gone to the cemetery with Lizi and my mom and the others, but I just didn't have it in me to care. No one spoke to me, not even Paul Duchênes or Yo Yo Ma. I suppose I had forfeited the right to any words of heartfelt condolence, but it still surprised me that no one felt obliged at the very least to congratulate me for my honesty. I waited for a few minutes in front, then I retrieved my knapsack from the coat check, went out the front door, and walked to school.

Mr. Dukakis, who had slipped out right after I was done speaking, was waiting for me when I arrived and together we walked down the corridor towards my locker. (I had about ten minutes before gym, my least favorite class of the week.)

"So how do you feel?" He actually turned to look at me.

"Okay, I guess," I said tentatively, not sounding even to myself like I meant it.

"Are you proud that you spoke honestly?"

"Not so much. All I did really was to dump on my father at his own funeral, which most people would think of as an example of precisely the kind of self-absorbed behavior I so eloquently attributed to my dad."

"That's not entirely fair, Jack. You didn't tell any lies at all about his death or about his life. Everyone else did, but you didn't."

"Mr. Ma didn't either," I said softly. "But only because he didn't say anything at all."

And then the bell rang and I went to gym class, which was the usual complete waste of time. I went right home after, but they were all still at the cemetery—it was going to take hours to drive all the way out to Farmingdale and then to get back—and I had the place to myself. I felt more numb than anything else. I spoke the truth, but it didn't feel anywhere near as virtuous in the remembering as it had in the planning. I hadn't wanted to speak ill of my dad, only to be honest. Wasn't he the one who was always telling me to be honest, that the only way to be a great musician—and he truly was a great musician—that the only real way to be a great musician is to play honestly, to play straight from the heart? So that was what I was doing, I guess, or trying to do. But it didn't feel right or good. If anything, I felt cheap and stupid, like I had somehow fallen into a hole that I had dug myself without realizing what I was doing, without understanding what the consequences of digging that particular hole might conceivably be.

The weeks passed quickly. My mom and I somehow managed not to discuss the funeral even one single time. I saw Lizi in a supermarket on Seventh Avenue once, but she made believe she didn't see me and I wasn't up to confronting her. (And besides...what exactly was I going to confront her about?) I went to school. I kept up with my schoolwork. Mr. Benson helped me through the details concerning my dad's estate, including the sale of his super-valuable 1720 cello. Lizi was in the will, of course, as were her kids. My mom got a small gift, enough to make her grateful but not to change her life. I myself inherited a fortune—by the time I was done paying all his bills and authorizing Mr. Benson to send checks to the other beneficiaries, I got the almost two million bucks that was left in the estate, which I invested in some mutual fund Mr. Dukakis recommended. Other than knowing I was super rich, though, my life didn't change much. I went to school. I did my homework. I read *Leaves of Grass* for the eight-thousandth time. I was a freak, I guess. But I was a really rich one and that kept me from being made too much fun of by anyone at school. Or anyone else, for that matter. Plus you get a lot of pity credit when you dad dies and you're only in eleventh grade.

In July, Mom rented a cabin in the Catskills in a place called Swan Lake. It was quiet and peaceful, but I was antsy and ill at ease. I read a lot that summer, including for the very first time both *Journey to the East* and *Under the Wheel*. (My obsession with Hesse, just beginning around the time of my dad's death, continued well into college and even beyond; even today I can feel the influence of his books on me in certain specific ways.) I was, as noted, rich as Croesus—my dad liked that expression, by the way, and used it all the time, always making me think of the creases in the folded bills in his wallet—but all my money was invested away and we ourselves continued to live as we always had. It was a quiet summer. Mom worked on her watercolors. I smoked the occasional Marlboro down by the lake but otherwise kept my nose clean and devoted myself to my books and, occasionally, to helping with the laundry or other chores.

I thought about my dad now and then, but mostly when my

mother put one of his CDs on and I could hear the music filling the cabin and flowing out the windows into the world. But then one night I was down by the lake smoking and thinking about Hans Giebenrath, the hero (so to speak) of *Under the Wheel* who gets kicked out of school when he starts screwing up under the influence of his malign friend, Hermann Heilner. He has no friends. He's lonely, disconnected, isolated. His family's solution is to get him apprenticed to a blacksmith so he can learn a trade, but all he really wants is a friend to talk to, to hang out with, to listen to him. It's a really, really powerful book with a terrible ending. Years later, when I was a senior in college, I actually re-read the book in the original German. But this was when I was still in high school and college was still a few years off. So there I was, just sort of standing there in the dark, smoking, looking out at the lake and up at the stars. I was feeling lonesome, I guess. Mom had said I could have invited a friend to come along, but I hadn't taken her up on it...and now I was sorry I hadn't.

I considered for the first time what it really meant that I had no brothers or sisters, and no dad. I had a mother, of course, but she and I were increasingly on different pages about...everything. She loved me, of course. I really did know that, but standing there in the dark smoking and watching the occasional shooting star I suddenly felt alone, fatherless, forlorn. And I felt something else too, something draped over me like a kind of unwanted cloak: embarrassment that I had spoken so shamelessly about my dad at his funeral, that I had outed him in public and in front of his stepdaughters as a drug addict and, even worse, that I had accused him of loving me less than he loved getting high. It was weird how little blowback I got for that speech— my mom never mentioned it, Lizi was completely gone from my life, Mr. Dukakis thought I had behaved admirably, and none of my friends from school had been there to react one way or the other. But now that I thought about it carefully, I felt truly ashamed of myself.

And then, completely unexpected (and totally uncharacteristically), I began to cry. Not to whimper either, but to cry like a big baby with big salty-tasting tears flowing down over my face. It felt as though some sort of gate had been opened that I was powerless to close as I sobbed quietly, not wanting my mom up in the house to hear. But it wouldn't stop...and as I cried I felt the loneliness enveloping me and making me as cold as my face was wet.

For the first time, I truly missed my dad, narcissistic crazy person that he was and all, and really couldn't imagine living on in the world without him. I heard myself praying for him to rest in peace, something I hadn't ever dreamt of doing, something I don't remember even *considering* doing. Once I started, I couldn't stop either...I wasn't even sure whom I was praying to, but I couldn't stop this deep wave of emotion from seizing control and making me—and trust me, I know how weird this is going to sound—from making me into this huge flesh-and-blood prayer for my dad's safety, for his peace, for his repose. I liked to think sometimes that he was in heaven playing duets with Casals or Jacqueline Du Pré, which fantasy I somehow found soothing even though I didn't really have it in me to believe in heaven. I certainly didn't believe in God. But it wasn't even as though I was praying, not really—it was really more of me myself being the prayer, being this vehicle of...of yearning, of this deep wish for his safe passage from this horrible world of lonely boys and dead dads to whatever there is on the other side. I know how crazy that sounds now, I really do. But it was totally real then and didn't feel at all like a dream or *just* some ridiculous fantasy.

Eventually, I calmed down. I smoked my last cigarette. I dried my eyes and my face with the bottom part of my t-shirt. I looked out at the lake one last time and stared into the darkness, then went back to the house.

I said something to my mother, then brushed my teeth and went right to bed. I fell asleep instantly, exhausted from that whole weird scene down by the lake. And then it was morning and the room was filled with light. If I had had any dreams, I didn't remember them. I pulled my boxers on and went for some reason to stand by the window and look out at the lake. And there, in the middle of the lake in the clear light of morning, I saw my dad. He was dressed in his normal khakis and this bottle-green flannel shirt I remember him wearing all the time. He wasn't doing anything, just standing on the lake, hovering over the surface of the water. I rubbed my eyes, thinking I was probably just dreaming that I was awake. But I somehow knew that wasn't true, that I was fully awake in a way I don't believe I had ever experienced before or have ever experienced since, fully *there* in the moment in a way that the word "there" doesn't even begin to describe adequately.

For a long time, nothing happened. I felt myself filled with regret so real it was almost palpable, with love for my father and anger at my father and, finally, a kind of acceptance I hadn't ever imagined I could bring to the contemplation of my father's story and particularly the story of his stupid, selfish death. For a long moment, I just stood there as the sea of seething emotions in my heart slowly calmed and, for the first time since I skipped going to the cemetery, let me be. And then my dad raised his arm to me in a gesture of reconciliation I hadn't really earned and certainly didn't deserve...and then he was gone forever from the world, never to return.

BABYLON AT
THE GATES

I knew him, of course. *Everyone* knew him, or at least knew of him. For one thing, Jerusalem was a pretty homogenous place back then and there weren't that many foreigners in our midst. For another, he was a head taller than the average man in the street, or at least in *our* street, and his dark brown skin didn't exactly make him *less* noticeable. There were other Africans in town, of course—the non-Judahite members of the royal guard were more or less *all* from Kush or Nubia. But Eved-Melech was the only one who frequented the ḥammam on the Street of the Lambs—the bath I and my brothers visited almost daily—with any regularity and, apparently, without feeling even slightly out of place. And he really was remarkably tall, even for a man from Kush.

I knew what I wanted to say. It wasn't that complicated a request. It is true that I had given some thought to the specific way I should broach the topic, but that was because I wanted to avoid sounding like I didn't fully understand the importance of what I was asking the man to do, or the possible implications for the both of us if he agreed to do it. But once I actually saw Eved-Melech climbing out of the cold pool and heading into the steam, all that well-thought-through planning flew right out of my head and left me more or less totally on my own. And so I just followed him inside into what I hoped would turn out to be a private moment for the two of us to speak out of the earshot of others.

He was sitting on one of the marble benches at the back of the room, a white sheet wrapped tight around his waist and his eyes shut as he leaned back against the wall and relaxed in a world of his own thoughts. I looked around to make sure that we were alone. And then, sitting down next to him, I cleared my throat and crossed my personal Yabbok into the next part of my life.

The story I want to tell took place during the reign of King Tzidkiyahu, the last king of Judah. But to get a running jump into that story, I have to start earlier on because first time I laid eyes on Jeremiah was years earlier when King Yehoyakim was still on the throne. Things had gone from bad to worse to even worse than that. The endless war between Egypt and Babylon was in full swing. The Babylonians had actually gotten as far as the Egyptian border when Nebuchadnezzar—called N.N. by all—got word that his dad had died back home and so put off the invasion and returned to Babylon to establish himself as his father's uncontested successor. That wasn't our problem, or it shouldn't have been, but then Y.Y. (as we all called Yehoyakim) got it into his idiotic head that N.N.'s withdrawal was basically about God sparing us from further disaster instead of it being about Nebuchadnezzar's interest in settling his huge behind securely on his father's golden throne. And it was that almost unbelievably self-serving piece of political lunacy that led to Baruch ben Neriah, Jeremiah's secretary and spokesman, entering the Temple precincts (where Jeremiah had been forbidden by royal edict to set even his big toe) and reading aloud from a long scroll in which he had stitched together some of Jeremiah's choicest and most condemnatory oracles regarding the sorry fate of our doomed land and its ill-fated residents.

It didn't go well. Those present were outraged. They sent Baruch packing, but the scroll they seized and brought to the king. It was wintertime and Y.Y. had already settled into the Winter Palace. And it was there that he sat perusing the scroll on his famous lion-throne with a huge butcher's cleaver in his hand, slicing each column off as he read it and flinging it into the blazing hearth. He ordered both Jeremiah and Baruch to be arrested, but they were both long gone from the city at that point. Even now I'm not sure where they holed up, but it was just over a year later that Jeremiah suddenly popped up in the city again, walking its streets as though he had never left and looking none the worse for his time away.

But Jeremiah's days of walking around the city unmolested as he dolefully announced its imminent doom and made it clear that only national *t'shuvah* on an unprecedented scale could possibly avert the severity of the impending doom—those days were clearly over. He was routinely trounced in the street, and not *just* smacked or stuck either, but truly thrashed. His bruises were visible to all. He more or less always had at least one black eye. The Hebrew words for "death sentence," *mishpat mavet*, became the city's regular catcall when the man passed by—I even heard of children knocking him down and calling it out as they ran off. And, yes, I myself succumbed as well.

I hated the man. Why wouldn't I have? Two of my three brothers were in the king's army. The city, its walls, its Temple, its palaces, its very existence were all on the line. Only the terminally naïve imagined that the Babylonians were gone for good. On top of all that, there were the Egyptians to worry about—and there was simply no way to imagine that they were just going to go away either. And every time the Egyptians and the Babylonians went to war, guess whose country they trampled through? And whose Temple treasury they raided to "find" the funds to underwrite the new war? Our only hope, it seemed, lay in maintaining a strong standing army, keeping our arms at the ready, using whatever intelligence we could gather effectively and insightfully, inspiring the citizenry with the need to remain alert and

TO SPEAK THE TRUTH AND OTHER STORIES 2011-2019

on guard, and trying to foster the kind of national unity that makes war seem like virtue rather than folly. But that was not at all how Jeremiah saw things.

For him, all our efforts at national defense were a joke. And not even a real joke, but rather an example of self-referential folly ratcheted up to the level of national suicide. For him, our sole hope lay not in military prowess, but in a return to the old ways: to the long-since-abandoned practice of letting the fields lie fallow every seventh year, of closing the *shuk* every seventh day, of cancelling real estate sales every seven-times-seventh year. He preached a kind of spiritual militancy. He never tired of pointing out that security against enemies the size of Egypt or Babylon was never going to be achieved by spending money on weapons or fancy uniforms, but solely by pursuing justice and by creating a society whose least powerful members are treated as valued citizens. For Jeremiah, reaching down to hand a crippled beggar a coin was going to be more effective in safe-guarding the nation than adding another thousand troops to the already swollen ranks of the king's army.

The people neither enjoyed the man's preaching nor took it at all seriously. And I was among them, always eager to sound more bellicose than even my own bellicose father when it came to taking pride in our nation's military. Did any of us ever pause to note that our army was less than a twentieth the size of the Babylonians' fighting force and only about a tenth of the Egyptians'? Did it ever strike any of us that victory was not going to be merely elusive, but actually impossible militarily if *either* of them ever truly set out to annihilate us as a nation or a people, let alone if they ever somehow joined forces against us? Let me answer that for you: not any of us, and not for a minute.

And so we focused our wrath not on our hapless king or his end-less array of pompous, self-important generals and advisors, but rather on the one man in our midst who was eager to tell us the truth.

No one remembers Pashchur ben Immer these days, but I was

present when he took on Jeremiah ...and I behaved disgracefully. In those days, Pashchur was the *pakid-nagid*, the head clerk in the Temple treasury. His neck was as thick as one of his thighs and his nickname, "Little Ox," derived directly from the degree to which he was grotesquely overweight. How such a prestigious position ever came to a slob like Pashchur ben Immer, I have no idea. But come to him it did, and with it came a retinue of armed guards.

I was just cutting across the Temple Plaza on my way to the *shuk* to buy some dinner when I suddenly saw Little Ox standing in front of Jeremiah and ordering him to shut up and move on. There was yelling, and then there scuffling as Jeremiah tried to stand his ground. Finally, I saw him being dragged off in the direction of the Upper Benjamin Gate and followed along to see how this would end up.

It was winter. Jeremiah was wearing a thin cloak, a kind of loincloth, and some cheap sandals. By the time they got him to the gate, the sandals were gone and the cloak was mostly gone, leaving him covered in terms of his personal modesty but not in any way protected from the cold. As they clapped him half-naked into the stocks, the crowd jeered and laughed. Pashchur first raised his arm and smacked his prisoner hard across the face, then gave an angry little speech in which he invited the prophet to repudiate his prediction that the Babylonians would raze Jerusalem to the ground and take its citizens off into exile, which act of self-betrayal (Pashchur called it "a coming to terms with reality") would earn him his immediate release from the *mapekhet*. Jeremiah, always the showman, responded so quietly that no one, not Pashchur and not any of us, could hear. Pashchur, insanely thinking he had somehow won, asked his prisoner to speak up. Again, Jeremiah said something that no one could hear clearly. Pashchur, preening for the crowd, came closer and bent down to hear his prisoner's confession. And it was then that Jeremiah looked up, spit in Pashchur's face, and, having nothing further to say, said nothing at all.

The crowd, myself included, went wild. They threw things at Jeremiah, including stones, until he was bleeding from any number of head wounds. And then I came forward with a group of other Levites and, acting as one, we spit on the prophet of God, reviling him, laughing as the gobs of saliva dripped off his face onto his knees. The crowd laughed too, many taking their turns to spit as well. By the time the sun set, Jeremiah was still there, still half-naked, covered in saliva, his arms and legs extended out in the stocks and the blood from his many wounds congealing in angry red splotches over his upper body and his head.

It was obviously going to be freezing once the sun set, but that thought only seemed to please the crowd. Eventually, there was no one left to mock the prophet but myself and some chums. My plan to buy dinner in the *shuk* forgotten, we all went off to eat in one of the taverns that surrounded the city-side of the Upper Benjamin Gate.

The next morning, Jeremiah was released. There was one final *contretemps* in the course of which Jeremiah formally cursed Pashchur and his household with death in exile. I had gone back in the morning to see if the prophet was still alive and I personally heard the curse…but it still failed to strike me that I had behaved shockingly poorly or even, really, that I had behaved poorly at all.

But that was all then. After Y.Y. died, his son Chunia came to the throne and lasted exact three months before being replaced by the boy's Uncle Tzidkiyahu, one of Y.Y.'s brothers. And it was this Tzidkiyahu whom Eved-Melech served.

"You are Eved-Melech?" It was an idiotic question, but I couldn't think of how else to begin. Who else did I think he was? Eved-Melech looked down towards me through the white steam and said nothing.

"I know we don't know each other," I continued, offering him the chance to respond by observing that we actually had met on a few occasions over the years.

He just looked at me as a few beads of sweat dripped off his nose onto his lap and waited patiently for me to get to my point.

I realized that this was my only chance, that it was entirely possible that we wouldn't ever be alone again with no one at all around, that blowing it now could possibly mean blowing it permanently. So I pulled myself together and, instead of trying to pave the path before walking on it, I just set forth into the unknown.

"I know you have a...a special kind of relationship with the king." That much was well known. Eved-Melech was always standing there right behind the king, always protecting him, always tasting his food for him, always sampling his drink. When the king went to bathe, Eved-Melech would position himself in the doorway leading into the pool so that any who would approach the king needed to get past him first. The fact that he was a full head taller than the next tallest member of the court, that his skin was almost the color of coal, and that he was reputed to be incredibly strong and superbly physically fit made it hard to miss him. And, trust me, no one did. And yet, for all he was feared, he was also respected. He spoke hardly at all, but when he did give forth on some topic or another it was in clear, precise, unaccented Hebrew. He seemed genuinely to have the king's best interests at heart. He was not married—he was widely called "the eunuch," but that was probably just a derisive way of referring to someone whose overt masculinity was so unnerving—and lived with his brother and his brother's family in a very nice home right behind the Spice Market, not far from the Water Gate. I had heard all sorts of stories about the "real" nature of his relationship with the king, but all that was, as far as I could tell, just so much gossip born of jealousy and prejudice. And here he and I were, all alone in the steam, and the floor was clearly mine.

Eved-Melech looked over at me now and nodded in tacit acknowledgement of my polite remark about the intimacy he enjoyed with the king. "Service to His Majesty," he said in a low voice, "is its own reward."

I nodded my head in agreement. "But such a level of closeness also entails a certain kind of responsibility," I said quietly.

This was clearly not where he thought we were going. "What kind of responsibility do you mean?" His voice was low but clear.

"Jeremiah is in prison. Again."

"I know."

"But maybe you don't know how things have changed. The king gave his tormentors leave to do with him as they wish."

"The king's wishes are my own."

"Look," I continued, buoyed by the fact that he was still sitting and listening, "the king is a trusting, decent man. When he sentences someone to death, then the person deserves his fate...but he specifically didn't sentence Jeremiah to die. And now they are about to kill him anyway."

"To kill him?" A raised eyebrow signaled his interest. "To kill him how?"

"They took him—don't ask me how I know this but I do—to the police station run by the king's son Malkiyahu and they put him in the pit."

"The pit is only used by the king's express command."

"Not this time. And that's why you have to step in. He's going to die down there. There's some chance he's already dead. No one can survive the pit for long." Everybody in Jerusalem knew about Malkiyahu's pit: a hole in the ground at least twelve cubits deep and filled with mud that most prisoners eventually drown in. You were thrown in naked. You were given no food. You could only breathe by standing on your tiptoes and looking up. (The mud levels were altered depending on the prisoner's height.) You stood there freezing to death for as long as you could and then, eventually, you sank back into the mud and drowned. Later on, Malkiyahu got his too—he was one of Tzidkiyahu's two sons who were beheaded in front of their father after the city fell to N.N. a few years later, after which the king was blinded so that the last thing he ever saw was the execution of his sons—but, of course, who could even have imagined something that horrific before it actually happened?

"How do you know any of this?" Eved-Melech asked, leaning slightly forward. Malkiyahu was an officer in the king's guard and, although what went on in his prison and its pit were well known, the specific identities of persons brought there were generally kept secret.

"My youngest brother works there."

"And he told you that Jeremiah is there right now?"

"That's what he told me."

"And what do you want me to do exactly?" Clearly, I had the man's interest, but only because he saw harm coming to his king and wished to head it off if he could.

"I want you to go to the king and tell him that the nation's future depends on Jeremiah bringing God's word to the people. We're probably doomed anyway, but that would seal the deal for good. If Jeremiah dies, we're as good as done for. You know that."

Eved-Melech said nothing. He made no promises. He didn't even look over at me, just stood up, retied the knot holding the sheet tight around his waist, and left. If he told the king to spare Jeremiah, I imagined that could somehow be an act of atonement for my behavior all those years ago. I felt sure he would keep my brother's name out of it, but if he denounced me to the king as a supporter of Jeremiah, I would be lucky if *all* they did to me was to throw me in Malkiyahu's pit. I watched the door close behind him. I lay back on the marble bench and let the steam penetrate my pores. Had I succeeded? I had no idea.

The whole "stocks" incident was back in the eighth year of Y.Y.'s reign. Then we had little Chunia for a few months and then Tzidkiyahu acceded to the kingship, and now we were eight years into his reign. Did any of us understand that we were thirty-six months away from the end of the world, from the end of everything? Or maybe the right way to ask the question would be to ask how any of us could *still* not have understood just how bad things were, how precarious our situation was, how completely and utterly damned we all were. Two infinitely powerful giants were engaged in a wrestling match to the finish, and we were a tiny flea that naively flew in between them as they struggled in the ring, thinking we were safe because of our insignificance. But no one could have imagined the horrors to come—the famine, the thirst, the violence, the blood—as we scurried around in those last years of Tzidkiyahu's reign and imagined that God would protect us and that Jeremiah was just a crazy old coot who imagined himself a prophet. Now, of course, it sounds idiotic even to write out those words. But we did think that at the time, and we didn't think we were crazy. Of course, what crazy people ever think that of themselves?

As the years passed, I grew more insightful. And Jeremiah sounded more and more right.

I was present when Jeremiah went head-to-head with that pretentious fop Hananiah ben Azur, just four years before he was lowered into the mud and left to die. That was a kind of a turning point for me too. Little Chunia was gone and Tzidkiyahu was installed on the throne. Jeremiah was still selling the same story in the streets, only now he was using props to make his point. There were several, actually, but at this particular juncture he had begun to walk around the city wearing a huge ox's yoke on his own neck, explaining his point to any who would listen: those who do not submit to the yoke of the King of Babylon will be punished with sword, famine, and disease. The more time that passed, the more honed the message became. And, even despite the public's general reluctance to take the man too seriously, there were also at least some few people in Jerusalem who were listening carefully and taking the prophet's message to heart.

This went on for years. J. didn't wear that thing on his neck all the time (who could?), but he wore it a lot. And people got used to seeing him that way, which was probably a good thing (because the message became familiar) *and* a bad thing (because it became ever easier to ignore). And then, in the fourth year of Tzidkiyahu, this pompous coxcomb Hananiah approached Jeremiah in the street and announced that he too was a prophet of God…and that *his* message, patriotic and glorious, was that God had broken—or at least was about to break—the yoke of the King of Babylon. Jeremiah listened, then almost politely suggested a simple way to find out who was right: whoever's prophecy ended up mirroring the reality soon to come would be entitled to claim the "real" mantle of prophecy and the other one could rightly be condemned as a phony. This did not sit well with Hananiah, who responded by yanking the yoke off Jeremiah's neck and throwing it to the ground, breaking it into pieces and explaining that God shall similarly break the yoke of Babylon. Having said his piece, Jeremiah just walked away. But then he returned with a message for Hananiah personally: "Oh, and by the way," he said, "the Lord God of Israel says you're a phony and a liar, and also that you'll be dead before the year ends." And that is exactly what happened: the man had a fatal heart attack on Erev Rosh Hashanah and so was dead before new year commenced.

That whole incident, everybody knew about. I was there too and saw it all come down. And it was probably then that the ember that had been smoldering in my heart for years was transformed into a steady flame: I loved my king and I loved my country, but I knew in my heart Jeremiah was right. I hated his message. I hated the future he could see before his eyes. I hated the certainty with which he spoke. But all that was because I knew he was right, not because I was sure he was wrong. And, that, in the end, made all the difference.

Early the next morning, three enormous men, all clearly armed, appeared at my door before sun-up. I was, to say the least, unnerved.

"You are the Levite Simon ben Daniel?"

I couldn't think of anything clever to say, so I just answered the question. "I am," I said.

"Please get dressed and come with us."

"Where are we going?" It felt like a natural question.

The larger of the two smiled slightly. "To jail," he said.

I knew better than to argue. Even if I did somehow outrun them, where was I going to go? And, I reminded myself, I did have at least some friends in positions of authority so I wasn't *irrevocably* doomed. I excused myself, went inside, pulled on some clothes. I told my wife that I'd be back soon. I took nothing with me.

Twenty minutes later, we were approaching Malkiyahu's pit. My spirits rose slightly when I saw Eved-Melech in full battle gear standing at the front gate. He looked right at me, then signaled with his eyes for me not to approach him.

"In here," one of my escorts said, showing me a doorway with a clear view of the pit and the holding cells behind it.

I took my place, then looked out at what happened. Eved-Melech had a dozen men with him. Cotton towels were produced from somewhere and thrown into the pit. Ropes were lowered. I could hear Eved-Melech calling down and telling its sole resident to put the towels under his arm pits, then to put the ropes under the towels. And then they raised him from the pit, almost from the dead. I hadn't ever seen anything like this in my life. He was naked, as I expected him to be, and covered in mud. He was skinny to the point of emaciation and looked mortally frail. He wasn't *that* old—Jeremiah was in his mid-fifties, I figured, but he looked ageless as they drew him from the pit and almost delicately rinsed him with warm water. Then, when he was almost clean, they produced white cotton clothing for him to put on—a pair of underbreeches, a pair of baggy pants, an undershirt and a *k'tonet* to wear over it, a white cap—and, while I watched, he dressed. They had food as well—olives and humus, *pitot*, cheese, a jug of pomegranate juice—and we all waited patiently while he ate a bit, then vomited, then washed out his mouth and tried to eat again.

He said a few words to the men who had saved his life, but I couldn't hear them. They seemed moved, though, and some bowed politely as he walked past them into the street.

As he passed the doorway in which I was standing, he stopped. His eyes were dark grey and piercing. He seemed to know me or at least to know who I was. For a long moment, we just stood there.

"You spat at me in the stocks," he said quietly.

I nodded, not knowing what to say.

He too said nothing, clearly waiting for me to respond.

"Yes," I said finally, "I did. But I was wrong to do that and I know it."

He stared into my eyes before he spoke. "You should have known it then," he said.

"Yes," I admitted. "I surely should have."

"And now you've saved my life."

"How do you know that?"

"Prophets know all sorts of things," he said and then smiled. "And Eved-Melech told me."

I smiled back. "I apologize for all the years I willed myself not to understand who you were or why you were sent to us."

"Sins can be expiated with a willing heart and a supple spirit," he said. "Bad times are coming, but not for you personally. The city will be destroyed. I won't leave, but you can and you will. And one day you will sleep in peace with your fathers."

And then he walked out of the police compound into the street and the stone that was set in my heart was gone.

THE BONES OF
A SLAVE

Rabbi Kalman Licht, born in 1820, was my grandfather's grand-father. What I know of his life, and what I am presenting to my readers, I know from his diaries and from decades' worth of detailed letters he wrote to his brother Sholom. (Both the diaries and the letters are currently in the hands of the American Jewish Historical Society, although they are technically speaking my personal property and are merely there on loan.) Here and there, I have reconstructed some of the dialogue that appears below. But every single detail presented herein derives directly from the man's own words as recorded by himself in one written document or another.

1838, the year my great-great-grandfather formally began to prepare for a career in the rabbinate under the tutelage of his teacher, Rabbi Asher Levitas, feels like a long time ago. It *was* a long time ago. Martin Van Buren, the first of our presidents to be born a citizen of the United States, was in the White House. The Seminole Wars were raging. The telegraph had just been invented. Mormonism had just been invented. *Iowa* had just been invented. It was, to say the least, a time of new things. But my great-great-grandfather, apparently unimpressed with the options modernity offered, chose instead to spend the choicest years of his—or any young man's—adolescence cloistered away in Rabbi Levitas' *yeshivah* (in those days housed in two adjoining rooms on what was then called Baxter Street in the Five

Points section of lower Manhattan) and to devote himself in the course of those years solely to his studies. And there he stayed put until, in 1846 at age twenty-six, he was ordained after eight full years of study. He was, by all accounts, a *very* good student. And he got a very good job too, being taken on almost immediately as the adjunct rabbi at the Manhattan Hebrew Congregation on Houston Street and then, upon the death of the incumbent, moving up to occupy the position of senior clergyperson.

In those days, the Jews were a tiny minority of fewer than twenty thousand in a sea of almost seventeen *million* Americans. Three-quarters or so lived in or around New York. The upscale Germans lived uptown. The rest lived downtown. My grandfather's grandfather lived just a few houses down from the synagogue he served in a manse provided for him and his family by the congregation. And he began, as far as I can tell from his letters, to make a name for himself almost immediately. He published pamphlets and he published books. He mainly preached in Yiddish, but occasionally—and to the delight of his younger congregants—in English. He maintained a strictly observant lifestyle, but not precisely in the old European way. He trimmed his beard. He had the panache occasionally to appear in public wearing a non-black suit. (Although the only surviving photographs of my great-great-grandfather are sepia-tinted, he specifically references a navy blue suit in several diary entries.) He did not require his wife to wear a wig. He prided himself on his knowledge not only of rabbinic arcana, but of current events. To the amazement of many, he not only voted in national and local elections himself but encouraged his congregants, or in those days at least the men among them, to do likewise. Even more daringly than that, he befriended local politicians and once actually invited Jacob Aaron Westervelt, then the mayor of New York City, to speak from his pulpit about the mayor's vision for peaceful relations between the city's religious and ethnic groups. And he himself preached regularly about current events as well, trying to frame the issues of the day in a way that would give his congregants a sense of how he believed Jewish people should feel about them.

He was already well ensconced in his position when Congress passed the Fugitive Slave Act as part of the Compromise of 1850. Understood by its supporters merely to constitute a return to one of the founders' principles *already* enshrined in law —they were surely thinking of the Fugitive Slave Law of 1793, signed by President Washington on the twelfth of February of that year, which very early on had made it a federal crime to assist an escaped slave—this renewal of that horrific law made it a crime punishable by a $1000 fine and six months' imprisonment for a Federal marshal *not* to arrest a runaway or for any citizen to offer a suspected runaway such elemental kindnesses as shelter or food, or even water. To say that it was not our country's finest hour is to say nothing at all. Yet it is that specific piece of legislation that provides the background for the story I wish here to reconstruct based on my great-great-grandfather's letters and diaries.

"You're being an idiot."

"I'm not. I'm being honest." Rabbi Kalman Licht rose from his chair, opened a window, then sat back down. Then he got up again, closed the window, and poured himself a glass of cherry wine. Then he sat down again.

"You're being an honest idiot, then."

"That's better than being a dishonest one, isn't it?"

Rachel's eyes softened slightly. "Maybe," she said, "but you're still making yourself crazy over nothing."

"Over nothing?" Kalman Licht lifted his eyes to meet his wife's, then quickly looked away. "A child's life is nothing?"

It was very late at night, late enough even for Manhattan to have quieted down for a few hours. And it had cooled off as well; the August heat had finally broken slightly and a cool breeze was coming in through the open parlor window. The rabbi got up again, then walked to the window and glanced out at East Houston Street. And then he looked down yet again at the envelope in his hands, a letter that had arrived with the afternoon mail but which he had yet to open. For what felt like the thousandth time, he scrutinized the outside of the envelope. His name and his address were *still* written clearly on the front. The postmark *still* indicated that the letter had been mailed in Baltimore three days earlier. There was *still* no return address. But Rabbi Licht knew its author's identity perfectly well. He recognized his brother's handwriting, for one thing. And he also knew why it had been written and what news it had possibly been sent to convey. There was, of course, some chance that the letter contained good news, that Thadd's freedom had been purchased, that everything had worked out well. But that was not the way the envelope felt in the rabbi's hands. It felt heavy—despite the fact that the envelope was too thin to contain more than a single leaf of paper—and ominous.

As his own unanswered question hung on the humid air, Rabbi Licht allowed himself quickly to review where things stood. Had it really only been a single week since David Goldwasser had asked for his counsel? It felt like months. As such, the whole scene—the one featuring himself seated with David and the lawyer and the little boy in the Goldwassers' library—seemed more like a play the rabbi had once seen than like an actual event in which he had personally participated.

"So what are you going to do?"

The rabbi sat down on the brocaded divan in the Lichts' parlor and looked at his wife. "I don't know," he said eventually, his voice quiet.

"You could open the envelope."

"I can't."

"Why not?"

"I can't face…I can't own up to my own folly. I've done a terrible thing, Rachel. A terrible thing!"

Rachel's face softened as she sat down by her husband's side. "Maybe it's good news," she said.

"I don't think so."

"You won't know until you open the letter."

"I can't."

"Yes, you can." Then, "Do you want me to?"

"No."

"Then you open it."

The rabbi stood up again, this time to check that the bolt on the front door was properly set in place. Then he went back to the open window and looked out at the street for a few moments. Then he sat down again. He wiped a tear from his left eye with the heel of his right hand, then picked up an ivory letter opener and slit the envelope open. Inside, as anticipated, was a single piece of paper. For a moment, Kalman Licht sat stock still. And then, his heart beating so wildly that for a moment he thought he could actually hear it, he took the paper from the envelope and unfolded it.

"What does it say?"

"It says I'm a fraud, a true idiot, and a fool."

"No, it doesn't."

"It doesn't? Read for yourself."

Rachel Licht took the letter from her husband's hand. "Hanged by his own hand and buried this morning. *Barukh dayan emess*," she read aloud. Then she refolded the letter and put it back into the envelope. "*Barukh dayan emess*," she repeated. Blessed be the Judge of truth. Blessed be the just God Who determines the fate of all.

"*Barukh dayan emess*," the rabbi repeated almost automatically, wondering if he was the first murderer to recite the traditional blessing upon hearing of the death of his own victim.

"You should go see Asher Levitas," Rachel said quietly.

"I'm too ashamed."

"Too ashamed to ask for advice, to ask for a way out?"

"You think I need a way out?"

"A way out of your own head, I meant. A way out of jail."

"I'm not in jail."

"Yes, Kalman, you are."

For a long moment, there was only silence in the Lichts' parlor. And then, his mind apparently made up, Rabbi Licht lay down on the sofa and closed his eyes. Rachel went to bed. The night passed. Instead of attending the morning service in his own *shul*, Rabbi Licht said his prayers at home. And then he set out to seek the counsel of Rabbi Asher Levitas, his teacher and mentor.

Rabbi Asher Levitas was an imposing man. Although he had come to the United States in 1818—more than thirty years before Rabbi Kalman Licht set off down East Houston Street to consult with him—he dressed just as he had in Europe, wearing a long black coat over his black trousers and white shirt even in the dog days of summer. Nor did he feel anything but pride in the fact that he had, at age eight-three, never read a book that could be considered even marginally suspect in terms of the orthodoxy of its theology. And yet, for all the Old World baggage that he felt personally committed to *shlep* along with him through the years of his very long life, he nevertheless projected a warm, avuncular demeanor that made all who came into contact with him feel respected and liked. That he was gaunt, even to the point of looking haggard, somehow only added to his unexpected charm. As, for their part, did his sallow cheeks and the habitual dark circles under his eyes that said to all—or at least to most—that this was a man whose life was devoted to endless study, to scholarship, and to the writing of learned commentaries on sacred books. This was clearly not a man who sunned himself in the park when he could be locked in his study. And yet, for all his earnestness, Rabbi Levitas exuded a friendliness to which almost no one, Jew and Gentile alike, was wholly immune.

Although it was not even ten in the morning when Rabbi Licht knocked at his door, Rabbi Levitas had already been up for many hours, having put several hours of study in *before* the morning prayer service he attended daily. Indeed, he was almost ready for his mid-morning meal when he set his pen down to receive his student and, for the last five years, his colleague.

The windows in Rabbi Levitas' book-lined study faced east and, as a result, the room was filled with warm, yellow light when Rabbi Licht stepped inside and, without waiting to be asked, sat down in one of the winged armchairs that faced Rabbi Levitas' writing desk. For a long moment, neither rabbi said a word as each waited politely for the other to begin. Bertha, the rabbi's housekeeper, brought a silver pot filled with hot coffee and a plate of fresh almond pastries, then withdrew. Both men, neither having yet said a single word, served themselves. A long moment passed. In one of the chestnut trees just outside the central window in the study, a crow cawed.

"So," the older rabbi said, turning to face his visitor, "what do you need?"

Rabbi Kalman Licht looked directly into his teacher's sapphire-blue eyes. "I need to know how to undo something I have done, a sin."

"A sin?"

"The worst sin."

"You could try to make right what you have done wrong."

"I killed a man. And not even a man, really—a boy! Can I bring him back to life? Shall I lie down on top of him and breathe life back into his lungs like Elisha did for that poor woman's son?"

"Elisha ben Shafat was a saint, a *tzaddik*. None of us can hope to accomplish in our lifetimes what he managed to bring about

TO SPEAK THE TRUTH AND OTHER STORIES 2011-2019

with a few breaths. But there's always another way...."

"Another way? Do we have cities of refuge then to which a murderer might flee? To which *I* might flee?" Rabbi Kalman Licht began to weep freely now but without sobbing or, indeed, making any sound at all as the tears flowed silently down his face onto the front of his shirt. Nor did he attempt to speak as he wept, preferring to sit still and to allow his tears to speak more eloquently on his behalf than he felt mere words ever could. After a while, his nose too began to run and, producing a linen handkerchief from some inner pocket of his jacket, he blew his nose into it.

For a long time, the room was perfectly still, but eventually the silence was simply too heavy to bear. "Tell me," Rabbi Levitas said simply.

Rabbi Kalman Licht looked up at his teacher and then, when he was ready and the tears he had shed had mostly dried on his face, he spoke.

"I made so many mistakes in one half-hour that I can't even count them. I should have come to you. I should have refused to answer on one foot. I should have requested—demanded—more time to think, to study, to consider the issue. But I did none of that. Instead, I listened for a few minutes, then—more eager to show how learned I was than to open my heart to a child in need—I gave an answer. And now the child whose life was in my hands is dead."

"Did you strangle him with those hands?"

"I might as well have."

"But you didn't."

"It was only a week ago. David Goldwasser was waiting for me on the sidewalk when I came out of the house on my way to *shul* that morning. He had to talk to me, he said. Could I come to his home right after the service? He'd have a carriage waiting for me. All I had to do is agree and he'd do the rest. He sounded desperate, so I agreed. And, indeed, when I came out of *shul* three-quarters of an hour later his carriage was waiting for me. And twenty minutes after that I was walking into the Goldwasser home on Madison Square.

"I was escorted into the library and was amazed to find myself in the presence not only of David and his lawyer, the latter also a member of our congregation, but also of a young Negro child of about eleven or twelve years of age. The boy stood when I entered the room along with the others, then stepped forward to shake my hand and to introduce himself to me as Thaddeus Carver. I took his small hand in mind, wholly unaware that within a week his blood would stain my palms permanently.

"Thadd, I was informed, was a runaway. How exactly he had managed to make his way from Virginia to Manhattan was not revealed to me. Probably that was all for the best. Nor was it made clear to me what David's specific role in the boy's flight had been or, for that matter, still was. This too was probably how things had to be.

"David's question was as simple as it was clear. He reminded me that the Torah itself forbids returning runaway slaves to their masters. (He hardly needed to recall those words to me—I've known them by heart since I read them aloud at my own bar-mitzvah.) And then, specifically *without* saying how he had come to this impasse, he asked simply what he should do. This boy, this Thadd, had come into his care through a circuitous route that he clearly wished not to describe in detail. He was wholly sympathetic to the abolitionist cause, he admitted freely, but felt uncertain how to honor that sympathy now that aiding a slave in flight was an actual crime punishable by a thousand-dollar fine and six months of incarceration. He knew the principle of *dina d'malkhuta dina* that teaches Jews everywhere that the law of the land in which they live is the law they must obey. But what, David wished to know, was our obligation when the law of the land requires us to disobey a direct commandment of God?"

My great-great-grandfather clearly had Rabbi Levitas' full interest at this point.

"And what was your answer, Kalman?" Rabbi Levitas asked quietly.

"My answer? A decent man would have looked at this poor child and taken pity on him, would have remembered the Israelite children Pharaoh murdered and the others he willfully enslaved. A *mensch* would have taken this poor, brave lad in his arms and kissed his forehead and promised him he would be safe. But I was afraid. Afraid to take a stand. Afraid to be involved. Afraid to face jail or a fine if some *goyish* court somewhere eventually determined that just by answering a congregant's question I was somehow abetting the flight of a runaway slave."

"And what actually *was* your answer?"

"My answer? My answer was to ignore the child whose hand I had just shook and instead to scramble to show what an *illui* I was, how I hardly needed a library because I myself was a walking basket of books. Preening like a peacock, I explained that the Torah law applies specifically to Gentile slaves who run away from their Jewish masters and somehow find their way to the Land of Israel. And then, because it wasn't quite impressive *enough* for me just to be able to dredge up an obscure Rambam and quote it from memory, I went on to cite the original source in the Talmud as well. And then, to impress even further, I added that, as far as I could recall, the *Shulchan Arukh* omits to specify that the master has to be a Jew and extends the law even to the Gentile slaves of *Gentile* masters who find their way to Eretz Yisroel. But even the Shulchan Arukh itself applies the law solely to runaway slaves who seek refuge in the Holy Land, not to those seeking safe asylum in New York."

"What did your host say to all that?"

"My host said nothing."

"And the lawyer?"

"The lawyer also said nothing."

"And the boy?"

"I'm sure he had no idea at all what I was talking about. But what did that matter to me? I had been asked a question and I answered it. Did I write the Talmud? Am I Rambam? Do I teach the law as I wish it to be or as I know that it truly is? That I was holding a child's life in my hand didn't strike me for a moment. The boy was in the hands of federal marshals within the hour. It was only later on that day that I began to feel guilty, that I suddenly realized the enormity of my error. I made some inquiries, discovered that the boy had been sent to Baltimore where he would be held until his master could retrieve him. I guessed the owner's journey would take a few days, but he would obviously only set out after being notified that Thadd had been apprehended. I sent a letter on the coach that evening to my brother Sholom—my little brother, the one who owns a tannery in Baltimore and who married that Belgian giantess—I wrote to Sholom and told him that I had erred grievously, that I needed him to swing into action and buy that boy from his master, then free him. Or at least to keep him in Baltimore until I got there to redeem him myself and bring him back to New York City. I had the idea that we could educate him, help him find his way into a brighter future, maybe even raise the funds to free his parents and at least some of his siblings. As stupid and dull-witted as I had been in David's study, that was how energized I was with the desire to help this waif, this innocent. Rachel was entirely behind me. We were not only going to help this boy, we were going to do it publicly and thereby set an example for kindness and for justice."

Rabbi Levitas, knowing that the story ended badly, spoke quietly now. "But your brother failed to raise the money?"

"Oh, no, it's far worse than that. *That* would have been some sort of excuse, but the truth is that he didn't need to raise the money at all. He *had* it. And he knew perfectly well that I was good for the sum. The next morning he went right to the bank and withdrew the four hundred dollars he was going to need to purchase

Thadd from his master...*if* he could be there waiting when his owner got to town and *if* he could talk him into selling. Those were two big if's, but in the end it was all moot—by the time Sholom got to the Baltimore City Jail, the boy was dead."

"How exactly did he die?"

"He hanged himself in his cell with his own trousers. "

Rabbi Levitas looked at his student calmly and kindly. "You could say that he died while your brother was trying to redeem him."

"You could also say that I killed him myself, that I was asked to be kind to a terrified child and responded by quoting Maimonides."

By the account in his diary, my great-great-grandfather broke down at this point and wept openly. His teacher said nothing, however, and merely waited for him to calm himself. And then he spoke.

"Kalman," Rabbi Levitas said, "you didn't kill the boy, but you plunged him into the despair that led to him taking his own life and for that you must answer. You recalled the first part of the verse—the part about not returning a runaway slave to his master and instead suffering him to live "wherever it pleaseth him to live," the part *everybody* recalls—but you forgot the last words in the verse, the ones that *also* forbid oppressing such an *umlal* by failing to come to his aid"

"And for me then there is no *teshuvah*, no way back?"

Rabbi Levitas sat silently for a moment. "There is always a way back, Kalman," he said quietly. "You know as well as I that the gates of *teshuvah* are never closed."

"So that's it—I regret my folly and resolve to sin no more, and I'm done? A boy is still dead at his own hand, but I'm done and back in God's good graces?"

"No," Rabbi Levitas said, still speaking so softly that his student had to strain to hear him, "that's *not* it." And then he stood up and pointed with the outstretched index finger of his right hand directly at my great-great-grandfather's heart. "To do *teshuvah* for a sin against another of God's creatures you must seek forgiveness from the party you have wronged."

"And if that person is dead?"

"Then you must do this," Rabbi Levitas said, his voice stronger now and unwavering. "You must first make sure the child is buried in a decent grave and then you must go to that grave. Bring a *minyan* with you and in their holy presence you must confess to what you have done and you must do so clearly and unambiguously. You must beg God to forgive you in their presence as well…and you must then offer up a sin offering to atone for your transgression."

"A sin offering? *Bi-z'man she-ein beis ha-mikdosh kayyom mai ikka l'meimar*? No one has offered up a *chattas* offering in a score of centuries!"

"You will offer to God not the life of a goat but your own life… which you will devote for the rest of your days to seeking redress for the wrongs of this nation with respect to the bondsmen held in service against their will. You will embrace the cause, Kalman. And you will make the slaves free."

"I will make free the slaves of America? How could I possibly do that?"

"If you were able to close your heart to one child in need, you should be able to open your heart to hundreds of thousands of them…and so you shall."

And that is exactly what did happen. Through the sheer force of his personality, my great-great-grandfather made the Manhattan Hebrew Congregation into a center of the local abolitionist movement. When Lysander Spooner, the nationally acclaimed author of *The Unconstitutionality of Slavery* came to New York in

1854, he became the first abolitionist leader to address the Jewish community from the pulpit of a synagogue and was introduced to the congregation and their guests by none other than Rabbi Asher Levitas himself. When Shadrach Minkins—a name now forgotten by most but briefly America's most famous fugitive slave—was arrested in Boston and put on trial, my great-great-grandfather traveled to Boston and managed to draw a good deal of attention to himself by sitting barefoot on the courthouse steps with ashes smeared on his forehead as he read from the Psalms aloud in Hebrew—he said he was mourning the demise of freedom—while Minkins' lawyers inside the building argued for their client's release. And later on, after Minkins had been abducted from his own trial and successfully spirited off to Montreal where he spent the rest of his life as a free man, my great-great-grandfather actually travelled to Canada to meet Minkins and to have a once-famous photograph taken together with him.

Rabbi Levitas died in 1862, but my great-great-grandfather lived into his eighties and died in 1909 just three months before he would have turned ninety. And when he died, it fell to my grandfather to fulfill his own grandfather's final request by traveling personally to Baltimore, finding Thaddeus Carver's grave in the Little African Cemetery there (its granite marker paid for by his grandfather's brother more than half a century earlier and still standing), and returning to New York to plant some grass on his grandfather's grave by rooting the seed in soil taken from the final resting place of the bones of a young boy who so valued his freedom that he chose death over slavery.

WHEN YOU CAN'T BREATHE AND GOD SENDS YOU AIR

My story begins the Tuesday before Thanksgiving in 2003. It was, as you surely can't remember but as I personally will never forget, a cold, blustery day in New York. I was at work when the phone rang. (My partner and I owned our first three auto glass repair shops at the time, but the main office was still in the Little Neck store. That was the first one we opened and that's where I was when the phone rang.) One of the secretaries answered, listened for a moment, then handed me the phone. Not knowing to whom I was speaking, I merely said my name. The police officer on the other end of the line introduced himself, then told me that Laura had been in an accident. The ambulance had just left, he said. He hoped she'd be fine. I jotted down the details, then jumped in the car and was at the hospital fewer than twenty minutes later. I don't know what I was thinking as I walked through the automatic doors that led directly into the North Shore E.R., but I realized the news wasn't going to be good when I said my name at the front desk and the nurse responded by looking away as she lifted the telephone to her ear, then pressed a few numbers, then said my name—nothing else, just my name—into the receiver. A moment later, two doctors appeared. One—it's funny how you remember stuff like this—one was a short, chubby Indian-looking guy with a mole on his cheek and the other was a tall black guy with an unusually pointy goatee. They both looked unhappy.

There wasn't much to tell. Laura had parked her car on Northern Boulevard near Little Neck Road and had just gotten out when she was hit by a passing car that was careening out of control. They tried to save her, but they were unsuccessful. My wife of three years and one month, they said, was dead. (They didn't refer to Laura as "my *pregnant* wife due to give birth to our first child in six and a half months," but I didn't hold it against them. How could they have known?) A police officer was waiting to answer my further questions. They were, they said, sorry for my loss.

I signed some papers, then went home. I called my in-laws, then each of Laura's four siblings. I planned the funeral. I bought a grave. (What kind of thirty-two-year-olds own ceme-tery plots?) I met with the rabbi. The funeral came and went. I sat on my mourning stool and endured a week's worth of visits. Laura's family—stiff, unfriendly Episcopalians from Gloucester, Massachusetts, who hadn't ever really made their peace with her conversion or, worse, with the fact that she appeared truly to have embraced her new faith and not just undergone the pro-cedure as a favor to me—had duly showed up at the funeral and continued on to the cemetery, but from there they went dir-ectly home. It seemed odd, but not entirely unpleasant, to think that I could conceivably never hear from them again. In the end, they did phone a few times. But *only* a few times and *only* dur-ing the two or three months after Laura's death. For one thing, my mother-in-law wanted to get back her own mother's pearls, an attractive triple-strand which she had given to Laura years earlier. I told her to stop by anytime. Eventually, they stopped calling. I did too. If anything, I was relieved. It's been years. And the best part is that my mother-in-law never did show up for her damn pearls either. Maybe there were irritated that I let them wait until the rabbi mentioned it in his eulogy to find out that Laura had been pregnant.

They arrested the driver a few days after the accident. (Some passer-by had had the presence of mind to write down the letters and two of the numbers on his license plate.) Possessed solely of a learner's permit, my wife's accidental murderer turned out to be all of seventeen years old. Perhaps imagining that it would explain his reckless driving, the young idiot told the police offers who arrested him that he and some friends had cut school to have a few beers in one of their homes. I suppose I should have been deeply interested in his fate, but I found myself strangely disengaged from his story and the details of his now blighted future. He had been arrested. Either he'd plead guilty or he wouldn't. One way or the other he'd be convicted, then sent to some facility for young offenders, then released. Or maybe he'd be tried as an adult. But Laura would still be gone forever, and that was the only part of the story that mattered to me.

My mother died when I was in high school, but my dad is around and he was great. He ran the *shiva*, scurrying around all day to make sure the coffee pots were topped off and that there was more than enough sugar in the sugar bowl and cream in the creamer. He's had a girlfriend for years, a lumberjack of a woman named Anne who before all this happened had always kept her distance from me. But now she too got into the act, coming to the house every single day and tidying up, cooking some meals, making herself genuinely helpful. I was grateful. But mostly I felt hollow. Not so much sad as empty. Bereft. Lonely in a way that I still can't quite express clearly in words. I didn't know what to do, so I didn't do anything. I sat on my stool and drank coffee and numbly listened to people going on about whatever it was they were talking about. I nodded now and then, made some vague effort to look interested. But I was a thousand miles away in some private space I couldn't name accurately or, to speak honestly, even really at all. Mostly I wanted to get back to work and perhaps find some comfort in familiar routines.

Years passed. Alex and I were good. We opened four more shops, one in Brooklyn and three in Nassau County. Business was great. Everybody has a car. Every car has windows and, more to the crucial point, a windshield. Most people are afraid to drive around with damaged windshields and insurance companies almost never give anyone a hard time about fixing or replacing cracked glass, which makes it extremely easy to sell potential clients on the idea of having a busted windshield repaired professionally. But I was lonely. I signed up for J-date, but never logged on. I went to some singles' parties at Alex's synagogue, but never stayed more than half an hour. I said I was ready to meet someone, but I never actually did anything that could conceivably *lead* to meeting anyone. And when people occasionally offered to fix me up with some specific woman they met somewhere whom they thought I'd enjoy getting to know, I'd thank them profusely, take the number, and never call. I suppose I wasn't ready. And then, one day, I somehow was.

I heard that there was a kind of support group forming at the Jewish Y that was being pitched specifically at young widows and widowers. At first, it sounded almost ghoulish. I needed to be with other miserable people? But then I rethought the matter and decided differently. Part of my problem, I realized, was precisely that no one got it, that no one my age seemed to understand what it means to bury part of yourself in the ground, to take your own heart and put it in a box and dig a hole and shovel so much dirt on top of it that you don't expect ever to see it again, much less again to feel it beating. I knew other people who had lost their spouses, obviously. My own father was a widower. But my experience felt unique, or at least too different from my dad's and his widowed friends'—all of them in their sixties and seventies—for me to expect to learn much from hanging around with them. But the idea of an actual group of people my own age who had also lost their husbands and wives—the more I thought about it, the more it appealed. So I signed up. Even more amazingly, even to me, I actually showed up.

I met Rachel within ten minutes of arriving. She had long red hair tied back into a ponytail and was wearing a pair of jeans and a green t-shirt. She looked great. And she was friendly too, inviting me to sit with her when the meeting was called to order. One thing led to another. We agreed to come back the following week. And then I asked if she'd have dinner with me and she agreed to that as well. Within a few months, we were seeing each other two or three times a week.

Rachel's story was similar to mine in some ways, but also very different. Amazingly, it turned out that I had actually known her husband. I didn't really know him well, but he was exactly my age—Rachel was two years younger—and we had gone to the same high school and been in some of the same classes. He—his name was Robert Rosenfeld—was one of those irritating people who excels both in academics *and* in sports. I knew him because everybody knew him. And he was handsome too, and tall. He was a Westinghouse scholar and a National Merit finalist. And he was on the varsity baseball team. We weren't exactly friends —we were, to speak more accurately, barely acquaintances— but we did know each other. Once or twice, we walked part of the way home together. I hadn't known what happened to him after Yale—the whole school knew that he had had to choose between Yale and Princeton—but now I found out. He had been diagnosed with leukemia in his senior year but had responded well to treatment and then stayed long enough in remission to marry, to complete medical school, to become a father, and to finish most of his residency before he began finally to succumb to his disease. For a long while it seemed that he was going to beat the disease, but in the end he lost his battle with cancer —Rachel actually said that, by the way, that he had "lost his battle"—and died the day before his and Rachel's fourth wedding anniversary. And that too had happened in 2003, just a few months before Laura's accident.

I hadn't ever met Robert's parents. Why would I have? But Rachel mentioned them many times to me, always stressing how kind they were and how devoted, how they never forgot her birthday, how they always invited her over for the holidays in the fall or in the spring for one of the Pesach seders, how they never came by unannounced and invariably arrived with generous gifts for her and for Carl, their only grandchild, when she would invite them over for a meal or for some coffee and dessert. Robert had been their only child, Rachel their only daughter-in-law. They hoped, they said over and over, that she would find happiness, that she would remarry. They *wanted* her to remarry someday, to find a dad for little Carl, to have more children, to move forward with her life. But then they'd begin to cry and then Rachel would cry and eventually they just stopped talking about the future in a way that was obviously too painful for any of them to bear. Was the unfortunate coincidence that both of us, Carl's father and myself, had the same name not at least slightly obviated by the fact that no one ever called him anything but Robert and no one, not even my dad, ever called me anything but Bob or, when I was much younger, Bobby? Would I have appeared less to be stepping into his shoes if we *hadn't* shared a name?

Laura died in the fall of 2003. I met Rachel in the spring of 2007. By the end of the year, we were fixtures in each other's lives and the time had clearly come to meet each other's families. I went first, inviting her to my dad's house for a Friday night dinner. It went well. Anne was there and Dad invited his sister and brother-in-law and their son and his wife and baby, so the house was full and the spotlight didn't shine too exclusively on Rachel. We both considered the evening a success. And then it was Rachel's turn. She invited me to join her at her parents' home for Thanksgiving. That too went well, although Rachel's parents were quiet and hardly spoke in the course of the entire evening. And then she invited me to her place for one of the nights of Chanukah because, she explained, she also wanted me to meet her "other" parents, by whom she meant the elder

Rosenfelds, the late Robert's parents. That thought stopped me in my tracks. She wanted me to enjoy an evening with the parents of the man whose place in her life I was devoting all my energy to attempting to replace? Was that really a good idea? Wouldn't they resent me? Or hate me? Or at least find the whole situation awkward and unpleasant? And what would they make of the way Carl was beginning to relate to me almost as a dad, or at least as a kind of potential stepdad? Wasn't that going to be intensely painful for them to see?

Rachel had her answers ready. They were, she said, lovely people. They had suffered the most unimaginable of all tragedies, the loss of an only child. Despite their own misery, they had it in them to wish the best for their daughter-in-law—she *never* said "former daughter-in-law"— and to understand, and even to say out loud, that they understood that the best thing for her would be to remarry and to have with whomever she was going to marry the kind of happy family life she might otherwise have had with their Robert. And they wanted only the best for little Carl, which they acknowledged meant having a father figure in his life. They had been only kind and loving to her, Rachel reminded me. And they were also very generous, including financially. She couldn't bear the thought of them thinking that she had any intention of shutting them out of her life now that she had, to use her own words, "found somebody." It all made sense. It was beyond noble, her desire to repay kindness with kindness. And she wasn't really asking too much of me, I told myself, just that I spend an evening with people she described as good-natured and friendly, and that I let them see how fortunate she was to have found me. And what was I supposed to do when she put it like that, argue with her? The die was cast. I would have dinner at Rachel's on the third night of Chanukah and in attendance were also going to be my girlfriend's late husband's parents. I asked if she could at least invite a few others to make the whole evening less intense, but she declined, saying it was going to be weird enough for the Rosenfelds as the plan stood without them having to deal with their emotions in the presence of other people. I suppose that made sense. I agreed to that part as well. It wasn't, I told myself, going to be such a big deal, just an opportunity to be kind to people who had only been kind, and endlessly so, to the woman I was dating and with whom I had long since acknowledged I had fallen in love.

A week before the dinner, Rachel phoned to tell me that her (former) mother-in-law had called and asked what kind of books I liked, or what kind of music. They were, Mrs. Rosenfeld had said, bringing Chanukah gifts for Rachel and for Carl and thought it would be unfriendly, perhaps even rude, for them not also to have something for me. I found the whole concept a little strange, but I more or less saw their point. I too had planned to bring gifts for Rachel and little Carl, who had had his sixth birthday only a month or so earlier, and now I realized they had only been kindly giving me the heads-up so I would not be embarrassed by their generosity and could have some small gift for them that would serve as a reasonable complement to the one they apparently were intent on offering to me. Eric Clapton had just published his memoirs, so I chose that for my gift. Rachel told me the Rosenfelds liked spy novels and mysteries, so I bought them the new James Patterson.

The dinner went reasonably well. There were some tears, but more or less everything went as we had all hoped it would. The latkes, served with home-made applesauce and brisket and bottles of cold beer, were exceptionally good. The presents were all perfect. I got the Clapton book and was pleased. The Rosenfelds professed to love the James Patterson. Little Carl was thrilled with his gifts too, as was Rachel with hers. By the time I left, I couldn't even recall why I had been so ill at ease about the evening. Rachel's former in-laws were good people, decent people. They loved their grandson and they clearly loved his mother. Was that a bad thing? I told myself I had been nervous about nothing.

The weeks passed. From time to time Rachel mentioned that

she had had lunch with her mother-in-law, or that both Rosenfelds had come by to babysit Carl while she had to stay late at work. She was, of course, eager to know whether I could make my peace with the elder Rosenfelds remaining part of her life even if she and I became a permanent item. What could I say? They were Carl's grandparents. They were friendly and generous. They were also charting a path into the future that they couldn't possibly have imagined was going to be theirs to chart, yet they were doing so gracefully and charitably. I told Rachel that I was fine with the concept: if she and I ended up together permanently I could not only live with the Rosenfelds being part of our lives but I welcomed the role they seemed so eager to play in Carl's life. Why not?

It was when Rachel and I became engaged that the weirdness began in earnest. The Rosenfelds came for a Friday night dinner and had not only a toy for Carl and a gorgeous bouquet of flowers for Rachel, but also a pair of silver cufflinks for me. They had, they said, seen them for sale somewhere and thought I would like them. I *did* like them and it seemed unimaginable to refuse to accept them, so I thanked them and promised to wear them the next time I wore a shirt with French cuffs. (To complete the *mitzvah*, I went out the following week and bought two such shirts and then wore one of them the next time Rachel had us all over for dinner.) It seemed excessive, at least a little, but I told myself they were only trying to signal to me the degree to which they were truly willing to accept me into their lives. And the cufflinks really were beautiful.

A few weeks later, a boxed set of twenty-five of Clapton's albums, all remastered and accompanied by a beautifully illustrated volume about the artist's life and music, arrived at my home. I told myself that it was I who had opened the door in the first place by mentioning my deep love of the man's music, that they were only trying to make me feel welcome in their world by stepping gently and generously into mine. And it was, actually, a *great* set of disks, one that included not only all the best of the Yardbirds' records *and* all of Cream and the Blind Faith album, but also the full set of Derek and the Dominos' CDs *and* a healthy sample of the great man's solo work including *Slowhand* and *Pilgrim*, my personal favorites. It was an extravagant gift. I went online to see what it cost and almost fell over when I saw the price; I phoned Rachel and asked what she thought I should do, but her response—that I should send a thank-you note and enjoy the music—left me feeling intensely ill at ease.

The trickle of gifts turned into a flood. Tickets to Broadway shows for Rachel and me to enjoy. A portrait—in a silver frame, no less—of Rachel and Baby Carl that had clearly been cropped to remove Robert Rosenfeld from his former stance at his wife's side. (Creepy beyond words was the fact that I could still see part of his disembodied left hand resting on Rachel's right shoulder. But creepier still was the way the photographer's error more or less mirrored the way he was only mostly absent in death from his family's life.) A set of roller skates that happened to be precisely my size—they must have asked Rachel—that came a few days after a dinner at which I had mentioned in passing that in-line skating looked like fun. (I had meant that it looked like the kids in the park who used skates like that looked like they were having fun, not that it would be fun for someone my age to undertake a sport clearly meant for teenagers.) And then there arrived one day at my front door a box containing the late Robert's apparently extensive collection of rock star t-shirts. He hadn't ever taken them from his parents' home, the accompanying note explained, but his mom and dad thought they would fit me nicely. And why should they go to waste?

It was the t-shirts that put me over the top. I weighed my options, considering whether it would be more kind or more evasive to leave Rachel out of this. I knew where the Rosenfelds lived. (I hadn't ever been inside their home, but I had picked Carl up there a few times.) So all I really had to do was to drive over, park in front, ring the bell, and ask politely for them to stop sending me stuff. But what was going to be my reason for rejecting their presents? I had long since fallen in love with Rachel and that was clearly going to mean *also* having the Rosenfelds in my life. It seemed crazy to risk alienating them. It made no sense to make Rachel choose between them and me. (For one thing, I wasn't yet confident enough to be entirely certain what her choice would be.) Still, I knew I had to act. And I knew I had to act alone. Did Rachel know about the t-shirts? I had no idea.

I drove over. I parked. It was drizzling and cold and I felt foolish, but not foolish enough to get back in the car and go home to try on some of Robert's t-shirts and enjoy communing with him through his old clothes. I approached the front door and rang the bell.

"Who is it?" I could hear Ruth Rosenfeld's voice from behind the door.

"Robert," I answered without a moment's thought. Was I crazy? I mean, I *was*—I *am*—Robert. But I'm always and only called Bob. Their *son*—their *late* son, the one whose place in his wife's and child's lives I was poised to take—was the one called Robert in this story. I knew that. How could I have *not* known it? And yet when Mrs. Rosenfeld asked her entirely normal question, I answered idiotically with the one name that should never have passed, of all the lips in the world, mine.

The door opened instantly. Did she really expect her Robert to be standing there? If she did, she recovered almost instantly and then politely asked me in. Was she curious why I had come? If she was, she certainly didn't show it.

I was ushered into the kitchen where, Mrs. Rosenfeld said, she had just put on a pot of coffee. There were freshly baked cookies on a tin baking sheet cooling on the counter. She appeared to have been expecting guests, but when I asked if I had come at a bad time she said that, no, I hadn't, that she had been hoping for some company. Bill Rosenfeld, she said, was playing golf. (In the rain? I said nothing, just nodded.) She was all alone, hoping someone would stop by. And, she said with a smile, here I was coming to her rescue!

I had a speech all ready, but suddenly couldn't remember a single word of it. To stall for time, therefore, I took a sip of coffee. It was excellent too, strong and rich, and for a long moment I tried to gather my thoughts. Ruth stood up. But then she sat down at the table. She poured herself a cup of coffee, then failed to pick it up. Instead, she looked at me intensely, almost piercingly.

"I'm not a crazy person," she said.

"I don't think that."

"Yes," she said, "you do."

"I don't."

"You lost a wife."

I said nothing.

"And you lost a child."

"Not really. Not exactly." Rachel must have told the Rosenfelds about Laura being pregnant when she died.

"Do you know what it means to pray?"

My eyes must have widened. "To pray?"

"Not to *daven*. Not to *shuckle.* Not to go to *shul* and open a book and read along. To pray for something—to pray to God for something—that not only you can't have but that you know perfectly well you can't ever have. And to pray with all your heart for it anyway...." Her voice trailed off.

I looked into her eyes, expecting her to be on the verge of tears. But her eyes were dry. "I really do know what you mean," I said lamely.

"For a long time," she said calmly, "my sole comfort was in being crazy. I told myself that Robert would come back, that he would be reborn, that I would eventually see a baby somewhere and somehow *know* that that was my Robert come back to the world of the living. Then I moved on to an even stranger fantasy, no longer hoping so much that Robert would be reborn as a baby poised to begin a new life but rather that he would reappear in the world and resume *his* life by piggybacking along

95

in someone *else's* life as a kind of ghostly addition to that other person's soul, what my own grandma used to call a *dybbuk.* No one but me would know, of course. No one would recognize him. But I would know it was him all the same and then I would be at peace. And then when you arrived and stepped into his life —you having the same name and being the same age and having gone to the same high school and reading to the same little boy and—pardon my French—sleeping at night in the same bed with the same woman…what else was I to think other than that God had finally answered my prayer?

Was that a rhetorical question? I couldn't decide, so I chose simply to nod my head slightly in assent. Besides, I did understand. What else *could* she have thought?

Ruth was not done speaking, however. "This went on for a long time," she explained. "And you were perfect! You were the right age. If you weren't as handsome as my Robert—please don't take offense—it was only because no one could be, not because you aren't nice enough looking on your own. You earned a good living. You seemed devoted to our Carl. And we truly did want Rachel eventually to remarry and to have a life! And so I prayed to God that I was right, that you were in some magical way both yourself and himself too, both your dad's Bob and also our Robert…and that the two of you—that sounds ridiculous, I know —that the one of you who was also the two of you would look after our grandson the way our own boy surely would have on his own had he lived."

I put down my coffee cup, not sure what to say.

"And now God has answered my prayer," she continued. "I feel at peace. My son is gone, but my grandson is alive and well and thriving…and he has a good guy watching over him—and believe me that I can tell what a good person you are—and my dearest daughter-in-law has someone in her life that she can trust and that I can trust too."

Suddenly, I found my voice. "You think that I'm Robert? Or that some part of me is? I have to tell you…."

Ruth broke into my sentence. "I know who you are," she said simply. "You are the man who brought me peace, who made me able to face the future. From you I learned what prayer actually is. Which is not at all what I thought—which was that you want something and pray for it and God gives it to you or doesn't give it to you."

"It's not that?" I asked quietly.

"No," she said, "it isn't. It's when you can't breathe...and God sends you air. I knew you'd come, by the way."

"You did?" She did?

"I knew the t-shirts would be too much, that you'd have to respond. I told myself I should just phone you and invite you over for this talk, but I needed to know that you—this will sound ridiculous, I know—I needed to know that you weren't part of the fantasy, that you were on the outside, that you were the answer to my prayer and not part of the prayer itself. If I summoned you and you came, that would leave open the chance that you were just part of *my* fantasy world. I needed you to be yourself, to step aside from my own craziness, to show up on your own as a kind of visitor from the real world of non-crazy people...and to assert that you were not Robert, but that you were you. That, I can live with. I want to live with it too. The answer to my prayer is that I want you to be you so that Robert can rest in peace. But I needed you to ring the doorbell on your own, to drop in from the real world uninvited so I could be sure that I didn't just make you up. This is all crazy, I know. I can't even begin to imagine what you must be thinking. Does any of this make sense to you? I was suffocating and I prayed to God for air and He sent me you. Does that make any sense at all?

"A little bit, it does," I said. And a little bit, it did.

THAT REALLY IS
THE QUESTION

Hospitals, like bridges and prisons, have a certain permanent feel to them. And mostly they actually *are* fairly permanent features of the cities they serve: in New York, for example, it's not at all unusual to meet people well into their senior years who were born in hospitals that are still fully functioning medical centers. But that hardly reflects reality: even excluding smaller hospitals that only vanished in the sense they were taken over by larger ones, there have been scores of hospitals that have simply vanished from the cityscape in the last century or two. Some, like St. Vincent's, live on as names easily recognizable even today by most New Yorkers. But others have just evaporated from public memory: it's the rare New Yorker today who can even say what borough Deepdale General was in, or St. Anthony's. But even hospitals forgotten by all live on in the records that somehow manage to survive the decision to close them down.

In New York, those records live on in The Vincent R. Impellitteri Archive, an immense building that covers more than three city blocks in the northeastern corner of the Bronx. For many years, such records were kept in several *dozen* different warehouses and storage facilities situated across the five boroughs and were thus accessible easily to no one at all. Indeed, it was only when the Impellitteri Archive was established in 1955 that the obligation to preserve the records of defunct hospitals was addressed in any sort of organized way at all. And creating the archive was a gargantuan undertaking even *after* the site was secured: identifying the various locations in which the records had been previously stored was one thing, after all, but contracting with moving firms capable of dealing not with millions, but with *tens* of millions of brittle paper documents, and then creating even a rudimentary system for keeping them retrievably organized was another. But bringing together these countless files into one storage facility and labelling them correctly by hospital of origin was *all* that was done: once the initial funding ran out, no effort made to preserve the documents other than by warehousing them. Scores of thousands must simply have crumbled to dust in their unairconditioned new home. Nonetheless, millions of records remain available onsite for researchers and interested parties to find and possibly productively to use.

St. Mark's was a major Manhattan hospital until it closed in 1930, but its building was razed and no trace of it at all remains today at the intersection of Second Avenue and East Eleventh Street. My father—or at least the man I have always considered to be my father—was born there on February 23, 1920. He died in 1999, but lives on in in my heart and in my memory. And also in one of the millions of brittle, moldering, yellowed folders housed at the Vincent R. Impellitteri Archive of the City of New York Health Department. This is the story, then, of how exactly —and why—I found myself in that place and what I found there in the course of my single visit.

This whole expedition into the past started on a whim. Julia asked me what I wanted for my coming birthday, the big six-oh. I told her, reasonably enough, that I wanted it to be the big five-oh. This, she responded regretfully, would not be possible.

Luckily, however, she had an idea of something I'd possibly like that she actually *could* arrange for me to have.

The conversation left no real impression on me. In fact, I had forgotten all about it until I came downstairs on the morning of my birthday and found, next to a pile of birthday cards from my kids, a smallish box from Julia wrapped up in what I recognized easily as a page from last Sunday's magazine section.

"What is it?" I asked as Julia joined me in the kitchen.

"The future is yours to see," Julia responded lightly in song, channeling Doris Day. "Que sera sera."

"The future?" I honestly had no idea what she was talking about.

"Or the past," she added mysteriously. "Aren't you the one who's always saying that the past is memory and the future is fantasy...and that all that exists in any real sense is the present?"

"I may have once said that," I answered tentatively.

"Well, then," she went on, "welcome to your past. And possibly to your future."

Resigned to my fate, I opened the box and found what in retrospect I should have already expected to find: a tube to spit into and send off to progenitors.com so they could analyze my DNA and tell me which part of the world my people come—or rather, came—from.

I knew about these tests. (It was, after all, 2013, well into the age of web-based DNA banks.) And I had thought about buying one too. But then I had decided against it on the supposition that the results could only bring me grief if it turned out that I was half-Samoan and half-Basque instead of 100% Ashkenazic Jewish, which is what the grandson of four *bona fide* Jewish immigrants from Eastern Europe, two from Poland and two from Belarus, should certainly be. As the doc always says when I ask about some test that I've read about somewhere, the reasonableness of taking any test depends fully on what you imagine you might do with the results. So I rejected the idea then as something best avoided. I realized now, however, that I may well have failed actually to tell that to Julia.

"Are you pleased?"

"I'm thrilled," I said, trying to sound like I meant it.

"The future is the only true mirror of the past," she said, trying to sound like me speaking from the *bimah*.

"Yeah, yeah," I said. "But what good can come from looking into a mirror"

"You can make sure your part is straight," she answered sweetly. "Or people with hair can."

"Hardy-har-har!"

"I knew you'd love it."

And that was that. The decision was made. I had no real choice, but was also intrigued by the venture and slightly pleased for the decision to have been made for me. The next day I deposited the requisite amount of saliva in the plastic tube, sealed it with the tape provided by the company, and, using the pre-paid-for mailing label, sent it off at our local UPS Store. And that, I thought, was that.

That, however, is *never* that. You'd think I'd know that by now. And yet the will to avoid confrontation, and particularly with ourselves, is one of the strongest of all human emotions. And so, now for a second time, I put the matter out of my mind and spent the following weeks working, writing, editing...doing what I do when I'm not obsessing about my family's history, which is never. I was therefore caught just a bit off-guard when, six weeks later just as we were about to leave for a month in Jerusalem, I received an email from progenitors.com. My spit, they informed me solemnly, had been successfully analyzed and the results posted on their website. I could log on at my leisure and begin, and here I quote directly, I could "begin my journey into my family's past." Did I know at that precise moment what a bad idea this whole venture was? I may have had an inkling, but the real answer is that, no, I had no idea. I opened my phone, retrieved my log-in information, and went to the site.

Given how remarkable the whole concept of on-line DNA banks actually is, it's amazing how simple the next part actually was. I logged on. I clicked on the "DNA Results" menu, then selected "Ethnicity Estimate." And almost instantly there I was, face to face, with my genetic past.

I look as Jewish as anyone ever could. When I walk up to the Kotel in search of a *minyan* for Minchah, no one *ever* asks if I'm Jewish. Why would they? When I was in Buenos Aires a few years ago and wanted to go to *shul* on Friday night, the same security guard who was demanding to see *everyone's* identity card or passport just waved me through as though we were old pals. I had a similar experience in Prague and, even more impressively, at the Great Synagogue in Stockholm, where the security—except apparently with respect to myself—couldn't really be any tighter. And that is the background to the next part of my story, which begins with me staring blankly at the screen and reading that my DNA heritage is half Ashkenazi Jewish...and half Irish. This, I told myself, was obviously an error. And, at that, a humorous one. Samoan would have been funnier. But not that much funnier!

I've known a few Irish people over the years. I had a good friend back in college, a good guy as fully Irish-American as I was Jewish, with whom I attended my first (and last) St. Patrick's Day Parade. But one of the touchpoints of our relationship was specifically how different we were, how we liked each other precisely because we were from such dissimilar worlds. So my first response was just to laugh...and to wonder if I should track Conor down to tell him the good news! And then I closed the window, filed the email away, and resolved to leave the whole matter to deal with after our time away. It was, after all, a busy week: we were leaving for Israel in just three days and I had a lot of last-minute errands to look after. By the time I was in the barber's chair later that afternoon getting my pre-flight haircut, I had almost forgotten about the whole thing.

But, as the song goes, almost doesn't count. And so, just two nights later, when we were having a pre-departure dinner with my sister and her husband *and* with my favorite first cousin and his still-new second wife in a vegan restaurant on Avenue B, I told the story. We had all been at my cousin's wedding not four months earlier, so we were still in "welcome to the family" mode with respect to our new cousin-in-law. (She was the vegan.) I guess I must have made it sound exciting, the whole mail-your-saliva-to-the-lab thing, or at least intriguing. Although it was obvious that my results were impossible, all present found the whole concept of on-line DNA analysis arresting. And that despite the fact that, after all, it hadn't worked for me in the desired way, that my results had been impossible to the point of being funny.

The evening ended. We drove home, went right to bed, and the next morning we were up early to pack and get the house ready for our departure. That evening we were on a plane for Tel Aviv.

Four weeks later, we were back home. And it was a few weeks after that that my sister called to tell me something that I hadn't even been prescient enough to fear hearing: that she had been inspired to send her own spit to progenitors.com and that the results that had come back were identical to mine: 50% Ashkenazic European and 50% Irish. I went on-line, logged onto my progenitors account, and found her easily under the "DNA Matches" tab on my screen, where she was described as my "certain" sibling, as someone whose DNA could only be interpreted with respect to my own as being that of a full sibling. In retrospect, I know this will sound crazy, but I *still* didn't get it. Of course we were siblings, I remember thinking. The Irish thing was obviously some sort of algorithmic hiccup in their system, I suppose I thought. What else could it be?

Julia was less amused when I told her about Lisa's results over dinner that night. "There *are* other explanations," she pointed out. "Perhaps one of your grandmothers had an affair with an Irishman and then forgot to tell her husband that he wasn't the father of her baby."

I pondered that for a while, then dismissed it out of hand. "But I had four grandparents, not two," I pointed out. "So to yield a result of 50% Irish, *both* my grandmothers would have had to have slept secretly with men whose own DNA was 100% Irish. And how likely could that possibly have been? They both died the year I was in kindergarten, but I remember them both as super-traditional Jewish women, both with silvery Benson-hurst-blue hair tied up in buns at the backs of their heads. Both had strictly kosher homes. Both spoke Yiddish better than English, and both were almost fanatically devoted—this part I had heard from my parents—*both* were intensely devoted to the memory of their late husbands." I hadn't known either of my grandfathers, as Julia obviously knew. "But even if you want to argue that that kind of posthumous adulation specifically *could* be a function of pre-posthumous infidelity, are you really going to suggest that they *both* committed adultery with unadulter-ated Irishmen and then passed the fruit of their extracurricular activity off as their husbands' children?"

The idea was crazy. Julia thought so too. One, unlikely but possible. Two, so unlikely as actually not to be possible. But if the results weren't in error, then there had to be a different explanation. Could two of my grandparents have been covert Irishmen masquerading as Eastern European Jews? That theory was even loonier than the double-adultery one! And then the other shoe dropped, or rather the third one. Stephen, the newly-wed cousin we had had dinner with before leaving, phoned a couple of weeks later to say that he needed to see me and to ask if I could find a spare half-hour that evening. It sounded serious, although I had no idea what he wanted: I think I thought he was going to ask my counsel regarding some unanticipated glitch in his new marriage. I've liked Stephen, whom I still call Stevie, since we were kids. We've been through a lot together, he and I. And so, because he was one of the people in my life I always make time for, I made time for him.

"I'm done with *minyan* around 8:30. Can you come over then?"

"I'll help make the *minyan* and we can talk after," he said without any hesitation at all.

And there he was in our synagogue's chapel at 8:00 PM when I got there for our evening service. I arrived just as the service was beginning and took note of his presence without greeting him formally. Fifteen minutes later, we were in my office. Stevie looked pale, worried. I really did think this was about his marriage.

"Mike," he began tentatively, "I have to tell you something."

"You know you don't have to tell me you want to tell me something, Stevie. You can just tell me. Is there a problem at home?"

He looked surprised. "A problem? No, we're good. Things are happy."

Now it was my turn to look surprised. "That's good to hear," I said encouragingly. "So what brings you out here?" Stevie was one of those Manhattanites who never leaves New York County except when unavoidably necessary. "Not that you need a reason to visit!"

He leaned slightly toward me in his chair, looking a bit grim. "I have something to tell you," he said again. I said nothing at all, just waited for him to get on with it.

"After we all heard your story, I had the test too," he went on. "I got my results back the other day and, guess what, I'm 100% Ashkenazic Jewish."

"There's a surprise!" I responded. If there's someone in the world who looks even more Jewish than do, it's my cousin Steve. "No Irishmen lurking in your closet?"

"Mike," he said, ignoring my question, "I paid extra to have our relationship explored in more detail. You specifically permitted that when you signed on, you know."

I had no recollection of that, but who knew? Maybe I *had* agreed that my genetic results could be made public to others. "I guess," I said, suddenly unsure where this was going.

"Mike," he began again, "there's no relationship between us. We are genetically disparate. Our fathers were brothers. We have two of the same grandparents. We *can't* not have any genetic link between us. But I had them repeat the test three times and the results were uniformly that we are fully unrelated, you and me. At least biologically. That doesn't mean I don't love you. But it means we're DNA strangers."

I didn't know what to think. It sounded like more erroneous data, but that whole line of explanation—that these were all mistakes devoid of any real meaning—that whole concept that everything unexpected was simply wrong, that was getting a little far-fetched as the implications of Stevie's test slowly suggested themselves to me. We wrapped up the meeting quickly—neither of us could really think of anything to say—and I went home. I didn't mention any of this to Julia, the one person in the world from whom I have no secrets at all. But it wasn't from Julia that I was hiding a truth I could sense but not really yet see.

Over the next few days, a plan evolved. Rosh Hashanah was two weeks away. It was a busy time for me. I had my sermons mostly written, but I still had a thousand other details to look after at work. I needed *some* personal time as well to prepare internally for the days ahead. I did my best to avoid pondering the implications of Stevie's test and of Lisa's, but I did find the courage to take at least one important step forward in the course of those last weeks of a waning year: I phoned my Cousin Ian, the son of my mother's sister, and asked if he would sign up and have himself tested as well. I told him the whole story. He listened and declared himself willing, said he had been thinking of doing it anyway. I offered to pay for his test, to which offer he responded by laughing and telling me he could afford to pay his own way. As well he could—Ian has worked for Goldman Sachs for decades and lives on Park Avenue in the seventies. And that was where we left things.

He phoned back a few weeks later. He had had his test and it came back, just like Stevie's, as 100% Ashkenazic Jewish. So no surprise there. He had asked for his results to be compared to mine and there was no surprise there either: progenitors.com declared us first cousins, the children of siblings—which was precisely what we thought we were. And that left me on my own to figure out where things stood.

I worked the data. Lisa and I were definitely siblings, our matched DNA indicating a half-Jewish, half-Irish genetic background. Ian, whose mother was our mother's sister and whom progenitors identified as our genetic cousin, was fully, 100% Ashkenazic Jewish. So that means the Jewish half of our half-Jewish DNA came from my mother. But Stevie was not my biological relative at all. We had *no* shared DNA. Which means that our fathers could not have been brothers. Which is what they were. Or what we had always taken them for. And what they themselves surely thought as well. The fact that his DNA was 100% Jewish meant that his father too must have been Jewish. And that left my dad in the spotlight. Or do I mean on the hot seat? My father died in 1999, but he was suddenly back in my life...and not merely as a supportive presence surfacing from time to time in my recollective consciousness, but as an actual daily companion whom I couldn't have shaken off even had I wanted to. Not that I wanted him gone at all! Or at least not until he came clean and told me his secret.

I pondered the situation daily and darkly. The holiday season was long behind us by now. The weather was becoming distinctly brisker with each passing day. I wore a jacket to work now instead of walking to *shul* just in shirtsleeves. Julia had already begun to make some tentative plans for Thanksgiving with the kids and their various others. But a seed had been planted. And seeds, once planted, grow in fertile soil regardless of whether their planter subsequently does or doesn't wish them to.

I considered the issue a dozen different ways. The test results only really made sense if I had one Jewish parent and one Irish parent. And if my father and his brother were not actually blood relatives, that opened the door to the simplest explanation of my test results and Lisa's: that out father was as 100% Irish as our mother was 100% Jewish. Now I was really in the soup. And I couldn't see any nearby *kreplach* to hold onto.

It really must have been 110° in that corridor at the Impellitteri Archive. The poor man assigned to ushering me along, a thin black man who had introduced himself to me as Mr. Wilson, said nothing as we walked. I also said nothing. It felt like hours had passed although I knew that we had only been walking for ten or twelve minutes. And then, suddenly, we turned a corner and were facing a door featuring a bulletin board displaying a single index card held in place by four colored pushpins. The card read "St. Mark's Hospital, New York County, 1890–1931."

My heart was pounding as Mr. Wilson calmly opened the door and walked inside. I followed. Inside were three walls of rickety file cabinets, a folding table under a light fixture, and a chair.

"Knock yourself out," Mr. Wilson said jocularly.

"Thanks. How do I let you know when I want to leave?"

"There's a push-door at the far end of the corridor that leads to the parking lot. Just leave and I'll come by to lock up later." He looked up at me directly. "Don't steal anything," he said, chuckling at the very thought that anyone could possibly want any of this moldering junk enough to steal it And then he was gone. It was 9:30 in the morning. The air in the room was stale and stagnant. There was a tiny window at the far end of the room, which I opened. I stood there for a minute, breathing in the cool autumn air. And then I turned on the light fixture, then took off my jacket, and got to work.

The rest of the story you can probably guess. On February 23, 1920, there were born at St. Marks—as I knew there must have been—two baby boys, one of whom grew up to be my father.

The other was Fergus Hugh Gallagher, whose weight and length at birth were recorded in his file, as were too his parents' names, their home address, and their own parents' names. This data, of course, was from 1920. The chances that the family was still living on the same street in the Bronx were, I figured, zero. But Fergus is not at all a popular name these days. And the fact that Fergus's father's name was Séamus—an even less popular name, particularly when spelled that way—seemed beyond promising to me. I felt buoyed by my day's work, but also seriously ill at ease. I was onto something, surely. But what exactly it was, I had not yet allowed myself to say clearly...even to myself. In retrospect, I suppose I really did know. But it didn't feel that way to me at the moment, even though my expedition to the Bronx *itself* only made sense if I had already understood perfectly well how things were and what the data more or less had to confirm.

I found him easily enough. Or at least I found his death certificate: born the same day as my dad, Fergus had died in the same year as well. A little bit of digging—some Facebook, some nyc.gov, a shake of Google, a dollop of Bing—and out from the cloud stepped the late Fergus's daughter, a woman named Eileen Gallagher Doyle, who turned out to live just a few blocks from my younger son's apartment in Sunnyside. A week later, I was sitting in Eileen Doyle's kitchen.

She turned out to be a lovely woman just two or three years younger than myself. She made coffee and, as we sat across from each other, she told me the outline of her story: two brothers, a mother currently in an assisted living facility in Westchester, a husband of thirty-five years, a daughter, and two sons. And then she produced a thick photo album of her parents' early years that her mother hadn't wished to take along to her tiny room in Westchester. Bingo!

There was no possibility of any mistake. Her father looked more like my grandfather than my own father did. A lot more. And then I saw a picture of Séamus, Eileen's father's father...and he looked more like my dad than even I did. They were born the same day in the same hospital and they were the *only* two boys born that day. They were almost exactly the same weight. They were *exactly* the same length. They both had blue eyes. I suddenly had tears in *my* blue eyes, so overcome did I feel with a set of emotions I couldn't even begin to name. Eileen, I noted, was wiping away tears in hers as well.

What were we to each other? It wasn't that easy to say. We weren't cousins. We certainly weren't siblings. But saying who we weren't was distinctly easier than saying who we were. I was the son of my father just as unambiguously as she was the daughter of hers. But my father, raised by his parents as a Jew from the day they brought him home from the hospital, was clearly originally someone else. And her father, brought up from birth as a proud son of Ireland, had just as clearly once been my grandparents' baby. Briefly. That much seemed clear. But what all this meant in the larger picture of things was dramatically less easy to ferret out. Was my father who he was or who he wasn't? I wasn't even sure I understood the question, let alone felt able to answer it cogently. My father was circumcised on the eighth day of his life, was called to the Torah as a bar-mitzvah on the Saturday following his thirteenth birthday, was married to my mother under a *chuppah* by the rabbi of my grandparents' *shul*, and lived out his days as a deeply engaged, committed Jewish man. Was it all a sham? Was he really someone else? He certainly wasn't Fergus Hugh Gallagher! But if he wasn't who he was and he wasn't who he wasn't, then who exactly was he? My dad lived into his late seventies, did much good in the world, labored with my mother to create the loving home in which Lisa and I were raised, worked hard his whole life to support his family (first as a typesetter for the New York Times and then, later on, in their advertising department), and died content with his lot and grateful for all he had. So how could be possibly not have been himself?

Eventually, I told the story to the rest of the players—to Julia, of course, but also to Lisa, to Stevie, and to Ian. And I told it to my kids as well, although not right away. As the months passed, it became a part of the narrative—a part of *our* narrative—that was more interesting than earth-shattering. There was, after all, nothing at all to do about it. My dad was gone. So was Fergus. Eileen invited Julia and me over to meet her children. Eventually, we reciprocated and had her and her husband over to meet ours. We said we'd stay in touch, but I think we both knew that wasn't in the cards for either of us. I found room in my heart for Eileen and her people, for her late father who could have been mine, and for her mother. I feel certain she wished the best for us as well. We had chuckled over the weirdness that her dad had always liked eating in Jewish delicatessens and my dad had always liked Irish music, but behind the chuckles were a set of deeply existential questions. Are we who we are or who we could have been? Are we the slaves or the masters of unfulfilled potential? Are we our genes or are we our deeds? Do history and destiny have to be functions of each other, or is that just how it usually works out? Is the fault in our stars or in ourselves? With all respect to the prince of Denmark, *that* really is the question!

AN ACCIDENTAL MAN OF THE HOUSE OF ISRAEL

It wasn't ever a secret. I always knew. And even if they hadn't been completely open about it, how could I possibly not have known? My dad is six-foot-three and has a thirty-two-inch waist. My mother is five-foot-eleven. Both have jet black hair. My dad needs to shave a second time if they're going out for dinner. I, on the other hand, grew up looking like a baby Viking. I'm short, blond, stocky of build, blue of eye, round of belly. I do not look like either of my brothers, both of whom are tall and thin, and shave daily. I shave, maybe, every third day. And if I don't, my eventual beard is reddish-orange. Theirs, like Dad's, is jet black.

The whole "adopted" thing wasn't ever a real issue. When I was very young, I'm not sure I even understood what it meant precisely and, if anything, it made me feel special to know that I had been chosen—in a way that my brothers were not—to be my parents' child. Nor did it seem strange that our family had one adopted and two non-adopted children in it—it was years before I understood that we were the living example of that classic story in which a couple try forever to have a baby, then make peace with their lack of success and adopt a child, only then to proceed almost instantly to produce their own children as though there hadn't ever been a problem in the first place. Like most children, I suppose, I accepted my family as I found it, took it for granted that we existed on the terms on which we actually did exist, and did not devote time or energy to the pointless contemplation of how we might have existed in some alternate universe in which our family was configured in some partially or totally different way.

I was thirteen when the concept of having "birth parents" came into my life and I can remember the specific context in which I acquired that added insight into things. I was in summer camp. The boys in our bunk had been together since we all began sleepaway camp together when we were nine, so this was our fourth summer together. (Unlike some of the other bunks, we had neither suffered attrition nor experienced accretion in the course of our years at camp and so were exactly the same nine Jewish boys that camp had brought together in our first year.) By thirteen, we were all immediately pre- or post-pubescent. And it was in the context of our endless yakking about the various aspects of what we referenced, refined young gentlemen that we were, as "doing it," that it first struck me that if my parents chose me from among the available children of the world to be their oldest son but themselves did not actually actuate my existence with some version of the activity under endless discussion in our bunk, then some *other* couple must have actually produced me in the way that my bunkmates were so intent on puzzling out in all of its forbidden detail.

For the rest of the camp season, the notion of "birth" parents just buried itself down deep in my psyche and stayed there without prompting me to explore (or even to identify) its various corollaries, let alone to ponder the specific way any of them might somehow impact on my sense of self. But when my parents came to camp to get me at the end of August, I surprised myself—and, I'm sure, them—by not even waiting for us to get halfway home before bringing up the topic.

"Can I ask an important question?" I was alone in the backseat, happy to be able to have this conversation without having to look directly at my parents. My brothers went to a different camp, one devoted almost exclusively to sports and which went on for a few more days. If I was going to open this up for discussion, this was clearly the right moment.

"Of course," Dad answered instantly. He was a big believer in Important Questions, and often labelled his to me in that precise way so that I knew to pay attention.

"Before you were my parents, who were my...you know, my *other* parents?"

"Your *other* parents?" My mother turned to look back at me as though I had suddenly started speaking in some foreign language she couldn't account for me knowing. "You don't have any other parents. We are your parents." She sounded certain.

"I meant my first parents, the ones who gave me to you." I knew I was skating on thin ice here, but I couldn't really think of not pursuing this now that I had started in.

I'm not sure what answer I expected, but when my father spoke —and without turning around at all as he drove—it was quietly and calmly. "No one gave anybody to anyone. You were put up for adoption. We wanted to adopt a child. We met you and decided on the spot that you were the boy meant for us, so we took you home and that was that."

I was sure there was some detail I was missing, but I lacked the vocabulary to ask my question clearly. "But, you know," I mumbled, "the people...you know, the *other* people...." My voice became slightly choked as I tried to formulate my thoughts without referencing the concept of *doing it*. "...the man and the woman who, you know...." I was dying to finish my sentence, but I couldn't quite find the words. "...who, you know...you know, who...you know, the man and the woman...." I gave up. I had no real idea what I was talking about. I was sure I sounded like a total idiot, but I was still hoping my parents would rescue me by asking the question for me and then answering it as though I had asked it myself. And then, suddenly, I had a flash of unanticipated insight. "The people who gave birth to me," I said semi-triumphantly. "Those people, who were they?"

My mother turned in her seat to face me. "We don't know," she said. "Whoever they were, they weren't able to raise a child. So they arranged with an adoption agency to place their child with a family that could. That's the whole story. We had registered with that agency, so they called us to see if were still interested, which we most certainly were. But who your birth parents were, there's no way to know that now. They were probably just children themselves...."

My mom's voice trailed off as this new thought—that children could have children—insinuated itself uncomfortably in my marginally pubescent consciousness. But when I spoke, it was with conviction born mostly of ill ease. "Well, then, I guess they're happy that their kid ended up with such great parents," I said despite the fact that my mother had just said that they didn't know my parents at all, those probable children who produced me.

But my mother seemed not to notice the contradiction, so eager was she to agree. "I'm sure they were thrilled," she said.

And that, more or less, was my introduction to the concept of my conception, my fledgling inquiry stalled in its earliest stages by my parents' conviction that my birth parents' interest in me was terminated shortly after my birth when they, my birth mother and father, gave me away to the kind of agency that places parentless children with childless would-be parents. It would be years before it struck me as odd to use the phrase "parentless children" to describe children who had, not none of either, but two of each.

The whole issue lay dormant for a very long time. I finished high school and went on to Duke, where I earned a B.A. in American history, and then surprised everybody (including myself) by taking the LSAT and doing well enough to get into Yale. And it was there, in the middle of my first year, that this issue bubbled up unexpectedly and presented itself to me in a way that I hadn't ever thought to anticipate at all, let alone to consider seriously.

It all began innocently enough with a letter that showed up in my mailbox one day. This was 2010. Anything important was sent by email, so my mailbox—the one in the front lobby of my New Haven apartment house—was generally crammed with advertising flyers and take-out menus. I didn't even bother emptying it every single day. But on the Tuesday before Thanksgiving, I did...and there, amidst all the takeout flyers, was a letter addressed to me personally from an agency of some sort that I was sure I had never heard of.

The name was unfamiliar, but the envelope had a semi-official feel to it so I opened it. My birth parents, I read, wished to hear from me. But, because of the specific laws that pertained in Wyoming—which I now learned to my amazement was the state in which I had formally been adopted—because the laws of Wyoming only allowed adoption agencies to notify adopted children that their birth parents wish to hear from them and then to do nothing else at all without that child's permission, the ball was entirely in my court. Nor, oddly enough, could such adopted children actually *be* children—adopted individuals had to be over eighteen even to learn of their birth parents' interest in meeting them and only then could they decide how or whether to respond. I could therefore make the whole issue go away either by not responding at all or by responding in the negative. And, besides, I told myself, who were these people to me? Probably some goofy teenagers possessed of no clear idea about contraception who got pregnant and then solved their problem by putting their child up for adoption. Had abortion been an option? I actually went online to check and learned that there were three facilities providing abortions in Wyoming in 1987, the year of my birth. So they could have terminated the pregnancy! I am pretty liberal about abortion, but it suddenly felt personal in a way it hadn't previously as I realized that my whole existence was predicated on some unknown woman's decision not to solve her problem in that particular way.

But none of that musing spoke to the actual question at hand. Did I want to meet these people? Related to that question, but also distinct from it, was its corollary: did I want to have these people in my life? Would it be possible, I wondered, to meet them, learn a bit about the circumstances of my conception, and then go back to having nothing to do with them? That, I thought, would be ideal. They'd tell me whether I had been conceived in the back seat of a Chevy or a Pontiac. I'd tell them I was fine, that I was raised by decent, loving parents who sacrificed so that I could go to camp, have piano lessons, go to Duke and then to Yale. They'd be happy I was well. I'd be happy they were well. We'd all be happy! And then we'd go back to having nothing to do with each other, possibly after exchanging photographs of each other that they would cherish and put in a silver frame on their piano, and that I myself wouldn't quite know what to do with. Such as it was, that was my plan! And so, without giving it much more thought than that, I filled out the form (which involved merely checking a box, signing my name, and adding the date) and sent it back in the pre-paid return envelope.

In retrospect, I should have told my parents. In another age, they would have had to be part of the story already...but the agency had simply found me on Facebook and written to me in care of Yale, where someone in the Law School office had forwarded the letter to my address. And so, having jumped off a cliff without giving much thought to what happens to most people who jump off cliffs, I dropped the envelope in a mailbox on my way to class the following morning.

It was the day before Thanksgiving when I mailed that envelope. I went home for the holiday, had a nice time with my parents and brothers, and with my brothers' girlfriends and some friends from *shul* that my parents invited to the house for the holiday. I slept in my old room, wore my high school pajamas, avoided reading anything to do with schoolwork, and basically just vegged out for a few days without doing much other than eating. And we ate a lot! My mom had a whole different crowd for Friday night—two of her girlfriends and their husbands, plus some of my brothers' friends in town for the holiday weekend and one of our recently widowed neighbors. So that was fun—more eating, more drinking, more staying up late. I actually went to *shul* with my Dad on Saturday morning, partially because he asked me to and partially because I myself was curious to meet the new rabbi and to greet all the people I knew would be there and who had been part of the cast of characters that formed the backdrop to my mostly happy adolescence.

I drove back to New Haven Sunday night. The next day I was back in class. Things felt totally normal. But the following Friday, just ten days after sending the form back, I opened my mailbox and had yet another letter from the Albany County Family Services Center in Laramie.

Finally taking the matter seriously, I went upstairs and made a pot of coffee, then sat down at the kitchen table to open the envelope.

Inside was a piece of legal-sized ruled yellow paper clearly torn off a pad. And on it was written a message for me: "We would like to meet you," the note said. "But we don't want to disrupt your life or upset you. If you would like to talk to us, please call us at the number below." That was the whole message. At the bottom of the page were two names, Bill and Betty, each followed by a telephone number. For some reason, I liked the fact that they hadn't given their last name. Again, the ball had landed in my court.

I waited a few days, then called Bill's number. He answered on the first ring.

"This is Sam Kaufman," I said.

"Who?"

"You wrote to me," I stammered, having assumed he would just somehow know who I was.

"Is this a sales call?" He sounded like he meant it, which was funny since I would probably have said the exact same thing had the shoe been on the other foot.

"No," I said, "this is not a sales call. The Albany County Family Services Center forwarded your letter to me and I'm calling you because you asked me to." I could feel the emotion rising in my voice. "This is probably a mistake," I said quickly and hung up.

I had no idea what to do. Should I call back? Would he know who I was this time? I felt like I had opened a door and then shut it in someone's face for no obvious reason. All I had had to do was to do nothing at all if I didn't want to speak to this man. So, really, this was all my fault. I filled out the form. I made the call. I told him my name. Why was I being such a huge baby about this? I redialed.

He picked up on the first ring. He apologized, although he surely didn't have any reason to. I also apologized, mumbling something about cold feet. And then we began to talk.

He and Betty were in high school when she got pregnant. She wouldn't consider an abortion. She gave birth, gave up the baby, and was back in twelfth grade less than ten days later. They didn't tell any untruths to anyone; everybody knew she had gotten pregnant unintentionally and given up her baby for adoption. It was all anyone talked about for a week or two. And then some new scandal broke, and Betty and her baby turned into old news. Eventually, everybody moved on.

Bill and Betty married when they were both in college and went on to have two sons, Albert and Arnold, currently in tenth and twelfth grades at Whiting High School in Laramie and both of them, apparently, related to me in precisely the same way as to each other. Albert had red hair like his father; Arnold had blond hair like their mother. I apparently had a full second family...or, rather, a first one that weirdly mirrored my second one, complete with two parents and two brothers. Where this was all going, I had no idea.

I told him a bit about my life. The whole Jewish thing seemed to land with a thud, but I couldn't think of what to say when he said that he hadn't ever considered that I might not be a Christian and so just moved the conversation along in a different direction.

He stopped short of inviting me to Wyoming, saying he needed to tell his wife about our call. I didn't ask if he was going to share the details of our conversation with his other sons and he didn't say. To say the truth, I was relieved—there was a lot of information for me to process as well, plus I needed to decide to what extent I wanted to involve my parents—my real parents—in any of this, or whether I wanted to involve them at all.

We hung up without making specific plans to be in touch again. But I think we both knew that neither of us was done with the other.

The weirdness started within a few weeks.

First, Arnold, the twelfth-grader, called. He sounded friendly enough on the phone, although he insisted on calling me Samuel even after I made it clear that I am only really ever called Sam. He asked me if I ever went to church, an odd question that meant either that his—our—father hadn't told him about the Jewish thing...or, more ominously, that he had. I told him, no, I didn't go to church. I went to synagogue.

"Synagogue," he repeated, stumbling over the word slightly as though he had never said it out loud before.

"Yes," I said. "Like Jesus," I added, I thought helpfully.

"Jesus?" he asked.

"Yes," I answered. "Wasn't Jesus a Jew? So where would he have *davened* if not in a synagogue?" I was almost enjoying this, but somehow without understanding how offended young Arnold was becoming with each successive misstep.

"Jesus of Nazareth was the son of God," Arnold replied. He sounded sure.

"Well then," I replied wittily, "then he was adopted into a Jewish family, wasn't he? Just like me!"

"Only his father adopted him; his mother bore him." This was getting weirder by the minute. I knew what he meant, more or less. But I wasn't an expert on Christian theology, just a Jewish guy in law school who liked going to *shul* with his Dad back home on the Island and occasionally in New Haven too. And he was sounding more and more peculiar as we moved forward in our conversation, almost as though he were reading from a script.

"Okay," I acquiesced. "But his dad adopted him, right? Just like mine!"

The conversation ended shortly after that exchange. And I *still* didn't quite understand what I had gotten myself into.

The next week it was Albert's turn, the tenth grader.

"Hello, brother," he began when I picked up the phone.

I had noted the area code and knew it had to be one of them. "Arnold, is that you?" I asked.

"No, this is your brother Albert."

That was "brother" twice in two sentences. I was getting a very uneasy feel about this whole thing and decided to be clear. "I have two brothers. Their names are Joseph and Joel. You are the son of my birth parents, but I'm not sure there's such a thing as a 'birth brother.' We are related genetically, but…" I inhaled sharply both to gain a moment but also to steady myself. "…we are not brothers. Not brothers at all! For one thing, I've never even met you. I wouldn't know you if I were standing in front of you."

Young Albert was not one to be put off easily. That, I had to hand to him. "Arnold told me that you are of the House of Israel," he said weirdly, avoiding the whole concept of "birth brothers." But I was focused on the "House of Israel" thing instead. Who talks that way? Was he so unnerved by the thought of saying the word "Jewish" out loud?

"Here's the story, Al. I am not your brother, nor am I your brother's brother. I am *my* brothers' brother. And, yes, I am of the House of Israel, a Jewish man who goes to law school and, occasionally, to synagogue." I sounded sure of myself, but deep inside I could feel some niggling doubts beginning to assert themselves. Was I entirely who I was—who I am—or was some tiny part of me also who I wasn't? Suddenly, I wasn't quite sure.

"Can we be friends?" He sounded a bit pathetic, almost as though he had gone off-script to say something from his heart. But he also sounded, for the first time, like a nice person, albeit like a very young one.

"No," I said, his niceness somehow prodding me back into reality. "We can know each other a little. We can stay in touch from a distance. But I have a family, just like you do. And I don't need another anymore than I suppose you do." It was becoming increasingly clear to me with every sentence what a huge error of judgment I had made starting in with these people. They were something to me, but not—I knew this clearly now—they were *not* my family. And no one's cause was going to be well served by obscuring that fact.

He hung up quickly after that last exchange. I thought I was done. I had now spoken with my two full brothers and with my birth father. Betty was free to call too, I supposed, but she hadn't and at this point that was entirely fine with me.

And then the bombardment started. Calls, including ones late at night, started coming from all sorts of local church groups near New Haven. Books, including bizarrely not one but several Hebrew-language editions of the New Testament, and an endless number of pamphlets began appearing in my mailbox at school. My Yale inbox was suddenly clogged with emails from all sorts of young men who thought that we could possibly to go church together or even, if I were inclined, just for a walk. I noticed after a while that I was hearing only from men, never from women. I suppose that was part of the concept—they were plying me with comradeship, with the prospect of bonding intimately with pals who would stick with me through thick and thin, with manly intimacy. Embedded in all their calls was a kind of mistrust of women, I thought—or, at the very least, the peculiar notion that friendship is at its most profound a same-sex thing and thus, in their (no doubt) homophobic minds, the precise opposite of romance. At first, I was amused by the attention. But as the phone calls and emails became increasingly creepy and unsettling, I knew that I had to take a stand. And so I called Bob's number, which went directly to voice mail. I didn't record a message. And then, before my courage ran out, I dialed Betty's number. She answered on the first ring.

"This is Sam Kaufman," I said clearly. "Do you know who I am?"

"I know," she said.

I was all ready to tell her why I was calling—to ask her to step in to prevent her boys or her husband or whoever had been masterminding this crazy effort to help me find my way to church—but before I could get a word out, she began to cry. At first, she was sobbing so hard that I couldn't really say anything at all. But then she calmed down and was apparently waiting for me to say something.

"Betty," I said, "I'm calling because I believe that Bill and the boys have embarked on something that I'm sure they think is very good, but which is actually very bad. And wholly unwanted. I don't know if they've actually committed any crimes by signing me up for this endless harassment, but I intend to find out if it doesn't stop." I knew I was sounding unkind, but I felt I had to be clear. I had begun to keep a log of phone calls and emails a few days after they began, and there were *already* over 100…and this was in a matter of less than one single month.

"Harassment," she half-asked, half-said, almost as though she didn't know the word.

"Harassment," I echoed. "It's clear to me that you bore me, that Bill fathered me. But you made a conscious decision to let other people raise me. And, guess what? Other people raised me. And they brought me into their faith, now my faith, which was their absolute right…and which, just for the record, is exactly what you and Bill would have done with a child the two of you adopted. This whole Jewish thing is not a role I'm playing in some play. It's who I am and what I am…and I'm not looking to escape into some alternate universe that could only exist if the one we actually inhabit didn't. And that's why this has to stop."

"Or you won't be our son?" Now she was sounding even more pathetic than poor little Albert who only wanted me to be his friend.

"I am not your son," I said, trying not to sound even slightly equivocal. "I'd like to come to Laramie and meet you. I'd like to exchange photographs and hear about each other's lives. But I don't need four parents."

"You won't believe this," she said, ignoring that last comment, "but I've prayed for you every single day since the day you were born. I didn't know where you were. I didn't know who was raising you. But I prayed every day that you were safe and that you were happy. And I prayed that you would grow up to be a man confirmed in his faith, a man *of* faith."

"I am not a man of no faith," I said calmly. "I'm just not a man of your *specific* faith. So your prayers actually *were* answered."

And now we got down to the real item on today's agenda. "I

don't want you to go to hell," she said quietly. "I'm praying for you to be saved."

"Saved? Saved from what?"

"When you die, I don't want my baby to go to hell," she said again, her voice turning teary.

"If I go to hell, it will because I wasn't a good Jew, not because I wasn't a good Christian," I slightly surprised myself by saying. "And certainly not because I didn't belong to your particular church." I was clearly on a roll. "And I'm not your baby," I added for good measure. "And don't tell me that you're praying for me. You're praying for yourself, for you to get what you want from a child you handed off to other people without knowing anything at all about them," I continued, the rising tide of anger in my voice audible now. "Prayer isn't when you ask God to undo your own past by altering someone else's future because you don't have a time machine and can't do it yourself. For prayer to be real, it has to be selfless." This, from a man who, up until about a minute earlier would have answered in the negative if anyone asked him if he took the concept of prayer all that seriously.

For a long while, she said nothing at all. And then she finally spoke. "Good-bye," she said. "I'll never stop praying for you." And then she hung up without waiting for me to respond.

I never heard from any of them again. Eventually, the phone calls and emails stopped. I dropped all the New Testaments off at a Goodwill Store not far from my apartment. Not seeing any good that could possibly come of it, I never shared any of this with my Mom or Dad. Nor did I tell the story to my brothers.

I was altered by the whole experience, and in ways I couldn't possibly have anticipated. My ears perk up whenever I hear anyone mention Wyoming. For a while, I wondered about the meaning of identity…and what the precise relationship was between who I am and who I could have been. I'm happy enough being myself. But when I look in the mirror, I don't always see just my own face—sometimes I can also see the ghost of the other me, the me who could have been and maybe even should have been, the one raised by high school sweethearts who married as teenagers and found a way to move forward in life with a baby they didn't abandon to his fate but whom they nurtured and embraced and loved. I see the ghost of that non-person, that non-Jew, that non-me...and then I blink a few times and he's gone...and in his place is just me, an accidental man of the House of Israel. I don't think of them all that often. But when I stand up to say my prayers in *shul*, I always pray for the family that might have been and never was, and for the people who accidentally gave me life and then stepped back so I could meet my own destiny. I suppose there's irony in the fact that, after giving poor Betty such a hard time about praying for me, I've ended up praying for them! And I mean it too, which surprises me still, even after all these years.

NOT WORDS, JUST NUMBERS

"That shirt you're wearing?" Aunt Lena sounded sure of herself. But then again, I reminded myself, Aunt Lena generally sounded sure about everything.

"Your aunt is right," my uncle chimed in, apparently feeling the need formally to agree with his wife despite the fact that he didn't ever disagree with her, or at least hadn't in the ten and a half weeks I had lived with them.

I looked at them both, then looked down at my arm. The radio was on. (The radio was *always* on.) The man on the radio had just announced another scorcher. It was just eight in the morning, the man noted, and the temperature was *already* in the mid-eighties. And it was going to be up over one hundred degrees by early afternoon, hot even by Brooklyn standards for this time of year. The air was going to be stagnant and oppressive. People with breathing problems, the man said, should stay home. Everybody, actually, who had no specific reason to go out into the heat should stay home. I myself suddenly *wanted* to stay home, only that was clearly not in the cards. And, I reminded myself quickly, it wasn't even true. I didn't *really* want not to go. Today, after all, was going to be the first day of the rest of my life...a cliché, to be sure, but in this specific instance entirely true: it was the day after Labor Day, I was seventeen years old, and I was about to begin tenth grade. I wasn't entirely sure yet who James Madison was, but I was going to his high school. And

I was going to succeed too, I told myself...even if my English was still a bit shaky back then and I was clearly going to be the oldest tenth grader the school had ever seen.

I was already nervous enough that morning, so the last thing I needed or wanted was a confrontation with my aunt. I knew no one at all at James Madison, not a soul. And although I really had learned a lot of English since my arrival the previous June, I hadn't actually made any friends my own age in New York. Aunt Lena and Uncle Nathan were grand people, to be sure. And generous ones too, taking me in and making me feel as though I belonged there, as though it was *they* whose great good fortune it was to have *me* living under their roof, as though somehow *I* had done *them* a huge favor by moving in with no specific plans to move out in the foreseeable future.

They were actually my great-aunt and my great-uncle. Aunt Lena was my grandfather's youngest sister, the sole survivor—other than myself—of their entire family. Their own children, my second cousins Steven, Lawrence, and William, were grown men out of the house for years. Larry and Willy lived nearby, were married, and had families of their own; Steven, divorced for longer than he had been married and apparently—and to his parents' ongoing irritation—in no great hurry to remarry or to reproduce, lived on his own in a studio apartment on First Avenue in Manhattan. They were all friendly towards me, and kind. None of them seemed irritated to think of me occupying the bedroom they had shared as boys in their parents' apartment. Just to the contrary, they appeared to be happy to have someone present in the flat to keep an eye on their aging parents. And someone who had no real possibility of moving out precipitously suited the bill to a T as far as they were concerned.

The boys—this was how they were invariably referenced, their adulthood not so much unnoticed as simply ignored, all three also understood all too well what it meant to my aunt to have me in her life. Aunt Lena's parents, my great-grandparents, died on their own years before the war, but she, my aunt, was the only one of her five siblings to emigrate and, in fact, the only one *ever* to have left Poland, let alone permanently. How I myself survived is an entirely different story that I am still hoping to write about one day in detail. But here I will just say that I was the only one who made it, the sole survivor among the forty-four of us put on the trains on October 23, 1943, and even *I* was half dead when I was finally liberated. (To sharpen that image, I was five-foot-eleven and weighed less than eighty pounds when I was first examined by one of the US Army doctors assigned to our camp. And I was among the more robust people still alive in that place when the cavalry finally arrived.) The rest of the story I'll also leave over for another time—but the short version is that I was interned for a while at Buchenwald itself, then transported to a series of DP camps (including Föhrenwald, where I stayed for a full eighteen months), then helped finally to make contact with my aunt and uncle in Brooklyn. I knew Aunt Lena existed all along, of course. My parents mentioned their American auntie all the time. But where she lived exactly and how I might actually go about finding her, I had no idea at all. (Nor, of course, did she herself have any reason to think any of us survived once the truth about the deportations and the camps became known.) But then, with the help of the Joint and the Red Cross, I eventually did make contact. At first, she could hardly believe I was alive. (For the record, I could hardly believe it either.) We corresponded, obviously, in some mash-up of Yiddish and Polish, but it was clear to me from her letters that she had lost her fluency in both—Aunt Lena had been in America for more than a quarter-century at that point in her life—and was only really comfortable in English. Maybe that was why I devoted myself so intensely to my language studies, particularly after it was made clear to me that my American visa would eventually come through and that I would be permitted soon after that to step through the golden door into a new world and a new life.

I was thirteen when we were deported and still not sixteen at liberation. (I've always been tall for my age and I survived partially because I was able easily to pass for older. But now that there's no need to lie about it, I can just tell the truth: I was born on the first night of Chanukah in 1929, which made me thirteen in October 1943 and fifteen when we were liberated in April of 1945.) I'm eighty-four now, but in the summer of 1947, as I sat in my aunt and uncle's kitchen waiting for my aunt to express herself more clearly, I was still only seventeen. To say that I was a fish out of water is really to say the very least. I was a citizen of no country. (I had a *laissez-passer* instead of passport, but it merely noted that I was a stateless person under the temporary protection of the European Command of the United States Armed Forces and its Supreme Commander, General Dwight David Eisenhower.) I had never been in an automobile other than a taxi. I had never lived in a home with a television set. I hadn't ever attended a baseball game or even held a baseball. I hadn't ever owned a necktie, and still didn't. In fact, I owned nothing at all, unless you counted the stuff my aunt and uncle had bought for me since my arrival and the Passover Haggadah that Rabbi Schacter had given me in Buchenwald to keep and which I had indeed kept with me ever since after using it one single time at that famous month-late seder the rabbi conducted in May of 1945 not for the descendants of slaves but for people who just weeks earlier had *themselves* been slaves...and, at that, to a Pharaoh far more diabolical than his ancient forebear could possibly ever have imagined.

And yet, despite everything, there I was at my Aunt Lena's kitchen table wearing a crisp, short-sleeve white shirt and blue trousers and drinking a cup of black coffee while contemplating my first day at school. (At seventeen, I really should have been starting twelfth grade, but, having not attended a school in years and not being perfectly fluent back then in English, the principal had determined that I should start off in tenth grade and see where that took me. Truth be told, I probably should have started in elementary school, but they could hardly send a boy my age to school with eleven-year-olds and tenth grade seemed like the most reasonable compromise. So tenth grade it was.) I was some combination of nervous and excited, but also a bit stunned: the last time I had had a normal breakfast at a normal kitchen table on my way to a normal school I had also had two parents, two sisters, a brother, and an army of aunts, uncles, and cousins. Were they really all gone? Even to me, it seemed unimaginable that of them all only I was left. I tried to put the catastrophe that had befallen my family—and every other family I grew up with—I tried to put it all out of my mind, to focus on the good, on the future, on my incredibly good fortune to have survived. I listened to the radio, tuned as always to WEVD. I ate a piece of buttered toast with my coffee, then another. I suddenly remembered Rabbi Schacter saying that the greatest of all the commandments was to choose life and I found myself hoping that our paths would cross again, his and mine, and that I would one day have a chance to show him that I had done as he had said. I had just put a third piece of bread in the toaster and was pouring myself a second cup of coffee when Aunt Lena appeared in doorway and, without pausing even to wish me a good morning or to ask how I slept or to wish me good luck in school, turned her withering gaze to my bare arms and said, in her inimical style, "That shirt you're wearing?"

Standing right behind her was my uncle, whose response ("Your aunt is right") made it clear that he too had understood her question to be far more of a command to be obeyed than a question actually to be answered.

Nonetheless, the path of least resistance seemed simply to answer the question. "Yes," I said, "I am." What other shirt did she think I might be wearing than the one I had on? It was a nice shirt too. More to the point, it was one that Aunt Lena herself had bought for me! Wasn't this how American boys dressed for school? Was I supposed to be wearing a tie? (She hadn't suggested buying me one and I hadn't thought to ask.) Or was there some sort of color code connected with the specific grade one was entering? Were white shirts only for teachers? I had no idea. But if that was the case, then why had she bought this particular shirt for me in the first place?

Aunt Lena sat down at the table, saying nothing. She poured herself a coffee, then stirred some sugar into it. She herself was dressed for the day in a powder blue blouse with a bow at the neck and a slim tan skirt. (Even in her older years, my great-aunt was a handsome woman with a good figure she had no compunction at all about showing off.) I wasn't sure what I was supposed to say next, if indeed I was supposed to say anything at all. She had asked a question and I had answered it. There was, however, clearly more to be said. She drew her chair close to the table, then reached up to turn down the volume on the radio.

"A horse can only move in one direction at a time," she said.

I nodded thoughtfully, but said nothing.

"Forwards it can move or backwards," she continued undeterred, "but not both ways at once."

Clearly, she was trying to tell me something. But what was it?

"You see my point?"

"No," I said honestly, "not really. I don't know much about horses."

Aunt Lena looked directly into my eyes. "About horses I'm not talking," she said. "I'm talking about you."

Slowly, I began to catch her drift. And when I lowered my eyes to my left forearm, I could almost feel her gaze joining mine as we both contemplated my number.

For as long as I was at Auschwitz, my number was my name. That was how it worked and that was probably also how it had to work—for the dehumanization process the Germans put in place to be as effective as they intended it to be, the inmates had to be reduced to mere numbers, to nameless ciphers in a ledger book, to cogs in a machine to be replaced without fuss, not repaired, when broken. I don't want to tell here about my experiences in the camps, and particularly not about my first days at Auschwitz. Years ago I did one of those Spielberg interviews and didn't hold much back, so here let me just say that having no name was emblematic, at least in my mind, of everything we had to endure: the prisoner had no possessions, no rights, no freedom, no dignity…and no name. I wasn't *assigned* my prisoner number, I *was* that number. And that number was embedded in my mind no less indelibly than it was tattooed on my forearm. It wasn't my name and it wasn't exactly *who* I was, but in a real and brutal way it was *what* I was. And it was fully visible on my forearm for all to see who cared to look from that first day on and ever since.

Thinking back on that scene in my Aunt Lena's kitchen after all these years, it's hard to believe so much time has passed. Nowadays we're used to thinking of Shoah survivors as older people, but there were huge numbers of us in the late 40's who were still teenagers, some who were really just children. We had seen more in our brief lifetimes—more misery, more brutality, more beatings, more torture, more death—than most normal people living normal lives see in normal lifetimes. That, obviously, is a good thing…for all those other people. But it also made us into freaks even in our own eyes. I remember feeling that way in a thousand different ways, and particularly *after* I found my place at Madison High and had a gang of friends I hung around with. They were nice guys, good guys. They had normal lives, had had happy childhoods. They had at least some living grandparents, and to a man they had parents and siblings. They liked baseball, liked talking about girls, liked choosing the cars they were going to own when they got older and made some money. They were, in short, normal American guys on the cusp of manhood enjoying each other's company for as long as they could stay together. Of the misery of the world they knew almost nothing. They thought they had lived through a war because they knew somebody—or at least *of* somebody—who had died fighting in Europe or the Pacific, but they themselves knew death only at a distance. They felt rooted to their place, comfortable in their skin, at home in the world that they were growing up in and truly *were* at home in. They were, in a word, normal citizens of their time and place. It was me who didn't belong, who couldn't quite figure out how much to say or even *what* to say.

Eventually, I tried to tell them. They were curious about my past—we were friends, after all— but they also didn't want to know. Or at least they didn't want to know much. For a long time, my feelings were hurt by their lack of more than formal interest. But now that I think clearly back on how things were, I realize that the whole thing had more to do with me being unrealistic than with them being harsh or cruel or uncaring. Even Sam and Izzy—who were my closest friends until they both died not eighteen months apart a few years ago—even *they* didn't want to hear my story, not really, not in detail. But now that I consider the whole scene from the vantage point not of years or decades but *scores* of years, I can see that the whole thing was simply unfathomable, and *way* too much for teenagers used to *schmoozing* away long afternoons over cigarettes and coffee to assimilate into their sense of what life was or could be. These guys were interested, in order, in girls, cars, and baseball. Were they supposed *also* to want to know what it was like hearing trains in the distance and knowing, especially towards the end when the ramp selections ended, that not a single passenger—not even the children—would still be alive by nightfall? I thought then that they should have wanted to know everything, but now I find it more amazing that they wanted to hear any of it at all. In my naiveté, I thought they were shallow while I was this sophisticated witness to history. But in retrospect I can see that they were just normal guys and *I* was the visitor from Mars whose ability to breathe at all on earth was the surprising part of the story, not my earthling hosts' capacity to breathe easily on their own planet.

And, of course, I was also—in addition to being a survivor of deportations and beatings and extermination camps and death marches—in addition to all that, I was also a seventeen-year-old boy. I too liked sports, liked thinking about girls, liked speculating about the car I was going to drive once I had the income to support that kind of extravagance. By rights I should have been several people rather than just one person. And yet I was just me, just one single person, just myself. In retrospect, I can say easily that it was that *specific* piece of complicated reality that constituted the real background to the talk Aunt Lena and I had over breakfast early in the morning on Tuesday, September 2, 1947, as I prepared to attend my first day of school in America and she wished to get me to change my shirt by observing, just a bit obscurely, that horses are able only to walk in one direction at a time.

"You're talking about me?" She was talking about me?

"About you I'm talking. About you and what you've been through."

"I have to leave in a few minutes." My aunt and uncle lived on East Twenty-Second Street between Avenue R and Avenue S. It was going to take me about five minutes to walk to school if I was going to get there on time and it was already eight o'clock. I had been told to arrive at 8:20 and not to be late.

"Change your shirt. Put on the blue one, the one we bought at Macy's in the city."

"I don't look good this like?" I thought I looked fine. "*You* bought me this shirt!"

"You look good. You *are* good. I bought that shirt for you to wear in *shul* under a jacket. But wearing it without one, like this, with your arm exposed...with that that number...that damned number...." Her voice trailed off. Together we looked at the outer side of my exposed forearm, at the six digits that somehow encapsulated everything there was to say about who I was, about *what* I was. I remembered everything about that first day, about being separated from the others and from my parents, about being shaved and having that number burnt into my flesh. I didn't fully understand that I was one of the lucky ones, that there was at least some chance I would live to see the next dawn, that I had somehow been chosen (at least temporarily) for life.

"It's who I am," I finally said, not sure if even I knew exactly what I meant.

"It's who you were," Aunt Lena said quickly. "But it's not who you're going to be."

"But I'm not who I'm going to be, am I? I'm who I am right now."

"You want to be more than that number."

I said nothing.

"People need to see you, to see your face, to see your eyes," she continued. "But who will be able to look past that number? And then you'll never stop being a prisoner."

We didn't usually use that word, "prisoner." Truth be told, we hardly ever talked about the war at all, preferring to trade stories about the people we both loved from when things were normal and life was good. But we did speak about it now and then. Uncle Nathan never showed any interest. But Aunt Lena knew the whole story, having made me tell it all from beginning to end shortly after I arrived precisely so that we could then not discuss it again.

I can still remember that day clearly even after all these years. It was a couple of weeks after I arrived. We were still communicating in some made-up language of our own, mostly consisting of Yiddish and Polish with some English and some German thrown in for good measure. (I had no idea how to say some of the camp words in any language but German.) Uncle Nathan was out for the day—I can't recall where—and it was just my great-aunt and myself at home. And I really did tell her everything, holding nothing back. She said nothing, preferring to sit in her chair and smoke cigarette after cigarette while she listened intently. And then I was done and that, more or less, was that. We occasionally returned to this or that detail, but we mostly left the topic be. It was what it was. I was who I had become. Aunt Lena needed to know what had happened to her family—you have to remember that there *were* no historians of the Shoah out there in 1947, no reliable authors whose books about the camps you could buy in a bookshop or consult in the library, nothing but the personal accounts of individual survivors you could listen to or not listen to, believe or not believe, accept or reject—but now that she knew she didn't need to hear it again. And yet the fact that she did not need or wish to hear my story a second time did not mean that hearing it that one time hadn't altered her dramatically. Her sense—I can see this now, although I'm sure I didn't fully get it back then—her sense of who *she* was had been permanently altered by learning who *I* was and what had befallen me. And from all that came her resolve not to let me exist as nothing more than the latter-day version of the prisoner I had once been, to insist that I somehow morph forward through the present into the future rather than to live on merely as a living echo of the past.

In her defense, it took us survivors a long time to figure this out, to make ourselves comfortable with being both who we were and who we eventually became. All these years later, of course, it feels inevitable that we were eventually going to find a way to integrate a past that involved worrying about the possibility of being murdered with a present that involved worrying about the possibility of not getting into the best college. But it didn't feel that way back then, not by a long shot. And one plausible avenue into the future—I can see this now clearly—one *rational* path forward could indeed reasonably have involved simply moving past the past and treating the whole thing like a bad dream to be woken up *from*, then gotten *over*, then forgotten. I'm sure there are plenty who chose to travel along that path into their new lives. I know there are, actually. But it wouldn't have worked for me and even back then I think I *already* knew that I myself had no choice but to allow the past to flow through me—and through my story—into the future, into *my* future.

"I stopped being a prisoner on April 11, 1945."

"So why look like what you're not?"

I thought for a long moment, trying to figure out how to say any of this in English. "Because it's not *about* who I am. It's about who I was, and who I was is who I'll always be. Because the present is a moment and the future is a dream—it's really only the past that truly exists." Where that came from, who knows? But it's stayed with me for all these years. And I still think that. I really do. "But what that all adds up to is that life…life *itself* can only be…that life is just a prayer."

Aunt Lena put down her coffee cup and looked into my eyes. Her own eyes were sapphire blue and it was just then that I finally understood how kind and how good she was. "Life is a prayer?" There was no trace of mockery in her voice and I could hear easily that she was asking her question guilelessly and without pretense, that she merely wished me to say what I meant more clearly.

"Life is a prayer," I repeated. "A prayer for the future, but also a prayer for the past. Or maybe the real way to say it is that life is both those things at once, that they're both the same thing, that we live for a moment in the present and by living forward into the next moment…by *surviving* into the future…we make our lives into prayers that the past be justified, that the future reflect the best of what we've lived through in the past, that the future come to justify the past and give it depth and purpose in the same way that the past explains the future and gives it its real meaning." Where any of this was coming from, I had no idea.

But I meant it. And the ease with which I was expressing in English ideas I could barely understand in any language only made me surer of myself and less willing to cave in.

"The past is gone." Aunt Lena's voice quivered slightly, but I could see that she had been waiting a long time to say that to me clearly and unequivocally.

"The past is never gone. If it was gone, where would my parents live?" My voice sounded strange, even to me.

My dear Aunt Lena reached out and took my hands. I could see that her eyes were brimming over as, finally, she wept for her sisters and for her brother, for their children and their families, for all who had lived and died. I rarely cried, but I too felt my cheeks wet with tears. It was a truly cathartic moment for me, and all the more so for having been wholly unanticipated.

"And this prayer," Aunt Lena asked me, her voice soft but clear, "this prayer that is your life, does it have words?"

"Not words," I said from some distant platform, from outer space, "just numbers."

With no fight at all left in me and more than aware that I was going to be late for my first day of school if I didn't walk out of the apartment within the next three or four minutes, I got up from the table. I went to my bedroom, took off my nice white shirt, and replaced it with a blue shirt my aunt had *also* bought me at Macy's on Herald Square in Manhattan. I unbuttoned the cuffs but didn't roll the sleeves up high enough to expose my number, telling myself—and, as far as I can recall, in that moment truly believing it—that some prayers really are best said quietly and in private.

There wasn't time for a long discussion. I had to go. I gave my aunt a kiss on the cheek. And then I was out the door and into the rest of my life.

That first day at school was confusing and a bit overwhelming, but I got the hang of high school quickly enough and by Thanksgiving could hardly remember *not* being an American high school student. By then, of course, it was already plenty cool enough for everybody to be wearing long-sleeved shirts anyway. But once springtime came and the weather began to warm up, I came home from soccer practice one day to find a gift from my aunt waiting for me on my bed: three *new* short-sleeved white shirts, each still in its Macy's wrapper and each one a reminder that we had both been wrong the previous fall, that prayers, like speech itself, can be *conceptualized* within the heart but only truly *heard* in public, in the world. And that that applies to prayers that cannot by their nature be spoken aloud at all, merely put out there so that the world—and the God to Whom they are addressed—can take note of their reality and possibly even respond.

KEEPING FAITH
WITH THE DEAD

It was a day of firsts for me. I hadn't ever been in Dannemora before. (I'm not even sure I knew where it was before I began to make plans to head up there.) I hadn't ever been inside a men's maximum-security prison. I certainly hadn't ever met James Donniger before. I'd been to the Adirondacks—my parents used to take me there for a family week after camp was over and before the school year began—but that was a very long time ago and I hadn't been back since I'd stopped going to sleepaway camp at age fourteen.

I drove into town from the east on route 374, then stopped at the Dunkin' Donuts on Cook Street. I bought a coffee and sat down on one of the orange molded-plastic benches to drink it as I attempted to gather my thoughts. It wasn't that complicated a message, I told myself. Just one that would either make a doomed man's life even more miserable...or grant him solace in a way he could surely not even remotely be expecting. Either possibility seemed plausible. It struck me that Dunkin' Donuts coffee used to be stronger and tastier, and I found myself floating away from the real issue I needed to consider and wondering instead if their coffee was just more weakly brewed now than it once was or if they were possibly using a cheaper coffee bean instead.

I've been at Prestigunquit now for six years. Before that I served congregations in Washington State and in California, but I began my career in the rabbinate in New York and it was in those first years of service, while I was still in Queens, that this story really begins. I was young and untried in the profession when I first began. Some of what I needed to figure out came more or less intuitively. Some stuff I just made up. For more vexing issues, I had a few older and more experienced colleagues nearby I felt comfortable calling for advice. So it wasn't as though I was *entirely* on my own. Plus, I had Deena to bounce ideas off of, and that counted for a lot, particularly in the early years of our marriage.

Slowly, I got to know the members of my congregation. Some were Shabbos regulars; others were far less frequently seen in the sanctuary. Some were faithful attendees at my classes; others came only rarely or never at all. And some were absent entirely, congregants who paid their dues because they wished to support the community but who apparently felt no compelling need ever actually to set foot inside the building. And then there was Jackie. Her mother, Shelly Zuckergood, was an active member. There had once been a Mr. Zuckergood, but by the time I arrived in my first pulpit he was so long gone that almost no one could even recall his first name. There was a son too, Danny, but he lived in Manhattan and showed up only on the rarest occasions. Jackie, on the other hand, never showed up at all...but for that she had an excellent excuse: she was at the time incarcerated in a state prison for having done what her own mother referenced only obliquely as "some stuff."

Shelly met me early on and asked me point blank if I could or would visit her daughter at the Taconic Correctional Facility up in Westchester. Not having the nerve to ask why a nice Jewish girl from Queens would be spending time in a state prison, I agreed easily. It was not even a full hour's drive away. Why *wouldn't* I go? Wasn't that my job?

The first time was the worst, but that was mostly because I had no idea what I was getting into. It wasn't the frisking or the metal detectors that unnerved me, it was the whole oppressive feel of the place, as though gravity was somehow more potent there than elsewhere on Earth. The air felt heavy and, even in winter, peculiarly warm. You have to go through a lot just to get through the front door. But I eventually got used to the whole procedure and I ended up hardly giving the matter any thought at all.

Our first visits were a bit stilted, but as we got to know each other the tenor of our conversations changed. Mostly, we talked about Eric, her son. He had only been nine months old when she "went away" seven years earlier and had been living with his Grandma Shelly ever since. He was, she said, adorable—which detail I could corroborate, having met the boy several times, even before my first trip to Westchester—and extremely bright for his age. That too turned out to be the truth—later on, I was astounded by the boy's insight and ability to recall even the least consequential information that he once heard or read somewhere. Jackie was clearly living for the day when she would get out and resume her life as Eric's mom, which hopeful sentiment I strongly encouraged.

Our visits became routine; once a month, I'd drive up. I'd allow the nice men at the front door to probe and prod me in ways that you could have someone arrested on the outside for attempting. I took it all in stride, making jokes and never complaining. And then Jackie and I would have an hour to visit, during which she'd tell me everything *except* how she ended up in prison. I never asked. And then, out of the blue, she asked me a question I should have anticipated but somehow never had.

"Rabbi, can you ever do right by doing wrong?"

That got my attention, but I wasn't quite sure what the answer ought to be. "I suppose it would depend," I said vaguely, "on the circumstances."

"What if doing the right thing for person A meant doing the wrong thing for person B? Does that make it not matter what you choose because no matter what there will be one winner and one loser?"

"I don't think that's right," I said tentatively. "It would depend on the details—in what way A would benefit and in what specific way B would be harmed."

"What if A were a child and B an adult? Would that matter?" We were clearly talking about something. But what? That was where I should have withdrawn from the conversation until more information was forthcoming. But, being naïve and trying to be kind, I persevered.

"You mean like stealing milk from an adult to give to a hungry baby?" I have no idea where that came from. From somewhere!

Jackie thought that over for a while before responding. "Not exactly...but tell me the answer anyway: *would* you steal a quart of milk from a 7-11 if a baby was hungry? What if the baby was dying of hunger? What if it wasn't *a* baby, but *your* baby, your own child...would you steal food to feed it?"

I felt a bit queasy. "I would, yes. But I'd know I had done wrong and I'd try to atone later on."

"After your baby was fed?"

"Yes, after the baby was fed."

"So it's right to do something wrong to do something right... if you feel bad after?"

"No, that's not at all what I said." But, of course, it was exactly what I had said, and I knew it too. The time had clearly come to talk about whatever it was we were really talking about. "Did you steal milk once when Eric was hungry?"

Jackie looked at me quizzically, as though she couldn't quite believe I thought she was talking about stealing milk from a 7-11. "No, I certainly did not," she said almost proudly. "But I did tell Eric's father that I had lost the baby so that he'd be permanently out of both of our lives."

My jaw dropped open. "You...you what?" I must have sounded like an idiot, but I couldn't quite fathom what she had just said. Then, without waiting for an answer, I suddenly found my bearings. "You lied to Eric's father and told him that you lost the baby? Why would you do that?"

"Because he was a violent criminal and a drug abuser, and because he was as hot-tempered as they come. He used to beat the daylights out of me when he got mad, so I just sort of guessed he wouldn't make the world's greatest dad either. And it wasn't like it took a lot to get away with it—he was already in jail by then, so I just stopped visiting once I began to show. It's not like we were boyfriend and girlfriend, you know. Not really!"

"Oh," I said, then fell silent.

"So?"

"So what?"

"So did I do the right thing? Eric is being raised by my mom while I'm away. She's a loving Jewish grandma; she dotes on him just the same way I would if I was there to do the doting. He went to a Jewish pre-school; now he goes to Hebrew School. He's well-mannered and smart and secure, and that's *with* his mom being in the slammer. If Jimmy knew where he was, how do I know he wouldn't claim his parental right to raise his own son and then sell him to the highest bidder?"

"He wouldn't do that."

"Oh yeah, he would. And I don't think he would be sending the boy to Hebrew School either."

And then she told me the whole story. Jimmy's full name. His background. His record. His history of bad acts. She told me about her relationship with Jimmy, such as it was. About how it had been something like fun briefly, but had turned quickly to him taking what he wanted and her either giving it up freely or getting beaten to hell until she did. Finally, he was arrested and confined at Rikers awaiting trial. And while he was there, she found out she was pregnant. Seven months later, she gave birth. And nine months after that, she was arrested "for doing stuff" herself, and ended up being sent to Taconic Hills. She made me promise that I would never reveal Jimmy's name to Eric. And, because I felt I had to, I formally raised my hand just as she asked me to and swore that I never would.

I finished my coffee. I used the restroom. I ordered another coffee, not because I wanted it but just to justify sitting on the orange bench for another hour. I was way early. Visiting hours only began at 11 AM and it was just nine-thirty. I wondered briefly if the donuts they sell in the kosher-certified Dunkin' Donuts shops are really any different from the ones they sell in every other one of their stores, then decided to show some discipline and to avoid a foodstuff that Deena would have a fit if she saw me eating anyway. I let the coffee get cold in front of me. I checked my mail. I checked my text messages. I read a little. Then I checked my mail again. Then I used the restroom again. And finally I went out into the cold air and got into my car.

You can't miss the Clinton Correctional Facility, conveniently located on the other side of Cook Street just half a block past the Dunkin' Donuts in downtown Dannemora. Rising out of the morning mist like a giant's castle in a Scottish fairytale, it is not just imposing, but truly intimidating...and that's just from the outside. Finding the front entrance was easy enough. Parking in the visitors' lot was not particularly daunting either. But then walking in...and knowing that this is where people who do really bad things spend, at least in some cases, their entire lives...something about knowing that I was entering some sort of earthside netherworld into which people vanish never to emerge again filled me with a kind of inner dread that will be familiar only to others who have walked through similar portals.

I submitted to a series of inspections not unlike the routine I knew from visiting Jackie in Taconic Hills, only twenty times more intense. Eventually, they were convinced that I hadn't come to smuggle drugs or weapons into the prison, and that I truly was who I said I was and whom the Warden had pre-cleared for this visit. A guard was assigned to me, which somehow unnerved me more than it made me feel secure, and together we made our way down a long corridor into the visiting area designated for lawyers and clergy. It was a large room with a scuffed linoleum floor, several dozen folding chairs standing haphazardly around the room, a single pay phone on the far wall, and a folding table set up in one of the corners. It was just the guard and me. I told him, politely, that I hoped to speak privately with the prisoner I had come to visit, which request elicited the information that our four hands had to be visible for the entire time we were together but that he would stand far enough away for us to be able to speak without being overheard. Clearly, this was a big deal, and I wisely decided not to challenge the rule.

A quarter-hour passed, then another. I had known to leave my phone in my car, so had nothing to read, no email to check, nothing at all to do. The guard clearly did not wish to talk. And so I sat there on one of the folding chairs wondering about all my favorite questions of late. Was I doing the right thing...or a terrible thing? Was this an act of true *tzedakah* or a sin I was about to commit? Was I dishonoring Jackie's memory by going against her specific wishes...or was I helping her, albeit posthumously, to do the right thing even if it wasn't something she herself ever felt able or willing to do? I was deep within the matrix of these unanswerable questions when the door suddenly opened, startling me out of my reverie. And there before me stood one James M. Donniger.

When I first met Jackie, she had been up at Taconic Hills for seven years. And four years later, almost to the day, she was released on parole. This part of the story is almost too painful for me to tell in detail, but the short version is that she was released on a Sunday and was dead of a drug overdose that very evening. I found her body myself. Shelly and Eric were away for the weekend at a family wedding in Boston. The plan was for Jackie to have a quiet evening alone to adjust to life on the outside, then for her mom and son to come home the next day and for their new life together to commence. It seemed to me personally like not such a great idea—that they not be there when she arrived home—but Shelly was adamant that this was the way to go: Jackie, she said, needed time to adjust to new surroundings and an evening to herself would probably make their reunion the following day go that much more smoothly. Also, she reminded me, Eric had not seen his mother since he was an infant. She had never permitted him to visit while she was "away" and, although they did speak on the phone almost weekly, he hadn't ever seen her other than in photographs. I wasn't convinced, but it wasn't my call. I would, I said, drop by to welcome Jackie home, and then leave her to get a decent night's sleep.

I walked over a little after eight. The lights were on inside, but no one answered the doorbell. I had a weird sense that all was not well, but when I tried the door and it opened easily I was suddenly overcome with a kind of preternatural certainty that things were terribly wrong. And they were: she had been dead for hours when I found her on the living room floor, the paraphernalia of serious drug use scattered all around. I phoned 911, then several women from *shul* whom I thought I could trust and asked them to come over. Then I called a colleague in Boston, really in Needham, and, locating the invitation easily enough on the fridge, asked him to go to the wedding in person, to find Shelly and to tell her to come home with Eric that same night. I told him what had happened, but assured him he wouldn't have to say more to Shelly than that I called and asked him to find her and to tell her to come right home.

A year later, I found myself in a courtroom in the Queens County Family Court in Jamaica in the courtroom of the Honorable Sheila Floor to offer my opinion regarding the reasonability of allowing Mrs. Shelly Zuckergood formally to adopt her grandson. I showed up naively expecting to say my piece and be on my way. But nothing happens quickly in court and we had to wait for hours until the judge even got to our case.

I had my remarks memorized. I was completely ready. When prompted, I declared my full name, my profession, and my relationship to the applicant.

The judge seemed unexpectedly interested in me. "You knew the boy's mother?" she asked.

I was caught a bit off guard. Wasn't this supposed to be about Shelly, not Jackie? "Yes, your honor," I answered politely. "I knew her well."

"You knew her only in prison."

"Yes, your honor. The only time I laid eyes on her outside of prison was after she had died."

The judge, who clearly knew the whole story, nodded slightly. "How often did you go to visit her?" she asked.

"Monthly," your honor. "Monthly for years."

"How many years?"

"Four, your honor."

"Did you ever discuss Miss Zuckergood's son?"

"Miss Zuckergood's son was often *all* we talked about. She was interested in everything about him—how he was doing in school, whether he was well-behaved, if he seemed well-adjusted. Things like that."

Judge Floor looked oddly at me for a moment, then asked her next question. "Rabbi Weissbrot, do you know who Eric's father is?"

If she had taken out a two-by-four and smacked me on the head with it, I couldn't have been caught more off-guard. I felt my heart pounding so loudly in my chest that I was surprised it wasn't audible to everyone in the court. My undershirt was suddenly drenched. I could feel drops of perspiration dripping down the small of my back. For an odd moment, I thought I felt my father's presence just behind my right shoulder, but he was gone almost before I was fully aware of it. And then my heart slowed down back to normal and I suddenly felt comfortable and secure. "No, your honor," I said calmly, "I don't."

The rest, you can imagine. Just to be sure, Judge Floor asked me the same question three more times. I answered it in exactly the same way each time. Eventually, she grew tired of asking. The proceedings wound down. I told the judge what a wonderful mother I thought Shelly Zuckergood would make and that was more or less that. By the end of the day, Eric's biological grandmother was also his legal parent.

Years passed. I took a much larger (and better paying) pulpit in Seattle, then another in southern California. And then, in 2007, I came to the Prestigunquit Hebrew Congregation after its previous rabbi was murdered in cold blood in front of Penn Station by some inept mugger who was arrested within an hour or two of fleeing the scene, and there I stayed. Deena was still keeping up with one or two girlfriends from my first pulpit and relayed their news to me, but Shelly and I hadn't been in touch for years when she died of a massive heart attack the year before last. And then, just a few months ago, I noticed a story in the paper that opened up a door for me to step through if I dared.

The story was in *Newsday*, Long Island's largest newspaper, in the human-interest section. A prisoner serving a life sentence for participating in what turned out to be a felony murder had been granted permission to donate a kidney to his own ailing sister ten years earlier, and was now himself dying of kidney failure. A successful kidney transplant would save his life, but he was refusing to put himself on the transplant list—this was the whole point of the Newsday story—because he felt that an available kidney should go to someone who could go on to do real good in the world, not someone highly likely to spend the rest of his life behind bars.

I recognized his name immediately. And as the world fell away, I could somehow see myself all those years earlier raising my right hand to swear to Jackie that I would never tell Eric who his biological father was. But I never promised not to speak to his father or to try to meet him. And it was that detail that was now looming front and center before me and daring me to look away. Was it a mere oversight? Was Jackie simply incapable of imagining a scenario in which James M. Donniger and I would ever meet? Or was her concern merely for her son and not even remotely for her son's father?

I read more. The article was a long one. Donniger had been, as Jackie had reported to me, a violent man, a criminal. He had done many bad things, but in prison he somehow found himself in a way that had eluded him earlier on. He embraced his Catholic faith. He got his high school diploma. He became a kind of father figure for younger prisoners, helping them find their way onto the path of repentance and atonement for their crimes. He expressed regret to the reporter that there was no way for him to become a priest and to devote his life to God's service in that capacity. He even joked about how unfair that was, given that he was at least as poor, celibate, and obedient as any priest on the outside could possibly ever be. But, he said, even if the priesthood was just an unfulfillable fantasy, he was still intent on doing what he could to make the world a better place even from within the confines of a prison fortress like Dannemora.

I shook his hand. He seemed slightly confused by my *kippah*, but not at all hostile. I told him I was a rabbi, then fell silent. When he finally spoke, it was to ask me if I was a prison chaplain. And that was the door I had needed him to open.

"No," I said, "I am the rabbi of a synagogue on Long Island. But once I had a pulpit in Queens and it was there that I met Jackie Zuckergood. Or not *there*, of course, because she was already 'away' when I got there, but I knew her mother and I went to visit Jackie regularly upstate."

There was still time to back off, to turn away, to make up some crazy story about "just" being in the neighborhood and thinking it would be a nice gesture to stop by and say hello. It would have sounded idiotic, but I could have babbled away for a bit, then beat a hasty retreat. It was just a six-hour drive to Long Island—I could almost be home for dinner, this whole crazy episode behind me forever. But then I saw a different path open up before me. I looked into his eyes. "You have a son," I said.

Donniger looked directly at me. "A son?" he half-asked, half-said.

"Yes, a boy. Eric. A teenager now. Nineteen. A sophomore at Stony Brook."

I told him the whole story from beginning to end, just as I've written it down here. I told him what I knew of Eric. But I didn't tell him what to do nor, in fact, did I offer any specific counsel at all. I simply told him the story, including the part about me swearing never to tell Eric who his father was. That he himself had no specific reason to feel bound by *my* promise in that regard, I left unsaid.

"I'd be proud of him, you think?" he asked in a shaky voice, his eyes wet.

"Yes," I said, my voice quivering too by this point, "I think you would."

James M. Donniger died three months later without, as far as I know, making any effort to contact Eric. And with his death, my own options were reduced back to a single one: to keep faith with the dead by honoring my solemn oath never to reveal to a young man his father's identity. And, being a man of my word, I never have.

THE DEBT

There are survivors who can't stop talking about their wartime experiences, but there are also those who cannot bring themselves to speak about the events that befell them at all. My grandfather fell in the latter category: for reasons never disclosed, he chose never to tell us—or at least never to tell me or either of my sisters—he chose *never* to share his story with any of us. Was there something shameful in his past that he wished for us not to know? For a long time, I thought that had to be it...but eventually it struck me that if there was anything truly dishonorable or disgraceful in his past, the way to hide it would have been with a flattering, made-up story rather than with no story at all. And that was what my grandfather offered us when we occasionally screwed up our courage, or one of us did, to ask about his wartime experiences: no story at all. "It's all the past," he would say dreamily, as though we had asked him about some unpleasant childhood disease he preferred not to have to recall in much detail. If we persisted, he would simply say that he did not wish us to fear the world and was therefore unwilling to tell us stories that would do just that—make us feel that our neighbors could turn against us, that the people we considered our friends in the world could wake up one morning redefined as our enemies, that our sense of security and rootedness in the world could simply vanish in the wake of a single election that went the wrong way and brought bad people to power.

Some small part of the story I knew anyway. That our family came from Germany and that there had been Speiers living in

Worms for more than a thousand years before the debacle. That my father and his parents had all been born in that city, in its day one of the jewels of medieval Jewry and among its greatest centers of learning. That there had once been a family jewelry business, but that my grandfather's father, Willi Speier, had been a physician. That my Grandpa Emil had somehow been responsible for finding a way for my grandmother and my father to escape deportation. And that they—my father and his parents—had somehow survived in hiding.

My other grandparents—my mother's parents—survived the camps and settled in Fresh Meadows not far from where we live today, but they died long before my bar-mitzvah and my memories of them both are, at best, hazy. But my Speier grandparents, my dad's parents Emil and Hannelore—they were the grandparents I grew up with into my twenties. My grandfather was a tall man with an aquiline nose and deep blue eyes. My grandmother was a handsome woman with a large, prominent bosom and long hair she wore in a twisted braid pinned up in a circle around the circumference of her large head. But of the actual story of their wartime survival, I heard nothing at all.

All that changed, however, after my father died and I found among his papers a small diary that I soon realized had been written by my Grandfather Emil. He wrote in English—my grandparents tried to speak only English once they arrived here, and particularly when any of their grandchildren was present—but the specific *reason* he wrote down his story in a notebook that he then did nothing with other than preserve among his papers, *that* he took to the grave. I still don't really know what he hoped would happen with it or to it.

The story has an ending too, and an interesting one that only unfolded years after my grandparents were gone. But first let me let my grandfather speak. I've fixed a bit of his spelling and some grammatical errors, but other than that what now follows are my grandfather's words as transcribed by myself from a notebook I found among the papers of my late father, Henry (formerly Hanns) Speier.

The deportations in our city began almost immediately. At first, it appeared to be by random selection that families were chosen for resettlement in the east. The S.S. men appeared at first quite bizarrely polite and willing to wait almost patiently as the Jews gathered their few things together for the trek to their as yet unspecified destination. But by 1942, when the killing machine was running smoothly and efficiently, the randomness disappeared and the municipal authorities mounted a systematic effort to rid Worms of its few remaining Jewish citizens. Our names were known. We were all registered with the authorities. Other than by taking one's own life, there was no avenue of escape.

Miraculously, days passed and no deportation notice appeared for our family. I watched in silent amazement as Jewish families all around us disappeared, often on only hours' notice. I stayed in the shadows all day, hoping to avoid arrest while Hannelore and our Hanns, then just an infant, lay low at home and awaited my return.

Out of work and without any visible means of support, I basically spent my days trying to conduct enough illegitimate business to provide some food for the family. We had had a jewelry shop before it had been destroyed on that horrific night in November back in 1938, but I had been clever enough to keep the best part of our stock at home and now, because of that bit of forethought, I was able to conduct a bit of trading with some local, mostly unscrupulous, characters with whom I was acquainted. Still, I was in a better position than the Jewish shopkeepers whose stock was impossible to keep anywhere but on site in their shops: I at least had something to trade once all Jewish businesses were formally closed and, at that, something I could carry around in my pockets. Business was difficult, illegal, and generally profitless. But I kept at it in the almost entirely futile hope of keeping the family afloat for as long as it would take the Allied armies to smash the Axis powers and bring peace and sanity back to Europe.

By the summer of 1942, however, even I had lost my nerve. The situation was too impossible and the scoundrels with whom I was obliged to do business had themselves mostly disappeared either into the army or prison. The only chance we had was to go into hiding all together...*if* a suitable refuge could be located and secured.

My father, Willi, had been a medical doctor until his death in 1932 and among his patients had been a certain Jutta Lich, a young woman whom he had saved from death by operating on a malignant tumor that every doctor she had previously seen had diagnosed as a harmless fibroid.

The woman had survived and gone on to marry, but she was never able to have children. This particular woman, now Frau Jutta Wiltsch, had remained in touch with my father until the day he died and she had attended his funeral in the great synagogue.

As she passed by the line of mourners, she had stooped over to whisper a private word into my ear. There was, she said, going to be trouble for the Jews of Germany. I must have looked as though I was going to argue with her, but Frau Wiltsch silenced me with a single raised eyebrow before I could say a word.

"Come what may," she whispered into my right ear, "*ich werde mich euer annehmen*—I will watch over you all."

Late in the summer of 1942, when the situation had gone from bad to bleak to fully hopeless, I had a dream. In my dream, I saw my own father's funeral much as it actually had been. The black, horse-drawn hearse, the black crepe bunting over the synagogue's northern portal, and the solemn assembly of the bereaved and the curious was more or less precisely as I recalled it.

But the dream was not precisely as the reality had been, for in my dream my father's coffin was open, not shut, and the corpse was clearly visible. Only it was not my father at all in the plain pine box—it was me. Looking desperately for myself among the mourners and seeing myself present only as the body in the box, I suddenly realized I was having not a dream but a vision.

Following the course of events closely from some sort of invisible aerial perch, I could see the line of guests snaking forward for the privilege of speaking some few words of comfort into the ears of the bereaved family.

There were dozens, perhaps even scores of former patients of my father's standing patiently in line and a smattering of other doctors. None seemed to understand that this was not my father's funeral they were attending, but his son's. Nor were all the attendees known to me. Some I knew personally and could easily recognize, but many others were unfamiliar to me and presumably dated from the years of my father's practice that had preceded my own birth. There were even some few city officials, despite the obvious political reasons for anyone interested in a career in the civil service not to attend a Jewish funeral. Clearly, these people all *thought* they were attending my father's funeral, not my own. But there was no way for me to set them straight, no possibility of communicating with them at all.

And there, standing towards the back of the line, was Frau Jutta Wiltsch. Frau Wiltsch was wearing a black dress that was a size, at least, too big for her and was obviously borrowed from someone else for the occasion. On her head, she wore a small black pillbox with a veil of black tulle pulled up over the hat. In her hand, she carried a single white rose. From my vantage point, I could see Frau Wiltsch waiting patiently for her turn to come close to the casket. Since this was my funeral, it was Hannelore, rather than my mother, who was receiving the condolences with her own mother, my mother-in-law, at her side. And little Hanns, our son, was there too, standing by his grandmother's side and bravely holding her hand in his.

Eventually, Frau Wiltsch came to the front of the line. Pressing Hannelore's right hand between both her own hands, Jutta uttered some banal words of comfort that I could somehow hear from my elevated vantage point.

And then, passing over to where young Hanns was standing, Frau Wiltsch crouched down and, putting the palm of her left hand on the ground so as to steady herself, leaned forward to whisper something into the young boy's ear.

By straining slightly, I found I could hear Frau Wiltsch's whispered words. "*Ich werde mich euer annehmen*," she said. "I'll take care of you all." And then she was gone, her rose left in little Hanns' hand.

I awoke from my dream with a start. In the grey dawn, I imagined I could hear the thud of S.S. boots on the cobblestones as those proud knights of the Reich defended the fatherland against feeble, elderly Jews, innocent infants, and their defenseless parents. But there came no knock at the door.

We had no food at home and no money. If we were going to survive even a few days longer, we had only two choices: to volunteer for deportation—which, almost incomprehensibly, some families had done—or to go into hiding. I made my decision. And as soon as there were enough people out on the street to provide at least *some* modest camouflage, I was on my way to the Kranzbühlerstrasse. For better or for worse, it was time finally to see if Frau Jutta Wiltsch was as good as her word or not.

Speaking with Frau Wiltsch was not as simple as I expected it to be, however. Marek Wiltsch, her young husband, had been conscripted during the first few months of the war. He had undergone his basic training at a base outside of Kassel and had been just selected for officer training when he was killed during the invasion of Russia. Whatever mixed feelings his wife had had about Marek's future as a Nazi officer vanished with his last breath; she had married a pharmacist, not a soldier, but her grief was no different than it would have been had Frau Wiltsch not despised everything for which her husband had died fighting.

But Frau Wiltsch was not a pharmacist herself and had no real choice but to sell her husband's business to the first reasonable bidder. This, however, was easier said than done. The most likely would-be purchasers—young pharmacists seeking to set up shop—had all also been conscripted and were busy enough plying their trade, if they were plying it at all, for the soldiers of the Wehrmacht. Pharmacists old enough to avoid conscription already had their own businesses and, once the Jewish-owned pharmacies were all closed down, could barely keep up with their customers' demands, let alone consider taking on full lists of colleagues' clients as well. Finally, frustrated by the situation and bored by her own idleness, Jutta Wiltsch moved from the apartment in the Kranzbühlerstrasse she and her late husband had been renting to her parents' home just outside Worms proper in the suburb of Pfrimmbach, in those days still its own municipality with its own town council and its own mayor.

All of this, of course, was completely unknown to me as I made my way as evasively as possible to the address I found among my grandmother's papers. (She had died a year or so after my grandfather, but only after having written formal thank-you notes to all who had attended his funeral or made charitable donations in his memory. The addresses of those people she had collated in a small notebook she kept with her other papers. And there, on the fifth page towards the bottom, I had found Frau Jutta Wiltsch's address.)

I located the building easily. Entering through the unlocked front door, I stepped into the building. Shuddering to realize that the Wiltsches' downstairs Jewish neighbors had already been deported—I could see the police seal across their front door only partially obscuring the Jewish star in white paint just beneath the paper and paste—I actually tipped my hat politely to an elderly dame I met in the stairwell as I climbed the stairs to the Wiltsches' apartment.

I rang the bell over and over, but no one came to the door. Since I knew that Frau Wiltsch could not have become a mother, I guessed that she must have been conscripted into some work brigade or another. But where precisely she might be found, I obviously had no way to know. I rang her neighbor's doorbell.

A young woman came to the door and asked politely how she could help.

"I'm looking for Frau Jutta Wiltsch, but she doesn't seem to be home. Does she still live here?"

I felt the woman staring at the place on my jacket where the yellow star had been sewn until I had ripped it off in a fit of rage, but I had the sense not to lower my own eyes to check for loose yellow threads or faded outlines.

The conversation only took moments. Herr Wiltsch, the young woman said easily, had fallen on the eastern front. Frau Wiltsch had given up her flat and moved back in with her parents. The young woman thought her parents lived somewhere in Pfrimmbach, but she wasn't entirely sure.

The door closed. I felt worried, but also exhilarated. I was on Jutta Wiltsch's trail and, with any luck at all, I would find her before the S.S. found me. That Marek Wiltsch was dead was not necessarily a disaster—that there was now one less Nazi soldier in the world could only be good news—and if it now meant that I could encounter Jutta Wiltsch without having to take her husband's feelings or affiliations into account, then so much the better! So far, I told myself as I wandered out into the warm air of the Kranzbühlerstrasse, so good.

Taking the streetcar was risky, but I was feeling daring. Just for good measure I made a point of not buying a ticket before getting onto the car, figuring that, if a conductor did stop me, I could always stammer that I didn't have a ticket and then run for it as though avoiding the fine for riding without a ticket was the biggest of my problems. I walked from the Kranzbühlerstrasse to the streetcar stop on the Alzeyer Strasse just north of the old Jewish cemetery, itself still miraculously intact despite nine years of Nazi rule, then climbed onto the next car that came, then changed cars once or twice on the chance someone might be watching and wondering why a man of conscription age should still be walking around free when everyone else was in the army. I made a point of limping as I got on and off the streetcar, hoping to suggest that I had indeed been conscripted and was merely home recuperating from an injury sustained in the service.

Forty minutes after leaving the Kranzbühlerstrasse, I was standing in front of a post office on the Ringstrasse gazing into the muddy waters of the Pfrimm. My courage somehow built up, I entered the brick building and inquired how I might best go about finding Frau Jutta Wiltsch, currently thought of by myself to be living with her parents somewhere in Pfrimm-bach.

The clerk gave me a strange look, rose from his seat, and disappeared into a back room of the post office. Well, I recall thinking, now I can only pray that he comes back with Jutta Wiltsch's address instead of an S.S. man.

The next few minutes were harrowing. All around me business was going on freely at the other wickets while my clerk remained absent. Every logical bone in me said to run for it before the man came back, but something even more powerful kept me rooted to my spot. Three minutes passed, then four.

I felt the sweat beading up under my shirt and dripping down onto the small of my back. I loosened my collar. My palms were soaking wet. And then, a full five minutes after he disappeared, the clerk returned. He was an older man who himself had probably only escaped conscription due to his age and had a distinctly uneasy look about him. His dark eyes seemed to have something of their own to say, but their message was unintelligible to me. My only thoughts were on what the next few moments were going to bring.

The old man leaned forward until his forehead was almost touching the brass bars that crossed the upper half of the wicket. "Hermann and Sieglinde Lich, Steingasse 18," he said quietly, almost inaudibly. Then, obviously wishing our conversation to be over immediately, he waved the next customer forward and even before I left the wicket was already asking in what way he could be of service.

The Steingasse, one of Pfrimmbach's oldest and most lovely streets, was only about eight blocks away. In ten minutes, I was standing in front of no. 18.

It was a lovely house, an old one with a grey stone facade and a well-tended garden in front. I knocked and then, almost immediately, the door opened and before me stood the widow Wiltsch, the former Jutta Lich.

She recognized me easily. *"Grüss Gott*, Herr Speier," she said politely. "Come into my parents' home."

I stepped inside and felt an immediate surge of relief. The house was spacious and light. Books lined the four walls of the living room and there wasn't a single bit of Nazi paraphernalia or art anywhere to be seen. "We need some place to stay," I said, not seeing any reason not to get to the point quickly.

"Ich werde mich euer annehmen," she said softly and without even a moment's hesitation. She must surely have understood she was putting her life and her parents' lives on the line, yet her voice was clear and strong. "Please don't worry about a

thing," she added, "I'll take care of you all."

That's as far as the story goes. She apparently did it, too, keeping her word and watching over my father and his parents until the end of the war. What exactly her parents' role in my grandparents' and father's survival was, I couldn't know. But I was curious about the after-story, about what happened to Frau Wiltsch after she selflessly risked everything to save my father and his parents. My sisters could not possibly have been less interested in pursuing the matter. What mattered, they said, was that our father and his family had survived, not the specifics of what may or may not have happened years ago. I wanted to see it that way too, but I couldn't. The story as my grandfather wrote it down was intriguing, but too brief to be satisfying. I wanted to know more, but I didn't know exactly where to turn. Eventually, I had the idea of mimicking my grandfather and knocking on the widow Wiltsch's front door. Could she still be alive? I wasn't sure. My father was born in 1938. My grandfather himself was not even forty in 1942. But I imagined Jutta Lich Wiltsch as being far younger than my grandfather, perhaps only in her early twenties when he knocked on her parents' front door. I did the math a thousand times. If she was, say, twenty-two in 1942, she would have been born in 1920. Surely she could still be alive, I figured—she'd be in her nineties, but it seemed at least possible that she had yet to abandon life to the living. I resolved to find out.

For some reason, I thought it was going to be complicated to find her. But, as thing turned out, it couldn't have been simpler. Google offered up five different women in Germany with the name Jutta Wiltsch, a sixth in Vienna and a seventh in Zurich. Five were on Facebook and were clearly far too young. That left two. One was the woman in Austria, but the other lived, amazingly, in Worms, just where my grandfather and his family had left *his* Frau Wiltsch at war's end. We live in an amazing world. I started the day with no idea at all if Jutta Lich Wiltsch was dead or alive, but before the day was done I not only knew that Frau Wiltsch was alive, but that she was living in some sort of old age home on the Kirschgartenweg in downtown Worms. The next day I spoke to the doctor in charge, Dr. Gerhard Lammers. I had studied German in college and his English was more than adequate to fill in the parts I couldn't manage, but more crucial was that he seemed to have none of the qualms about sharing details about his patient that the HIPAA laws would have inspired in one of his American counterparts. Frau Wiltsch, he said, was very old and very weak; she was not suffering from any specific disease, just a lack of stamina and a deep, lingering depression that was robbing her of her will to carry on. She had never married, the doctor said. (He ought to have said "remarried," but, since she had apparently never mentioned her late husband, I also said nothing about her marriage to Marek.) She had given up her room in the "regular" part of the home, he explained, and was now living in the hospice wing. As far as he knew, she had no living family.

I'm not by any means a wealthy man, but I do own my own business—we are book designers and manufacturers—and I can take time off when I must. More to the point, I have a partner who has two elderly parents in Los Angeles whom he goes to visit regularly while I hold down the fort and who therefore didn't say a word when I said that I needed a week away "to go see someone." Then, once my decision was made, things just fell into place. Three days after I spoke with Doctor Lammers, I was on a plane to Frankfurt. And from there it was an easy train ride to Worms.

I'd never been to Germany before. My father, there one single time to make some presentation at the Frankfurt Book Fair, pronounced the experience weird and unsettling. He never went back. My grandparents refused even to speak German in public, let alone to return to their former homeland. Yet, to my amazement, there I was getting off the train in Worms, taking a cab to my hotel, then stepping out into the sunshine and walking the four or five blocks to the nursing home that housed the hospice wing in which Jutta Lich Wiltsch lay dying.

I found my way easily enough. I asked for Dr. Lammers by name and was ushered directly into his office. We shook hands. If he wondered what my specific relationship to his patient was, he didn't ask. And I didn't say, preferring to allow him to imagine whatever he wished. Probably he thought she was some distant relative I had somehow managed to track down.

Finally, the time had come. I walked down a long corridor, following the signs to room 2035 (which was unexpectedly on the ground floor). I felt my heart pounding in my chest as I approached the room, not sure what I would say. As noted, I had taken German in college—there had been a language requirement at Bowdoin and I figured I might have some genetic predisposition towards German—and had kept at it for three years, but it was one thing to speak with someone like Dr. Lammers, who could fill in my missing vocabulary with his own sturdy English, and something else entirely to speak with someone who, as far as I knew, knew no English at all! But it was too late to turn back and then, amazingly, I was standing outside Frau Wiltsch's door. I waited for a long moment while I gathered my thoughts, then knocked. There was no response, or at least none that I heard. But the door was not even latched shut and swung open from the force of my knocking. Feeling both bold and timid at the same time, I stepped inside.

It was a tiny room, barely large enough for what it contained: a bed, a table, a chair, and a floor lamp. In the bed was a woman, but she appeared to be sleeping. Not wanting to disturb her, I sat down on the chair. I had a few books on my phone and began to read.

It took a while but she eventually woke up. I expected her to find it alarming that a strange man was sitting in her room, but she seemed totally unsurprised and completely at her ease.

Using my best college German, I asked how she was feeling.

She looked at me, but did not answer.

Was she possibly hard of hearing? I asked my question again, this time speaking louder and more distinctly.

She stared at me and still said nothing. But then, just as I was about to repeat myself again, she finally did speak.

"*Wer sind Sie?*" she asked. Who are you?

"*Ich bin der Sohn von Hanns Speier. Emil Speiers Enkel.*" I am the son of Hanns Speier. Emil Speier's grandson.

She smiled, appearing to recognize the names. "*Wo sind sie?*" she asked. Where are they?

On the spot, I decided to lie. "*Sie sind in New York,*" I said. "*Sie wohnen in New York.*" They are in New York. They *live* in New York. Why risk upsetting her by pointing out that my grandfather would be 110 years old if he were alive or by mentioning that my father died of a brain aneurysm at age seventy in 2008?

Frau Wiltsch closed her eyes. For a moment, I thought she had fallen asleep. Her breathing was shallow. I could see her chest rising and falling, and could tell easily how weak she was.

And then she opened her eyes. "*Und Sie?*" she asked. And me? Was she asking for me to say again who I was? Or did she want to know why I was in Germany or why I had come to visit her? It was hard to say.

Overcome with emotion, I stepped towards her bed. I could smell some sort of scented talcum powder in the air. Her skin was pale, but her hand felt cool and smooth as I took it in mine and paid my family's debt to an ancient woman who had once risked everything by taking them all in when the alternative would have been deportation, degradation, and death.

"*Keine Sorge, Frau Wiltsch,* I said. "*Ich werde mich deiner annehmen.*" Don't worry about a thing, Frau Wiltsch. I'm going to watch over you now for as long as you live.

IN ROOM 808

I was alone at home because my mother taught an evening class at C.W. Post on Tuesday nights. I had finished all of my written homework and but still had to read the scenes from *King Lear* that Mr. Bergman had assigned for the following morning. (Like half the college-bound twelfth graders in my school I was taking A.P. English, except that I was more or less enjoying it.) There wasn't anything on television I was interested in watching. I fooled around with the Wii, then turned it off and was making a chicken sandwich when the phone rang. I have no idea why I answered it. My own friends never used the land line. I usually let messages for my mom go to voice mail. But for some reason I picked it up. Maybe I thought it was my grandpa phoning. But I'm getting off track and I haven't even begun to tell the story. The phone rang. I lifted the receiver.

A woman's voice. "Is that Thomas Sugarman?"

No one calls me Thomas, not even my mother. I'm Tom in school and Tommy at home, but Thomas only to people who don't know me. My driver's license says Thomas, of course. So does my passport. Could this be the DMV phoning, or the Department of Homeland Security? It seemed unlikely. "Yes," I said, "this is he."

"My name is Sherry Sugarman," the voice said. "I'm your father's wife."

"My...my what?" I must have sounded like an idiot and in retrospect it seems funny even to me that I didn't understand instantly who Sherry was. But I don't think I did. I mean, I obviously knew I had a father. And I knew he was married. I knew the whole story, actually. My mother went to Barnard and ended up pregnant in the middle of her senior year. My father, then just her boyfriend, tried to do the right thing. Or at least that's how she always tried to depict him when the story was told (which it in any event hardly ever was): as a guy in a bad situation trying his best to do the right thing. Graduation was in May. They married in July. I was born in August. He stuck it out for a while, but then he realized—this is my mother speaking again—he realized that he had only compounded one error of judgment with an even bigger one and they had the marriage annulled. The guy hung around New York for a few months after that, but then he got a job in Los Angeles and that, more or less, was that.

Years passed. My mom got a job at Macy's, went to grad school at night, and ended up working as a teacher in some middle school in Queens. But she continued on in school too and eventually finished her dissertation, then moved up to teaching English at Post. And then, when I was about ten, my bio-dad moved back to New York.

In the meantime, he had become a lawyer. He knew his obligations. More to the point, he knew he'd be even more completely screwed than most dead-beat dads if he failed to pay up. So he did, making child support payments monthly and on time but never exceeding the amount owed by even a single penny, not even for my birthday or for Chanukah. Nor did he ever show any actual interest in me, not in getting to know me or even in meeting me. He had, my mother told me, remarried. And to go with his new wife he also had two new sons. He had, she said, moved on. And it would be best for us too to move on, she said, sounding like she meant it and was pleased to be doing it. How *exactly* my mom knew any of this, I never thought to ask. Even now, I'm not entirely sure how she kept tabs on my father's life. But move on we nonetheless did. Mom occasionally dated men, notably a dentist about twenty years her senior whose own wife had died on 9/11. That lasted for a few years and he was always nice to me. But they never married and he never seemed to want me to think of him even as a father *figure*, let alone as an actual father. Eventually, they grew apart. My mom somehow kept an eye on him too and told me when he finally married some-one else, also a single Queens mom with a teenage son. (He was, she said, a specialist!) But what did that have to do with us? I shouldn't complain, though. I grew up in a nice apartment with a really good mom. I was happy. Or happy enough!

I knew that my dad was a successful man. When I would ask, my mom would point out that we didn't need to beg for money, that we were making do quite nicely on our own. So he could make all the money in the world—which he apparently did—but all that we ever saw of it was exactly what some judge once decided that he owed us. And even those checks stopped when I turned eighteen. Realizing that my mom was going to have to borrow the money to send me someplace fancier, I applied only to City University schools and to Stony Brook. When I picked up the phone just after eight o'clock that May evening, I was eighteen years old. I was starting Queens College in the fall. (For the record, I got into Stony Book too.) I still owed Mr. Bergman two scenes of *King Lear* by ten o'clock the next morning, how-ever. And now my father's wife, Mrs. Sherry Sugarman, was on the phone. My mom reverted to her maiden name, Reich, after the divorce. But for the moment it was just us Sugarmans on the phone: the first son and second wife of my non-dead-beat dad, Donald Arthur Sugarman, Esq.

"Your father's wife. We've met. Maybe you don't remember." I remembered. Seven years earlier, when I was eleven, my mom —apparently having forgotten for the moment how nicely we were doing on our own—sued my dad to see if his child sup-port payments could be increased. I had to appear in court. So did my dad. His wife came too. We had met, but only briefly. I couldn't even really remember clearly what she looked like. Tall, I thought I remembered, with long black hair pulled back into a ponytail. Or maybe not. I was eleven. It was a long time ago. I'm not even sure who won in court. If it was us, it didn't make much of a difference in the way we lived.

"I remember," I said mostly honestly. I suppose I should have asked her what I could do for her or if she wanted to speak to my mom, but I couldn't bring myself to say anything at all. Suddenly, I really needed to use the bathroom. I waited.

"Your father asked me to call," she said.

"He did?" I must have sounded like an idiot, but I honestly couldn't imagine that this was for real. He asked her to call me? Why wasn't he calling me himself?

It would have been a first. In the course of our non-life not together, I had on that April evening spoken to my father exactly one single time on the phone. When I was twelve, I sent him an invitation to my bar-mitzvah. My mom told me not to bother, but I wasn't dissuaded. I went straight to the library from school and found his number—not his private home number, but the number of his office on Park Avenue South in the city— in the Yellow Pages. Then I ran home and called it. The receptionist put me through to his secretary when I said I was his son. The secretary, a man—I remember that surprising me, since I hadn't realized that there even *were* secretaries who weren't women—was friendly and asked me which son I was. When I gave my name, he hesitated. (Later, I realized that he must have known the names of my father's other sons and not been sure what to make of one of whom he hadn't ever heard.) He put me on hold. I waited. He came back on a few minutes later and told me my father was on a conference call—I'm not even sure I knew what that meant, but it sounded important—and that I could wait or call back later. I said I'd wait. Where did I have to go? It took more than twenty minutes, but he eventually picked up the phone. He must have thought my mom had died or something like that, because he asked me right off if she was okay. I told him she was fine. Silence. What did I want? I was too naive to understand just how profoundly cold and creepy he was being towards me; I think I thought he actually wanted to know. I told him my bar-mitzvah was in four weeks and that I'd like to send him an invitation but I didn't know his address. He hesitated for a moment, then told me to send it to his office. He gave me the address. I didn't want to tell him it was in the Yellow Pages ad and that I had already copied it down, so I wrote it down again. He wished me good luck. I said thank you. He told me had had a "four o'clock," which meant nothing to me. It was, at any rate, only ten to four. I said good-bye. He said it too, then hung up. I got out an invitation from the box of printed invitations my mother had picked up a few weeks earlier from the printer's and an envelope, then carefully wrote my father's name down on the envelope and his firm's name (which consisted of only his—my!—last name and two other people's), then the address on Park Avenue South, then New York, New York, and then the zip code. I found a stamp in my mother's desk and put the invitation inside the envelope, then sealed it and put it in my knapsack. The next morning, I put it in a mailbox I passed on the way to school.

He didn't respond. Not a filled-out "So sorry but I'm having open heart surgery that day" response card. Not a check. Not a less-flat present. (When I was a kid, the checks you got for your bar-mitzvah were called flat presents.) Not a letter. Not a note. Not any response at all. Being an idiot, I took his silence to mean that he was coming. My mother, of course, knew nothing of this nuttiness and was therefore unable to explain to me what a gigantic error of judgment that was and how all I was doing was setting myself up to be miserably disappointed. On the day of my bar-mitzvah, I couldn't believe he wasn't there. When I told my mother that he was probably on his way but must have been stuck in traffic, she made me tell her the story. I confessed, more proud of having dared phone him than I was ashamed of having made a fool of myself. Then she started to cry. Then I started to cry. This all happened in the sanctuary during the actual service in synagogue while they were reading the Torah out loud and we were waiting for me to be called forward to chant my *haftarah.* It was a mess. People actually started shushing us. Eventually we both calmed down and we never referred to the incident again. But it was always there anyway, always stuck in my mind, always framing any thought regarding my father that for some reason popped into my mind. And now it was back as I uttered my pathetic "He did?" and the *exact* way I felt turning around over and over in my seat in the synagogue to see if he had walked in rose within me and unbidden became the sorry backdrop against which this almost unbelievable phone call was taking place. *Now* he calls? I thought. Does he need directions to the synagogue?

"Yes," my father's wife answered, "he did. He's not...look, Thomas, your father is not well. Do you know anything about this?" Her voice was quivering slightly. I felt a little sorry for her.

"No one calls me Thomas," I said. "Call me Tom."

"Tom," she said, stretching it out into almost two syllables as some sort of compromise. "Tom, has your mother mentioned to you that your father is ill?"

"No," I said, "she hasn't."

"Then I'm sorry to be the bearer of bad news, but your father has lung cancer and he is not responding well to treatment. He's a sick man, Thomas. Tom. Tom, your dad is very...the situation is serious. He asked me to call and ask if you'd come in."

"Come in? Come in to where? Is he in the hospital?"

"Yes," she said, "he's in the hospital." Suddenly, she sounded weary. "He's at Mount Sinai and I'm not sure...." Her voice trailed off. Then she cleared her throat. "Tom, if you want to come you should come now. Maybe even tonight. Or tomorrow."

"It's pretty late. And I have school tomorrow."

"Then come after school. Check with your mother to make sure it's okay, then call me on my cell phone." She gave me the number. "When you call, tell me the address of your school and when you're done and I'll send a car service to pick you up." She paused. "This is what your father wants," she added, almost as though she understood just how unbelievable I had to be finding this conversation.

"I go to Francis Lewis High School," I said, ignoring her insulting suggestion that an eighteen-year-old guy might still need his mommy's permission to go into the city and see someone. "It's on Utopia Parkway just north of the LIE. I'm done at 3:45. Send the car service to the front of the building then and I'll come out as quickly as I can. Tell the driver I'm six feet tall and have black hair and a goatee. I'll be wearing a blue jacket and carrying a leather knapsack."

She thanked me for being so agreeable. I thanked her for calling. She thanked me for listening. I thanked her for talking. It was entirely clear that neither of us knew how to end the conversation, so I eventually just told her I had to go. Then I hung up. I ate the chicken sandwich. I washed it down with some ginger ale. When my mom came home, I was reading *King Lear* on the couch. She told me about her day. I told her about school. I really wanted to tell her about the phone call, but I knew it would upset her and I somehow ended up not telling her. Eventually, I got into bed, read another few lines of *Lear*, and went to sleep. If I dreamt that night, I woke up not remembering a thing.

The car was waiting when I walked out of school the next afternoon. The driver was actually holding a cardboard sign with my last name on it just like in the movies! I thought he'd want to see my school ID or something, but he didn't ask and I didn't offer. An hour later, I was getting out in front of Mount Sinai. I felt I should probably tip the guy, but I had no idea how much was the right amount. Nor did I have any idea how much the trip itself cost. I offered the guy a five, but he turned back my hand and said that he had already been "taken care of." Not knowing what to say, I stuffed the bill back in my pocket and got out. He told me to have a nice day. I told him to have one too. He drove off. Alone on the sidewalk, I was suddenly nervous. I felt summoned. I *had* been summoned. And I had obeyed. Suddenly, I felt unsure of myself. But I was way too far into this just to go home.

Mount Sinai Hospital is located on Fifth Avenue, New York's most elegant street. Where else would a man like my father choose to die? (I later found out that he lived there too, just about twenty-five blocks to the south.) It's a huge, sprawling place with a thousand buildings, each with its own entrance and its own name. Having no idea where my dad was—and not pausing to wonder why his wife hadn't told me exactly where to find him—I just went into the building I was standing in front of and, finding an information desk just inside, asked for my dad's room.

Amazingly, my father's room was only two buildings away. I went back outside. I found the building—and not *just* a building for a patient as fancy as my father either, but a *pavilion*—then went inside and took the elevator up to the eighth floor. Suddenly I could feel my heart beating hard in my chest. Would my father even recognize me? I'd find out in the minute. As far as I knew, the last time he had laid eyes on me was when I was eleven. I'd changed since then. Had he? I'd find out as soon as I found the courage to push open the door to room 808. It was ten past five. The sun was setting. I knew that I should have told my mom where I was going. (I had texted her from the car that I was going into the city, but without saying why.) My heart was really pounding. There were some nurses and some old people in wheelchairs at the other end of the corridor, but the part of the hall in front of my dad's room was completely empty. I was suddenly roasting. I pulled open my jacket. I told myself to stop behaving like such a wuss. I hadn't done anything wrong, so why should I feel weird? A line from *Lear* suddenly came back to me so imposingly that for a moment I actually thought I heard Mr. Bergman speaking it aloud. "Time shall unfold what plaited cunning hides," the voice said. I pushed open the door to my father's hospital room and stepped inside.

It was a private room. (What else?) My father, recognizable but haggard, was lying back in a large hospital bed surrounded by monitors and machines of different sorts. In two identical chairs by the window sat two boys, apparently my half-brothers. Their faces were sallow and they both looked tired. The older one glared at me. The younger one, only about twelve or thirteen, looked away. Neither spoke. Seated in a larger chair on the side of the room by the door was a tall woman with long black hair twisted into a braid. She was wearing a navy blue dress with square black buttons going down the front and a thin golden necklace. She stood up and extended her hand. "You are Tom," she said. A statement, not a question.

I admitted it. She extended her hand. I shook it. She said her name—just her first name—and thanked me for coming. I thanked her for calling. Then, silence. The younger boy got up and walked out of the room without saying a word. The older boy picked up a magazine and pretended to read. He looked remarkably like I did at sixteen. I turned to face Sherry, not sure what to say and not wanting to sound like an idiot.

She also appeared unsure how to proceed. She approached my dad's bedside and touched his bony shoulder. "Don," she said softly.

No response.

"Don?" Louder this time.

No response.

"Donald, Thomas—Tom—is here. To see you. Tom's here in the room." Her voice broke off, but she didn't cry. I suddenly realized that I had no idea what to call my father. "Dad" seemed weird for a parent I had met—other than as a baby—exactly once in my entire life, "Don" or "Donald" even weirder. For a long moment, I thought the whole question was going to be moot, but then he opened his eyes and appeared to be taking in the scene unfolding around his bed. And then, almost unexpectedly, he spoke. "Thomas?" he asked. Was he asking his wife if I was there? Or was he asking me if I was Thomas? I felt my heart beating so hard I imagined it had to be audible to the others in the room. I looked over at half-brother and saw that his eyes were filled with tears. I looked back at my dad. Sherry stepped back. Now it was just me standing by the bed.

"It's me," I said. "It's Tom."

My father seemed lucid. He was certainly fully awake. I looked carefully at his face. Whoever had shaved him hadn't been careful enough to include the moustache hairs adjacent to his nostrils. I stepped in slightly closer. Surprised to realize he was wearing aftershave, I somehow stepped out of the moment long enough to find it amusing that as elegant and wealthy a man as my dad would use a brand as ordinary as Old Spice. Maybe, I told myself, that was just what the hospital provided. I had a bottle of my own in my medicine cabinet at home. I even used it now and then when I shaved, which was not too often. I realized I was floating away from reality and drew myself back into my father's presence.

"Dad?" I said, forgetting my uncertainty about what to call him. To his credit, he didn't flinch.

"Thomas?" he responded, turning his head to face me directly.

"Yes," I said. "Thomas."

He shifted to one side and, as I contemplated his bony face more with curiosity than horror, I realized he was smiling. "You came," he half-said, half-asked.

"I'm here." My half-brother—his name turned out to be Joseph —put down his magazine. I had no idea what to say. Was I supposed to launch into some sort of complicated soliloquy about the inviolate bond between sons and their fathers, about how none of his poor behavior mattered, about how it had been just fine growing up in our little apartment in Fresh Meadows with a single mom who had to scrimp and save even to send me to the day camp at the JCC or to pay for that cheesy uniform so I could join the Little League? Was I supposed to assure him that I had turned out okay, that his hard-earned child support dollars had been used wisely, that I loved him more for those checks than I hated him for his coldness, for the cruelty he showed me when I sent him that damn invitation, or for his apparent willingness to have absolutely nothing at all to do with his own son? Perhaps, I thought for a peculiar moment, I should have brought along my transcript and read out to him my fabulous grades and my stunningly good SAT scores so he could die proud of me. Should I tell him I got into Stony Book?

My father turned to his wife. "Leave us alone," he croaked. Then he turned to young Joe. "You too," he added, his voice hoarse with phlegm.

Without saying a word, the boy stood up and followed his brother out of the room. His mother left too, also without comment. It was just my father and me now. I had the peculiar sense that my life had somehow led me to this moment. I came close to the bed and looked down at him. He had been a handsome man. I had seen pictures of him at his and my mom's wedding and I could still see that man in the flesh-covered skeleton that lay before me in the bed. I wasn't sure if I should speak or wait. I waited.

"You're in the will," he said finally, each syllable an obvious strain. "For a fair share, same as Joe and Ian."

I said nothing.

"Your mom's taken care of too."

I nodded, tears filling my eyes. I knew I had to say something, but couldn't imagine what.

"I have to do something," he now said.

I found my voice. "Do what you have to do, Dad."

My father took my hand in his. It felt cool and smooth, almost like parchment. It looked like parchment too. I didn't pull back.

"With all my heart," he said, turning to look directly into my eyes, "I regret what I did to you. And also what I never did for you and also what I should have done for you. I was trying to be loyal to my new family, but I was wrong. In every way. About everything. About them *and* about you. And about your mother as well. I accept all that. But even if I can't fix any of it—not really, not in any way that could ever really matter—I still need you...I need you to find it in your heart to forgive me."

Over the years, I had imagined this scene a thousand different ways. He'd show up out of the blue at our apartment one day begging me to be his boy, to be his son. We'd meet somewhere by accident and he'd see what a great kid I was and beg me to let him into my life. He'd show up unexpectedly at my graduation or at my wedding and kneel down in front of everyone and apologize for not showing up at my bar-mitzvah. There were a million fantasy lead-ups, but they all ended with me spitting in his face and telling him to go to hell. Then, glancing over at his wife and kids, I'd add, "And take your whore with you. And your bastards." I can't remember when I started developing these fantasies, but it was definitely after my bar-mitzvah. In middle school. I guess. Sometimes I spit in his face, sometimes on his feet, sometimes in his kids' faces or his wife's. Sometimes I called them even worse names. Sometimes I even fantasized about smacking him hard across the face and daring him to raise a hand to defend himself. Even despite all that endless fantasizing, though, I never really expected this moment to come. Not really! But now that it had, I suddenly realized that all I really wanted to do was to ask some questions. There were a million of them too, each one a variation of some sort on the same theme and all of them about what it takes to walk out on a child and never look back. And now my chance to ask whatever I wished had finally come. Clearly, I had his full attention. It was, I realized, now or never. For a moment, I think I actually considered selling him my forgiveness for one single honest answer to just one question. But I also knew that the time for that kind of dialogue was past and that the man in the bed before me was using every ounce of his strength just to say the few sentences he had managed to speak out loud. I'm not sure I could have held up my end of the conversation either.

I leaned over my father's bed. His eyes were fixed on me. He said nothing. I pressed my lips down on his forehead. For a long moment, I kept them there. And then my eyes filled with tears and as they fell silently onto the side of his face I allowed them wordlessly to speak what was in my heart.

AFTER AARON DIED

Even all these years later, I can still see Ray Valensky's face the way it looked through the cut glass window in our front door as he stood outside and watched nervously as I walked down the hallway towards him.

Robbie Valensky was on the same Little League baseball team as our son Benjamin and their Lilly played soccer with our daughter Rebecca, so it was not *that* unusual for either of the Valensky parents to drop by the house unannounced to drop off something one of our kids had left behind or to retrieve something one of their kids had left at our place. But the evening Aaron died was certainly not the kind of night that anyone would just drop in for an unexpected visit no matter what anyone had left behind in someone else's home. For one thing, it had been snowing all day in Prestigunquit and the snow, which had been expected to taper off towards evening was, if anything, becoming worse. I myself had been home for hours, busying myself with housework and half expecting Aaron to phone at any moment to announce his intention to spend the night in Manhattan. If I force myself to try to remember, I think I must have been supposing that he was going to crash at his friend John's apartment in Soho rather than take a chance on the train. It would have made sense. I myself would have stayed over in town if I had a friend with an available sofa. But the bottom line, especially in retrospect, was that I hadn't heard from him. I had tried his number a few times, of course, but it had gone straight to voice mail. But even that hadn't struck me as especially ominous.

It was snowing. Cell phone service this far out on the North Fork isn't great at the best of times. That I couldn't reach him by phone, therefore, didn't seem too worrisome. Frankly, even once the doorbell had rung and I knew that Ray Valensky had come around for *some* reason—I do distinctly remember looking out our bedroom window down at the street, still totally clueless, and seeing the cruiser parked at the curb—even when I saw the cruiser I *still* hadn't the faintest premonition of trouble to come. I vaguely recall thinking that if Ray had come out on a night like this to tell me in person that the girls' practice for that Sunday was cancelled due to the weather then he was even crazier than Aaron always said he was. Probably, I told myself far more rationally, Nancy just wanted him to borrow some eggs or a quart of milk. What else could have brought him out in person? Well, I told myself as I approached the door, I'd know soon enough. As it happened, I did have plenty of both in the house, more than enough to share.

He told me quickly and, unlike on television, without telling me first that he had something to tell me. When I finally registered what he was saying and asked what hospital Aaron was in, Ray answered simply that he was at Saint Vincent's. I guess it must have been obvious that I still hadn't really heard what it was he was trying to say, however, since that was when he took my hands in his and repeated himself even more clearly. "He's at Saint Vincent's, Sarah," he said softly. "But he's not a patient there. He was D.O.A. and it's his body that's in the hospital's morgue. I wish I could tell you to rush down there and to hope for the best, but there isn't any best to hope for. He's dead, Sarah. And they're waiting for someone to tell them what to do with the body. The normal procedure would be for an autopsy to happen almost automatically, but I think you can probably talk them out of it. Look, he was hit with one single bullet and the bullet was recovered at the scene. So what do they need to cut him open for? To find out that he was killed when somebody shot a bullet into his heart? I mean, they're *always* supposed to do an autopsy when the deceased is a victim of a violent crime, but I know they bend the rules sometimes. Just get every rabbi in the tri-state area to phone in and insist." He paused, then spoke again. "And you insist too, Sarah. They'll listen to you."

I was only vaguely listening to him. He was talking away. My hands were in his. The television was clearly audible from the den and the smell of roast chicken was wafting over our heads out onto the street. But I was a million miles away in a secret place, in *my* secret place, in the crawl space behind the eaves of my parents' house in Larchmont. That was my hiding place, the secret spot I could always run to when I was in trouble or scared. It was there, lying in that narrow space, that I had first read Anne Frank's diary as a girl. If only the Franks had had such a great place to hide in, I used to think, then maybe they would have survived.

When I looked up, Ray had finally stopped speaking. Later, he surprised me by commenting that I had a look on my face that he could only qualify as serene. (I wouldn't have thought Ray would even know the word, let alone be able to use it correctly in a sentence.) But I was wrong about that. I was, it turned out, wrong about a lot of things. And I'm willing to suppose that it may well have been obvious that there was a certain noticeable calm mixed in with the first stirrings of grief, a certain satisfaction borne of true love that can only have been flowing directly from the realization—it really is amazing how many different lines of thinking your brain can follow at once if the shock is sufficiently great—*directly* and *not illogically* from the realization that my dear Aaron was finally safe, that nothing could harm him or scare him ever again, that Aaron's life-long fears of dying in a pogrom or in a gas chamber or in a hastily dug execution ditch had come to nothing. He was gone, I was thinking, but he's finally free.

And then, reality set in. Aaron was dead. I was alone. And not *even* alone alone, which would have been bad enough, but alone with four children. Alone in a house that belonged to my husband's employers—or rather to my *late* husband's *former* employers. Alone with no career, with no income, and with about twenty thousand dollars' worth of credit card debt. Alone in a cold doorway spending the first few minutes of the rest of my life with, of all people, Ray Valensky.

Even years later, I could never quite reconstruct the rest of that evening. I must have told the children. I must have phoned my parents. I must have been the one who phoned my in-laws' rabbi to ask him to go in person to their home to tell them their only son was dead. I know I'm the one who phoned Sam Ryback and asked him to retrieve Aaron's body from Saint Vincent's as soon as possible and bring it to the chapel out here that he and his family have owned and operated forever. And I was also the one who opened the door when my in-laws arrived a few hours later, the pain on their faces so profound that the children actually cried when their grandparents entered the room in which we had all been sitting quietly and almost calmly in stunned disbelief. And then my parents also arrived too and there really was no more room at the inn.

Aaron was shot and killed on a Tuesday evening, but it was impractical to schedule the funeral until the question of an autopsy was settled one way or the other. For some reason, I couldn't bring myself to care. And since the synagogue's lawyer was dealing with the autopsy situation and since she had assured me repeatedly that she'd call the moment it became clear that I was going to have to put my two cents in as well, I spend Wednesday running around doing a thousand errands in preparation for the week of mourning that would follow the funeral. I phoned the head of Aaron's rabbinical association and asked him to send out an e-mail announcing Aaron's death. I summoned Daisy Kogan to the house and asked her to lengthen the black dress I wanted to wear to the funeral and to let it out where it felt tight. I left the kids with their grandparents and went to the store on my own to pick up some groceries, but I had to return empty-handed once I realized that I could neither face encountering people who had heard the news nor dealing with people who hadn't. Nancy Valensky ended up doing my shopping for me, but the truth was that it was hardly necessary to purchase anything at all. By evening, the house was overflowing with more trays of food and cakes and fruit and cookies that we could have eaten in a dozen *shiva* weeks.

In the end, there was an autopsy. The New York County Medical Examiner insisted. I didn't have the strength to object. Almost to my surprise, I found that I didn't care, didn't even *want* to care. Some friendly officer from the N.Y.P.D. kept in touch until it became clear to both of us that Aaron's assailant, apparently a talentless mugger who probably shocked himself as much as Aaron by pulling the trigger on his Saturday night special and who ended up running off without even taking Aaron's wallet or wristwatch, was never going to be identified or located. I didn't much care about that either. I didn't really care about anything except my children. And their grandparents, all four of them, seemed to be channeling their own misery into watching over my kids so intently and intensely that there really was nothing left for me to do.

Sam Ryback's people went into the city to retrieve Aaron's body. The funeral came and went. Because I insisted, my mother stayed at home with the baby and I took the other children to their father's funeral in the company of my father and my in-laws. Over seven hundred people showed up. In retrospect, it seems like a reasonable number. But at the moment I was astounded by the size of the crowd. The funeral itself, I actually do remember quite well. The eulogy was spoken with surprising eloquence by Michael Pressburg, the rabbi of Prestigunquit's only other Jewish house of worship. Aaron hadn't really liked him at all, but he somehow managed effectively and eloquently to deliver a eulogy in the classical style Aaron had always admired so much. The cantors of his and our *shul* offered up a long, mournful setting of the Twenty-Third Psalm set as a duet. Aaron's Uncle Stanley, a self-trained and self-styled "cantor of

MARTIN S. COHEN

the people," sang the memorial prayer with unexpected talent. Who knew he could sing at all? I remember thinking that it was too bad Aaron wasn't present to revise his opinion of his uncle's musical ability.

After the funeral, came the *shiva*. More like a week-long Roman circus than a traditional week of Jewish bereavement, the *shiva* was extraordinary even by Long Island standards. By the end of the week, there may well have been over twelve hundred people in the house and I am certain there were more than a thousand. I had enough cake in our (and our neighbors') freezers to open a bakery and enough cold cuts to open a delicatessen. If the house wasn't a total shambles, it was because we put in at least an hour every evening of the *shiva* week tidying up and trying to make the house look presentable for the next day's hordes.

By the last days of *shiva*, I had had enough. Enough of crying. Enough of being condoled with. Enough of being spoken kindly to. Enough of everything. The week had been deeply emotional in its own way, though, and I recognized the usefulness of that kind of intense catharsis for someone trying to deal with the sudden, brutal death of a loved one—but I also knew that I would explode if one single person brought me one single cup more of tepid tea and told me that he or she wanted to be there for me. For their part, the directors of the synagogue had politely informed me that I was not even to think of vacating the manse until I was ready, as they put it, "to move on." They hadn't even begun the search process for a new rabbi, they observed oh-so delicately, and the whole procedure could conceivably take an entire year. They had put it semi-kindly, but I hadn't needed to listen too closely to get the message all too clearly: I had less than a year to get out of my home and on with my life.

My parents had been almost completely useless during the *shiva*, sitting like lumps of solidified misery on the living room couch as they accepted the condolences of scores of people who took them for Aaron's parents. My in-laws, on the other hand, were anything but inert. Perhaps because their grief was so much the harder to bear, they threw themselves into the rhythm of the *shiva* with something approaching gusto, staying seated on their mourning stools as little as possible and insisting on looking after the baby almost to the exclusion of any of our neighbors or friends. Almost as though they could keep their only child from being dead by refusing to accept any words of consolation on his passing, they scurried around the house endlessly, straightening up the kitchen, keeping a careful inventory of supplies, making sure the coffee urns were all relatively full and fresh and, above all else, looking after Levi.

The children were in their own world of disconnectedness. Too stunned to express—or even really to acknowledge—their grief, they perceived themselves as bored rather than dazed and spent most of the week hiding in their rooms playing Nintendo. This, I told myself, was probably all for the best. And, honestly speaking, how could it have been otherwise? Benjamin himself, our oldest, was all of nine during his father's *shiva* week. And the others, even younger, were that much less able than he to take in what had befallen them.

Eventually, the *shiva* week ended. In retrospect, I suppose I must still have been in shock. Indeed, as the delegation of rabbis from the Suffolk County Rabbinical Association appeared on the last morning of the *shiva* week to escort us on the traditional walk around the block that concludes the week of heavy bereavement, I could hardly believe that I was going to return twenty minutes later to a widow's house. Later that day, my parents finally agreed to go home. My in-laws, on the other hand, simply refused to leave and insisted that they be allowed to stay on just a little while longer "to help out with the children." More than aware of the fact that I might never get rid of the elder Rakmans if I didn't push them out the door before they really settled in, I *still* couldn't find the energy to insist.

Shiva ended on Wednesday morning, but I refused to take the children to school that same afternoon. But Benjamin, Rebecca and Nathan were all up by seven o'clock the next morning, fully dressed and sitting at the kitchen table waiting for breakfast. Seeing them all together, I realized that I had no choice. Screwing up my courage, therefore, I awakened my father-in-law and asked him to drive them to school. Strangely overwhelmed with the excitement of finding himself needed (and their decision not to go home immediately therefore at least slightly validated), he agreed almost before I had the words out of my mouth.

By ten past eight, the children and their grandfather were gone. My mother-in-law had yet to emerge from the guest bedroom. Levi was playing in his crib with a plastic horse that someone had brought over as a gift. The house was reasonably neat. I resolved to have the carpets cleaned before the weekend, but found even that much decision-making tiring and unexpectedly upsetting. I found the carpet cleaners' number, then stuck it on the refrigerator with a magnet for future reference rather than calling to see if they were open yet. I made a pot of coffee. I retrieved the newspaper from the front lawn. I put some bread in the toaster, then spent a ridiculous amount of time foraging in the pantry for some jam. For the first time since the funeral, I felt my face wet with tears. As I reached for a paper napkin to dry my eyes, though, I was visited neither by grief nor by self-pity, but by the sudden realization that I was alone in the world, that I was a single mother of four with no income and enough insurance money to keep things going for somewhere between a year and eighteen months. And then I heard the door to the guest room open and close. So much, I thought, for any private time to think things through.

"You're up." Esther was barely up herself, the after-effects of her sleeping pill both audible in her voice and visible on her face, but at least she was mostly dressed.

"I guess." I was hardly in the mood to face my mother-in-law, but I felt I had no choice but to respond somehow to what had clearly been more of a question than a simple observation.

"The children?"

"Gone to school. Max drove them."

"You woke him up?"

"I knocked on the door gently and he came right out. He must have been up."

"He doesn't sleep."

"No one sleeps."

"Only my Aaron," Esther groaned. "Only my little boy sleeps forever."

That was enough. I needed strength, not pity, if I was somehow going to get my life back on track—and endless references to Aaron sleeping forever in the earth were the very last thing I wanted to hear now that I was finally finding the courage to face the future. Wiping my eyes with vigorous efforts more appropriate for removing make-up than for drying tears, I waited until I calmed down a bit. And then, after a long while, I began the conversation I knew I was eventually going to have to have with my mother-in-law.

"I've been thinking about things," I began.

"So who hasn't?"

"And I've been thinking...."

"I can't stop thinking."

"I've been thinking about going back to..."

"To where?"

I fought down the impulse to tell my mother-in-law to shut up long enough to hear me out. "To school, Esther," I said calmly.

"To school?"

"You make it sound like I'm thinking of joining the circus. I liked nursing school when I started and I wouldn't have left if I hadn't gotten pregnant. And now I need a profession and I think maybe I'd like to be a nurse. That was Plan A, after all...."

"A nurse? Nurses make *bubkes*."

"I could specialize."

"There's such a thing?"

"Yes," I said, "there's such a thing." I sat down at the kitchen table.

"Doctors do better. A lot better."

"They do," I agreed. "But I don't have the science to apply to medical school and I'm not going back to take undergraduate science courses on the chance I might get into medical school after that."

"You're plenty smart enough."

"I think so too," I answered immediately, warming to my mother-in-law's unexpected confidence in my abilities. "But I don't have the time to pursue that kind of long-term plan. I'd need a year or two of undergraduate work. Then I'd have to apply to medical schools. And then, if I somehow did manage to get in, I'd need to spend four years in school. And then there would be years of training on top of that. The whole thing is just too impractical—it would be almost a decade before I would be earning a living—and nursing isn't just for people who can't get into medical school, you know. There's something that calls me to nursing, something about the whole concept of working as a nurse. I think I might like to do psychiatric nursing, to tell you the truth. Or else maybe Emergency Room work. Look, I did good work that first year. If I can get some nursing school down here to count it, I think I could probably be working in eighteen months. And then maybe I can continue my training while I'm already working."

"Eighteen months is a long time."

"Yes and no. I think I can stay here until at least next summer."

"They wouldn't dare throw you out."

"It's not like that. This is their house, not ours. The new rabbi will almost definitely want to live here. And they'll want him to live here too. Look, that's just how things are. But if the new guy starts next fall and we don't have to move until June or July, then I think Aaron's insurance money will last long enough for me to get out of school and start earning a living as a nurse. Look, we won't starve. And I think I still qualify to borrow the tuition money if it comes to that."

Esther Rakman looked directly into my eyes. "You're going to borrow money? Not as long as your father-in-law and I are alive, you're not. We had one son and he was our sole heir. Now your children are going to be our heirs and, as far as we're both concerned, you can have the money now if that's what you think best. What do we need? We own our home. We have the clothing we need. I need more jewelry? I wish I could get rid of what I have. All we want is for the children to grow up well and happy. Whatever comes, we'll be there for you as long we either of us is alive. And whatever we have left when we die will be for you and the children anyway. Look, darling, you're not alone in this. For as long as we breathe, we're in it with you and we'll do what you say you want. Whatever it is, we'll do it if we can afford it. And if we can't afford it, we'll just do it anyway. And if you decide that you really do want medical school, not nursing school —we'll just write a bigger check, that's all."

I was too amazed to speak. Truth be told, I had always found my mother-in-law irritating to the point almost of being grating. She was always pushing Aaron to negotiate harder, to demand more money from the *shul* than he was getting paid, to insist on them being more generous with us or giving us more vacation time or doing more in the house or the garden. She must have told him a million times not to let them bully him around. That was her favorite expression to use in this regard, in fact, but the irony was that it wasn't they who were bullying us, it was she who was bullying him. She was the one who was never satisfied with anything Aaron did or accomplished, the one who never gave him a break, who could never be unambiguously proud of any of his successes. And she wasn't above criticizing me either, including in the children's presence. I suppose I always imagined that she thought that Aaron could have done better, that she always wished I was prettier or smarter, or that my parents were richer, or that I was a better, more devoted wife to her perfect son. (I had a miscarriage after we were married for just eighteen months and she actually had the nerve to tell Aaron not to feel bad, that it wasn't *his* fault. And just whose fault did that imply it was? She didn't need to say!) But now that she was saying precisely what I had hoped she would *eventually* realize needed to be said I found myself overcome by emotion. "Thank you," I said softly, trying to keep my voice level.

"You're welcome," came the choked reply. And then the dam burst open and we both simply sat opposite each other at the kitchen table and cried until neither of us had any tears left.

SONS AND BROTHERS

My father's heart attack in the summer of 1966 had more far-reaching consequences for myself than it did for him. To be sure, he was chastened by the experience. He went on a diet and lost a full forty pounds. (His doctor has suggested sixty—after which loss he would still have been about twenty pounds more than when he first came to newly British Palestine in 1922—but forty was an amazing achievement that no one, and saintly Dr. Maisels least of all, wished to minimize. What man of seventy-four can fit into his wedding suit anyway?) To demonstrate his commitment to the project, he joined the YMCA on King David Street and actually went to exercise class from time to time. Even though my dad hadn't smoked more than a cigarette or two a week since he was in medical school, he now gave up even that sporadic pleasure and seemed relatively untroubled by the sacrifice. And after a lifetime of drinking Turkish coffee so thick you could stand a knife up in it, he switched to herb tea with nary a whimper. I was amazed. My mother was amazed too... times a million. In a dozen ways, my dad's first myocardial infarction brought him only good things. And that's in addition to it not killing him!

The story I want to tell begins a few weeks after my father's release from the then-almost-new Hadassah Hospital in Ein Kerem. He was feeling better, had begun the regimen of physical exercise he would eventually, if sporadically, continue at the Yimka (which is what the locals, Jews and Arabs alike, invariably call the YMCA), and seemed somehow to have escaped the depression that they say so often threatens the myocardially infarcted. My mother was out shopping, but my dad and I were drinking tea and coffee respectively in my parents' kitchen. (I had put my foot down about the herbal tea thing and a special stock of coffee was retained for me to drink when I was over.) I didn't work on Fridays in those days, which allowed me almost always to begin the weekend by dropping by my parents' beautiful home on Rashba Street at the edge of Rechavia, then as now Jerusalem's most elegant neighborhood. And so there we were, hanging out on a rainy morning in November, when my father, who just a moment earlier had seemed lost in thought, turned to me suddenly.

"David," he said, "I have to tell you something but we're not going to discuss it."

"Okay." What else was I going to say? I had no idea what we were talking about, but I was game to play along. So we wouldn't discuss it, so what?

"This is not the easiest thing for me to say."

I said nothing.

"This is a little complicated," he began again. "But it's also simple." My father's English was perfect, but when he became agitated I could hear a bit of Lodz behind some of his less secure vowels.

"Go on," I said encouragingly.

"When I was in the hospital, I had time to think about a lot of things. I had a heart attack. I could have another. I could have died. Probably I *will* eventually die." Probably! "And when that time comes, I imagine that you will end up going through my papers."

I said nothing as we veered into wholly unexpected territory. Before he mentioned his papers, I had thought he was going to tell me how much he regretted not being present when I gave the valedictory speech at Gymnasia Rechavia in 1948, thereby becoming the school's first valedictorian to deliver his speech not only in the Land of Israel, but in the State of Israel as well. He had a good reason, of course—he was living in the O.R. for days at a time in the summer of 1948, coming home almost never and dealing as best he could with an endless parade of wounded soldiers while retaining his personal certainty—even despite the massacre of almost eighty doctors and nurses just a month and a half earlier—that the Mount Scopus hospital campus would remain a viable part of the Israeli medical system. Does it sound pathetic that almost two decades later, that's *still* where I thought we were going? I suppose it must, but I quickly moved on, nodding thoughtfully and hoping he would take that as a sign to continue.

"And when you do," he finally said, "you'll find out that I was married before I met your mother. It lasted three years and we got a divorce. I moved to Haifa for a few years, then came back to Jerusalem. I should have told you years ago...."

As he fell silent, I was clearly supposed to say something. But what? I was thirty-six years old in 1966, a bit old to hear such a basic detail about my father's life for the first time. Clearly, I was better off knowing than not knowing, *even* at this late date. But I had no idea how he was hoping I'd respond. Perhaps, I thought, he just wanted me to ask the obvious questions so he could answer them without having to bring them up himself.

"Did you and your first wife have any children?" I asked.

My dad looked stricken. "You think I could have kept a child of mine hidden all these years? Or that I would have?"

I didn't know what I thought. "I think that sometimes people get divorced and move on," I said neutrally.

"We're done," Dad now said, the tone of finality in his voice unmistakable.

"What was her name?" I asked, I thought, entirely reasonably.

"Done."

"Does she live in Jerusalem?"

"Done."

"Did she ever remarry?"

"Done."

And with that he stood up, retreated rather dramatically into his and my mother's bedroom, slamming the door and not re-appearing by the time I had to leave. Clearly, we actually *were* done. Left on my own, I did the math. My dad was seventy-four in 1966. He married my mother in 1928, when he was thirty-six. So he must have gotten married in his twenties and was possibly even *still* in his twenties when the marriage ended. What did any of that have to do with me? People, I reminded myself, get divorced all the time.

Later that afternoon, I phoned Sarah-Dina and told her the news. She was unimpressed.

"So what?" she asked, successfully masking whatever emotions she was feeling. In any event, I knew all too well that she found my father irritating and imagined she found this newly revealed detail just one more reason to mistrust him.

"What so what?" I asked. "Out of the blue, my dad tells me he was married before he met my mother and that doesn't surprise you?"

"Darryl is studying in Nepal to becoming a Buddhist monk. Nothing surprises me."

I had to hand it to her that having a kid brother leave his law practice in London—his extremely lucrative law practice, I should say—to move to the foothills of the Himalayas so as to be able to devote himself to the pursuit of his own spiritual path probably trumps having a dad who was married one more time than I had previously thought.

"Aren't you curious if he had kids? If they did, I mean."

"Did they?" I could almost hear her ears perking up.

"He says not."

"You don't believe him?"

"I believe him."

"Why wouldn't you?"

And with that unanswered question hanging on the air, we ended our conversation. I had the idea of telling the boys— Sarah-Dina and I have three sons, one married, one engaged, one still in the army—but in the end decided not to. Why should I have? It was a private detail, one their grandfather was clearly uninterested in discussing. So I said nothing and the whole matter eventually became less important or interesting to me. So he was married before he met my mother. So what?

And now we must skip forward almost a full decade. Dad's second heart attack, which he rather dramatically had in synagogue on Yom Kippur during Yizkor, was worse than the first. Someone dialed 100. The ambulance got him to the hospital remarkably quickly. (There really is *no* traffic at all on Yom Kippur in Jerusalem.) Dad lingered for a few days, then succumbed. His last expressed thought, slurred but fully understandable, was that he regretting giving up coffee. And with that ridiculous thought still hanging on the air, he had his third and final heart attack and died. He was eighty-three years old.

The funeral came and went. We sat *shiva* on Rashba Street at my parents' house. The place was filled from dawn to dusk (and then some) with relatives and friends. My mother seemed calm, finding solace in making sure her guests were comfortable and guaranteeing to her satisfaction that the countless trays of food and cakes that arrived were either set out for guests to enjoy or else properly packaged discreetly to be sent home with one or another of her girlfriends. Eventually it was all over. My mother seemed ready to see what new direction her life would now take. I went back to work, leaving her house on that last day of *shiva* and proceeding directly to my office, which I found filled to overflowing with that day's patients plus a selection of those rescheduled from the week I was away. That first day back passed in a moment. Then I went home for eight seconds and was back the next morning to deal with the bedlam that is the daily lot of any successful urologist. The days melted into each other. I went to *shul* each evening to say Kaddish. (My first patient was almost always at 6:45 AM, so mornings were out. And besides, who needs that many Kaddishes? One or two a day seemed more than ample for the repose of any normal person's soul!)

This is how the world works. Time passes. The dead stay dead. The widow flounders around for a few months, then finds herself in…something. Or in a series of somethings—my mother joined a bridge club, then, to my slight surprise, a tennis club as well. And then she found volunteering and ended up serving as a volunteer English teacher in a rather rundown school in Kiryat Moshe, where she met Gadiel Caspi, her eventual second husband. But I'm getting way ahead of myself…and the real point here is that, except for Dad, we all moved on successfully to the next chapter of the book that is our lives. A year later, we (including by then Gadiel Caspi and his two daughters) gathered at my mother's home to mark my father's first *yahrtzeit*. It was a sunny day. The mood was upbeat. My oldest son read a chapter from the Psalms. I told some a funny story my father used to tell about his brief return to active service at age sixty-four during the Suez Crisis of 1955 to participate in a mission so top-secret that he himself had no idea what it was about. My oldest son read a poem by Bialik that my father particularly liked. There was a moment of silence and not an hour later we were all having lunch, including the Caspis.

So that was in the summer of 1975. Two full years after the Yom Kippur War, Israel hadn't fully returned to normal. People were still in a skittish, uncertain mood; things felt good and not good at the same time. (We did win the war, after all. But the price was very high, not at all something the nation was used to or wished to become used to.) And then, a few weeks after the second anniversary of the war passed, I was at work one evening working on patients' files when the phone rang and, because I was alone in the place after hours and assumed it was Sarah-Dina or one of the boys, I picked it up myself.

"Is this Dr. Sonnenschein?" The caller was speaking in fluent Israeli Hebrew, but his voice was unknown to me.

"This is he," I said, already regretting having picked up the phone.

"David Sonnenschein?"

"Who is this?"

A long silence. "My name is Paltiel Barr," the voice finally said. "And I believe myself to be your brother. Well, your half-brother at least."

He had my full attention, but I couldn't think of anything intelligent actually to say. "You believe yourself to be my half-brother," I repeated idiotically.

"Yes, I do."

"What makes you think that?" A plausible question, I thought. But one I already wasn't sure I wanted him actually to answer.

"It's a long story, one I'd like to tell you in person."

"I'm a busy guy," I said quickly, now more sure than ever that I was speaking with a crazy person. "I don't have that much leisure time."

"Perhaps I could come by right now?"

"Now?"

"Or in a half hour? I'm not far away."

"You're not far away?" I had to get rid of this guy, but I was too flummoxed to think of *how* exactly to end the conversation. So, as though I were *already* somehow in his thrall, I asked the obvious question instead. "Where are you?"

"I'm actually in Bayit V'gan, near Shaare Zedek. I could be in your office in twenty minutes. Or, could I..." I heard the hesitation in his voice now and began to wonder if he might possibly not be a crazy person after all. "If you want," he began again, "if you'd be willing, perhaps we could have dinner. If you're free."

I was free. I was heading home to any empty house. Sarah-Dina was in having dinner with two of her girlfriends in Baka somewhere and wasn't going to be home until at least ten or eleven. I had been planning to eat leftovers from Shabbat. I must have been crazy even to consider agreeing, but something in his voice called out to me—although it only struck me much later on that evening that it may well have felt that way because he sounded incredibly *like* me on the phone—and I heard myself agreeing to meet him at the Café Yinon in Katamon, just down the road from the then-brand-new Islamic Art Museum. I was, he said, to be his guest. At eight, I left my office on foot—my practice is on Ussishkin Street in Rechavia, not far from my mother's house—and was there in less than a quarter of an hour.

And there he was, waiting for me just inside the front door. I shook his hand. He looked normal enough, an Israeli man either my age or perhaps a bit older in khaki trousers and a short-sleeved white shirt. We were the same height. He had reserved a table, so we didn't have to wait. We ordered a bottle of iced vodka, then sat almost shyly in each other's company and waited for the bottle to come, which it eventually did. We both poured healthy doses into our glasses and then, as though some invisible curtain had just gone up on a production featuring him as the company and myself as the audience, he began to speak.

The short version is that his mother was my father's first wife. They divorced, Paltiel told me openly, because his mother was unfaithful and got caught in the act. Today, they would probably have been encouraged to see a counselor and try to find a way forward as a couple. But this was a different world, not just a different decade. The Jews of British Palestine in 1924 took marriage seriously. No husband would have had it in him just to look the other way after coming home unexpectedly at one in the afternoon and finding his wife *in flagrante delicto* with the greengrocer from around the corner on Alfasi Street. This, Paltiel assured, me was what had happened to my father's first marriage.

There was, however, more to the story...and Paltiel clearly knew this other part as well. My father, known to all (and surely to myself) as an essentially non-violent man, apparently turned on his heel and left the flat, never to return. He sent his brother, my Uncle Shimshon, to pack up his clothing, had his lawyer write to his wife with the bad news that she was about to become the former Mrs. Sonnenschein, and had his rabbi prepare the *get* that would end their marriage just as surely in heaven as my father's solicitor was going to get some mandatory magistrate to end it on earth. As far as Paltiel knew, they never met again...not even one single time. Which would explain why she did not feel particularly obliged to tell him when she found out that she was pregnant a month or two after the *de facto* end of their marriage, thus obviating the need to explain how she knew that the baby was my father's—which, Paltiel assured me, it most definitely was. For one thing, he said, the greengrocer was a very diminutive, dark-skinned Yemenite, whereas the fruit of my mother's adulterous fling, with whom I was apparently dining that evening at the Yinon, was as tall as me and had eyes as deep blue as my own.

Later, Paltiel explained, his mother went to nursing school, joined the army, and ended up making a career in the IDF, during the course of which she met Ephraim Barr who became her second husband and who duly adopted her son and raised him as his own.

Paltiel was obviously not told any of this as a child: his mother, understandably eager not to bring the greengrocer (or, apparently, my dad) into the story, had simply told him that she was unable to have children and that she and Paltiel's father had adopted him. A child of nine or ten when he first heard the story, Paltiel had been far too young to ask to see his adoption papers and simply accepted that he was adopted, which was at least half true, and that his parents had chosen to adopt because his mother was unable to bear children. The Barrs, conveniently for the story as told, did not have more children. Neither did my parents, choosing for reasons that even today remain unclear to me to close up shop after I was born and to be content, as they always said they were, with one perfect son. And so there we were seated across the table from each other at the Café Yinon, two only children *and,* at least in some peculiar sense, two brothers. Or half-brothers. Or something like that. Only children *and* siblings. Is that even possible? Apparently, it is!

And why, you are probably wondering, did Paltiel chose this particular day to find me? Well, that's the question, isn't it? And the answer is really where the interesting part of this complicated story really begins.

Eventually, Ephraim Barr died. Paltiel's mother at ninety-six was an ancient lady suffering from a dozen ailments and just enough dementia to keep her confused without being totally disconnected from the world. And *now,* her internal censor finally fully gone, she had finally told her son the full story of his birth, revealing his biological father's name as though she *hadn't* spent a lifetime diligently keeping that information from him. At first, he said, he thought she was just making it all up. But then he began to do the math—figuratively *and* literally—and he began to realize that she was telling the truth, that his biological father was not the faceless, nameless impregnator of the nameless and faceless young girl who had delivered her newborn up to some unspecified adoption agency for placement with a childless couple, that his mother *was* his birth mother, and that his birth father was none other than her first husband. Once possessed of all that information, he said, finding me was almost simple.

I listened carefully, then decided to move the conversation off in a new direction. "Where's your mother living these days?" I asked.

"She's still in the apartment I was raised in."

I was surprised. "Is that safe?"

"It's safe enough because she has a fulltime aide in the flat with her."

I was impressed. "She can afford that?"

Paltiel seemed uneasy. "My mother is a wealthy woman, David. My father—the man I've always thought of as my father, I mean —my father was a lawyer—I am too—but he was also an investor and he had a remarkable knack for buying just the right stocks at just the right time."

"And for selling at the right time too, I suppose."

Paltiel smiled. "He hardly ever sold anything until it was trading for twenty or thirty times what he had originally paid for it."

"So your mother has no financial worries in her old age."

He smiled. "None at all."

And now the time had come to get to the point. The main course lay half-eaten on the plates before us. The bottle of Finlandia was down to its final quarter. "So what does any of this have to do with me?"

Paltiel looked surprised and slightly taken aback. "You mean, aside from learning that you have a brother in the world? That you aren't an only child after all?"

I felt a weird surge of almost electric energy work its way down my spine. "Yes, aside from that," I said.

And now, both from the way his eyes narrowed and the way the color in his face became a shade more intense, I could tell that we had come to the crux of the matter. He wasn't drunk, I didn't think, but all that vodka had clearly loosened him up sufficiently to say what he had apparently wanted to say all along. "My mother is consumed with guilt," he said. "She loved my dad. She really did. And they had a great marriage. But now that he's gone from the scene, she's living more and more in the past. And she is sinking under the combined weight of some unhealthy mixture of remorse, guilt, and shame."

"Shame? What is she ashamed of?"

I had mentioned earlier in the evening that my father had died fifteen years earlier. Paltiel had reacted to that information emotionally, which at the time had seemed a bit exaggerated to me. But now, as the alcohol took over and Paltiel, his inhibitions shed, answered my question openly and clearly, I began to understand. "What she's ashamed of? Of what she did with the greengrocer. Of what she did to her marriage. Of how she denied your dad the knowledge that he had a son. Of how she deprived us both of the pleasure of growing up with a brother...if not by our sides then at least in our lives. Of never having had the courage to tell the truth. Of being responsible for the burden of loneliness that I bore as a boy and still bear, even now." I was amazed —but also not amazed—to see tears on his cheeks. "Of having committed a truly terrible sin, or possibly even the worst...."

I leaned in over my dinner plate. "The worst?"

"She betrayed your father's trust—*our* father's trust—and denied him his son. And now he's dead and gone, and that wrong can't be made right."

"She denied you a father too."

"I had a father."

"And my dad had a son."

"He had two sons, David."

What could I say to that? "She knows my dad is dead?"

"Yes and no. I told her. After she told me the story—this was just weeks ago—after she *finally* told me the whole story, I investigated a bit and found out that your dad had died in 1975. There hardly seemed any reason *not* to tell her."

"And she wants to make this right?"

"To say the very least."

"You understand that I can't bring my father back to life, right? I'm not *that* good a doctor."

"I want you go see her," Paltiel replied, finally getting to the point. "I want her to see that you're okay, that you grew up to be a fine man, that your dad didn't have me...but he had you. I could have been your older brother. Maybe it's too late for that now. Probably the best we could hope for now is to become friends. But who knows if even that's possible...we're strangers, after all, just strangers who happen to share half our DNA. If she sees that your dad ended up with a son whom he loved, she'll feel better. Maybe even at peace. And she needs to be at peace, David. She's dying, I think. Or maybe not dying exactly...but she's clearly coming to the end of her road. She's confused most of the time. She has to be dialyzed three times a week, but can't seem to understand why. She's a breast cancer survivor too, but who knows when that could return and what it could do to her? And she's suffering from congestive heart failure. Is that enough? She needs to be at peace. She did a terrible thing. But she needs someone to forgive her...and the only man left standing is yourself."

I felt queasy, as though I had eaten something bad that was only now beginning to churn and roil around in my gut. I reached for the water glass, but somehow managed to knock it over instead. I righted it, ignored the puddle on the floor. I tossed down the end of my drink, then thought I might vomit. But then I suddenly calmed down and felt better. For the fleetest of moments, I thought I saw my dad at the door of the restaurant. But when I looked again, the doorway was empty.

"I'll go see her," I said.

And then he started really to cry and so did I. The waiter must have thought we were both crazy. The room was filled with other diners, but no one seemed to notice or care that two fully grown men were sitting across from each other in a fully public place and crying. It was, to say the very least, a strange moment.

And then it was all over. We dried our faces. We ordered baklava and Turkish coffee. I suggested that we should split the bill, but he wouldn't hear of it and, because he had after all invited me to dinner, I backed down. As a big brother might, he walked me home, then waited on the sidewalk in front of our home until I disappeared through the front door. When I got inside and looked down from our living room window at the sidewalk below, he was gone.

As he promised he would, Paltiel phoned me the following week and gave me his mother's address. I suggested a time I could stop by and he said he'd confirm within the hour, which he did. And so, just a few days after that, I drove to Mevaseret Zion to meet my father's first wife.

I walked up the path, rang the bell, was admitted by Irit, Paltiel's mother's aide, who shook my hand and thanked me for coming. She knew why I had come, she said. Irit ushered me into the living room. And there she was, my father's first wife and the mother of my half-brother, stretched out on a *chaise longue* with a checkered afghan over her lap. She was frail-looking and pale, but her snow-white hair was neatly pulled back into a ponytail and she was dressed in a sky blue satin dressing gown. Irit stayed in the room briefly, then left us alone.

For a few long minutes, she seemed unaware of my presence even though she was looking directly at me. The obvious thing would have been to introduce myself, but I found myself uncertain how to begin or what to say. And so, sitting down on the couch, I said nothing for a few long minutes. And then, by that point almost unexpectedly, she spoke.

"Daniel?" she asked.

A good start, except that Daniel was my father's name, not mine. I said nothing.

"I didn't do right by you, Danny," she continued. "I denied you what was rightfully yours. You deserved to raise your son...or at least to know that he existed. Can you ever forgive me?"

Now I really didn't know what to do. Clearly, she was watching the right show on the wrong channel and, apparently having forgotten to remember that my father was dead, she seemed to imagine I was he, that I had come to allow her to apologize for the horrific error of judgment that had cost a son his father and a father his son. I reminded myself that she had last seen my father sixty-five years ago when my dad had been thirty-two years old, about twenty years younger than I was as this whole strange scene unfolded around me. So maybe she was just imagining that my dad had aged into looking like me.

I had to say something. But what? It was too late to ask forgiveness because the only person she seemed to want to ask forgiveness *of* was gone from the world. Would it be helpful to point that out? Or pointless? Did honest trump cruel? I wasn't sure.

So far, I hadn't said a single word. For an odd moment, I thought I caught a whiff of Arturo-Neff No. 6, my father's signature cologne. For a strange few seconds, I felt myself floating off and had to make an actual effort to draw myself back into the moment. In the meantime, though, her question was still hanging on the air. And then, suddenly, I knew how to respond.

"Yes," I heard myself saying quietly in my father's name if not quite in his voice, "I can."

GUILTY AND
NOT GUILTY

The last day in November was full-bore New York autumn: leaden skies, damp air when it wasn't raining (which was never), cold wind, and sunset encroaching more on the afternoon with each successive day. It was only ten to four in the afternoon, but the electric lights in the office were blazing bright. I was with a client, but we had finished up most of our business and were just chatting about a few final details when Dara came into the office, knocking with one hand while opening the door with the other.

"I'm with a client," I observed unnecessarily since she herself had brought the client into my office fifty minutes earlier.

"There's a call you need to take."

"It can wait until we're done. You know I never interrupt billable hours with other people's business." I must have said that same sentence to Dara a thousand time, but the point really was just to assure the client that he or she wasn't going to end up paying for my time on the phone with someone else.

Dara caught my eye. "You should take this call, Eric."

A chill raced down my spine. "Is it my wife?"

Dara smiled slightly. "Nothing like that," she said. "It's William Witherspoon."

"The Deputy Attorney General of the United States?" I noticed my client's eyes widening slightly.

"Yes, *that* William Witherspoon."

"Did he say what he wants?"

"To speak to you."

"Tell him I'll call him back..." I glanced at my watch. "...as soon as I'm free. Within the hour. Be polite."

Dara narrowed her eyes. "Yessir," she said, her tone matching her withering gaze. "Polite. I'll try to remember."

I wrapped things up with my client—we were really almost done anyway—and picked up the receiver to phone the Deputy Attorney General of the United States, formerly my roommate in law school. I dialed his cell. He picked up immediately.

Bill and I were together in the dorm for three years and were the best men at each other's weddings. When we were both still starting out, we spoke all the time to compare notes or to seek each other's professional counsel. As the years passed, though, we spoke less and less frequently, eventually settling into the easy pattern of phoning each other on our birthdays. On the November evening in question, in fact, we hadn't spoken since I had called him the previous February to wish him a good year and to ask after his family.

"Is everything okay?" My birthday is in December, so he was calling almost a month early.

"Everything's fine," he said quickly. "This is business."

"Business?"

"I need to ask you to serve your country." He sounded serious.

Even though I knew full well he would never ask for a favor he didn't truly need, I still responded warily. "To serve my country how?"

"To take on a new client."

"I'm not really looking for new...."

He cut me off instantly. "This is something different," he said. "The client in question is an old man. A very old man!"

I was intrigued, but still wary. "How old exactly?"

"Ninety-six. Exactly."

"What's he been charged with?"

"First-degree murder. The kind you execute successfully by successfully executing someone."

"And taking him on as a client would be serving my country in what specific way?"

"Well," he said, "that's a bit of a complicated story."

"I'm listening."

"Are you free for dinner later? I'm in New York."

"You're not at work?"

"I'm always at work. Come in for dinner. My treat."

I told him I could be in the city by nine and, remembering our shared predilection for Indian food, suggested a place on East Twenty-Eighth Street not too far from his hotel. He agreed, said he'd have his "guys" check it out and that, unless I heard from him first, he'd see me there at nine.

I was a few minutes late, but I knew that Bill was in place even before seeing him at a back table because of the two giant men with wires in their ears and bulges beneath their left shoulders sitting at a table near the front of the restaurant nursing mango lassis and trying wholly unsuccessfully to blend in. Bill, on the other hand, in a pale blue shirt and no necktie, really did look like a regular person having dinner out in the kind of Murray Hill eatery that mostly attracts people who don't travel with their own security.

For a few minutes, we had a normal conversation, quickly racing through the regular topics: our wives, our children, our health, and, briefly, the Rangers. (We met at Yale but were both originally from Queens, hence our interest in local hockey.) And then we got down to business.

"The man's name is Judah Augenwehtig," he said abruptly.

"Do I know him?"

"I doubt it. He came to this country in 1949 and settled in Eureka, Montana."

"I've been to Montana a few times," I said. "But I don't recall running into him."

"It's a big state. And he's hardly ever left since settling in about seventy years ago. Have you even *heard* of Eureka?"

"No, I don't think so."

"There's no reason you would have. It's a town of maybe a thousand souls a few miles south of the Canadian border. Near Kalispell. Due west from Glacier National Park. An out of the way place, to say the least."

"And that's where this Augenwehtig chose to settle? How did he support himself?"

"He worked for a local butcher."

"He had a family?"

"A wife. But she was killed in a hit-and-run after just three years in Eureka and he never remarried. No children."

"I take it he was Jewish. Is there any sort of Jewish community there?"

"Yes and no."

"Yes he was and no there isn't?"

"Correct. Or maybe it would be more right to say that there *is* a Jewish community in Eureka and he's its sole member. At least until we deport him, that is."

"We're going to deport him? I thought you said he's been indicted of first-degree murder."

"He's been indicted, all right. But not by ourselves. By a court in Germany, in the city of Frankfurt an der Oder. Not the Frankfurt with the huge airport. The other one."

"There are two Frankfurts?"

"Three, if you count the capital of Kentucky. That one is spelled slightly differently, however."

And then, having dispensed with the preliminaries, Bill told me the story in detail. Angela Merkel's party formed the current government in Germany, but all the opposition parties together hold more seats than her own coalition does. That makes it necessary for Mrs. Merkel to do what it takes to keep those opposition parties from bringing down the government, among which parties the far-right Alternative für Deutschland is by far the most aggressive in terms of its demands. That much I knew, more or less, from reading the newspaper. And now we got down to the real point of our meeting and I began to hear Judah Augenwehtig's story in detail.

"He was," Bill said, "born in this lesser Frankfurt. Today it's a border city right across the river from the Polish town of Slubice, but up until the end of the war they were one single German city. As a result, the troubles for the Jews began even before the war broke out. At first, it was all about deporting Polish-born Jews to Poland. But then the synagogue was destroyed on Kristallnacht and the distinction between Jews based on where they were born was made irrelevant. By the time the real deportations began, however—the ones to the camps—the Augenwehtigs—Judah, his parents, his maternal grandmother, and his three sisters—were in hiding, taken in by a dairy farmer and his wife on the outskirts of the town, good people motivated solely by their Christian faith. And hidden in the loft of those good people's barn they would have remained, except that the farmer's son-in-law, a confirmed Nazi, learned of their presence and betrayed them to the authorities. Kurt and Luise Hermann were executed on the spot. And once they had their guns out, they shot Augenwehtig's parents and his grandmother as well. The children, however, they shipped off to Theresienstadt where they were together until the sisters were sent to Auschwitz and never heard from again. Judah, the Nazis put to work building roads around the camp for a while, but he too was eventually sent to Auschwitz. What exactly happened next I'm not sure, but Augenwehtig ended up as the sole survivor of his entire family, including something like forty aunts, uncles, and cousins."

And now the story got even more interesting. "After liberation," Bill went on, "he was interned in a DP camp in Bavaria on the Czech border. He applied for permission to emigrate to Palestine and was turned down by the Brits, so he applied for a U.S. visa and we agreed to take him. We booked him passage on a ship leaving from Hamburg too. Things moved quickly in those days. What choice was there? There were scores of thousands of refugees to deal with, almost all destitute and stateless, and almost all eager to start new lives anywhere but in Germany. I doubt he garnered too much attention. He applied. He was granted asylum. We booked his berth on the boat. He had all of ten days to kill before heading north to Hamburg. But young Augenwehtig—he was *still* only twenty-three in 1946—young Augenwehtig wasn't quite as done with Germany as it was with him. And so, in the course of those few days he had left on German soil, he returned to his hometown to find out if his family's betrayer had survived the war."

The rest, Bill, said, I could probably imagine easily. He located Jürgen Nieland easily enough—after being discharged, Nieland had simply collected his wife from his own parents' home in Leipzig where she had been living and took her back to what had originally been her own parents' farm and was now their own property. And that made things almost remarkably simple for Judah, who simply walked on foot from his hotel in the center of town to the farm on its outskirts and, secure that he wouldn't be recognized after all he had been through, introduced himself as a reporter for one of the big German dailies. The son-in-law, fully unrepentant and only too eager vocally to lament the decision to capitulate after the Führer's suicide, was just thrilled to meet someone who wanted to listen to his rant. And so they were alone, just the two of them in the man's front parlor, when Judah took a knife from his pocket, opened the blade, and, without fanfare, warning, or explanation, slit the man's throat.

I was slightly amazed, slightly aghast. "And then what?"

"And then nothing. He walked back to his hotel, retrieved his suitcase, took the train to Hamburg, got on the boat, and came here."

"And no one ever knew?"

"Nieland was making a lot of the locals uncomfortable with his fervent post-war Nazism. No one could say for sure who had killed him and, as far as we can tell, no one cared. It wasn't a big news item—we found a few articles in the local press and one single one in a national paper. The police, most of whom were probably thrilled Nieland was dead, opened a half-hearted investigation. They asked around. The murder weapon was lying on the floor next to Nieland's body, but it had been wiped clean and bore no identifiable markings. They had no suspects, therefore, *and* no meaningful leads. The case was never formally closed, but neither was it pursued: the last thing anyone in the Soviet Zone of Occupation wanted was an un-denazified Nazi running around stirring up trouble. And that, more or less, would have been that."

"So how *do* we know all of this?"

"Well, that's the funny thing. Augenwehtig lived briefly in Newark, which is where he met his wife. They got married quickly —this was 1947, when they were both twenty-four—and went off to Montana, which he seems to have concluded was the state in which he was the absolute least likely *ever* to meet anyone who knew him from Europe. Why specifically Eureka, I'm not sure. The wife was killed a few years later by a drunk driver. But things otherwise worked out as he must have hoped they would and he was never taken by the locals as anything other than a refugee determined to earn his keep and fit in. And no one who had known him in Europe *ever* showed up to renew their acquaintance."

I felt completely drawn into the story. "So what actually happened? *You* seem to know all about it."

"Well, that's just the thing. The man is ninety-six years old. About seven months ago, he was diagnosed with something called Acute Myeloid Leukemia. His doctors told him it was serious, that he wasn't going to survive for long. I guess he had been waiting all these years to get it all off his chest, so he responded to the doc's pronouncement by—this is so twenty-first century —he responded by getting the kid next door to help him make a video in which he told his story, including the part about slitting Jürgen Nieland's throat, and then to post the damn thing to youtube. Which the kid did."

"It's impressive he even knew what youtube is."

"Agreed. But he was a savvy guy. Very bright, lots of time in Eureka to read, to plan things out, to practice the flute...."

"The flute?"

"He was apparently almost virtuoso-level. He certainly had enough time to practice! But the flute isn't the point. The point is that the video went viral. And not only in this country, but in Germany as well. And that brings me to his indictment. Mrs. Merkel was pressured by the righties to seek his extradition— and they had a leg to stand on: the man had basically confessed to what we in this country would call first-degree murder, fully premeditated and as intentional as murder comes, and specifically *not* in wartime or even close to it since this all took place in August of 1946, a full fourteen months after V-E Day."

I was stunned. We take a dim view of premeditated murder in this country as well, but I couldn't recall any instances of people in their upper nineties being indicted more than seventy years after the fact. Mind you, we too have no statute of limitations for murder. So how could we insist that too much time had passed for Augenwehtig to go to trial?

"And we've agreed?"

"What else could we do? We've certainly encouraged the Germans to indict, try, and convict Nazi war criminals in *their* nineties, you know. Oskar Gröning, the so-called accountant of Auschwitz, was ninety-three when he was convicted of war crimes in 2015. Reinhold Hanning was ninety-four. There have been others too. I realize the parallel isn't precise, but it's really close enough."

"And the AG has signed onto the idea of deporting an American citizen to face a trial for a crime committed more than seventy years ago?"

"He has. And that brings me to you. We'll arrange for a German lawyer to represent him in court. But we need someone to prepare the case here before he's sent to Germany, someone sympathetic who will work every conceivable angle—both in public and in private—to find grounds for acquittal. It's not going to be easy with that youtube clip out there for all to see. But we are committed to doing our best. Look, if it had been my family that had been completed annihilated and I had a chance to take out the person responsible, I'm not sure I wouldn't have done the same."

I couldn't quite think of how to respond to that last part, but one detail remained unresolved. "I thought you said he did this because the doctors told him he was dying of...what did you say? Leukemia?"

"Acute Myeloid Leukemia."

"So how come he's still alive."

"Because he hasn't died yet. How should I know?"

And with that, the intense part of our evening was over. The crispy pakoras and samosas were already on the table as the waiter approached with our bowls of mulligatawny soup. Clearly, it was time to eat our meal and go back to talking about our children. Which we did. For a good hour. And then it was wrap-up time.

"So you'll do it? You'll take this on? It's not much, when you get down to it: you'll have to fly to Sioux Falls...."

"In Iowa?"

"You're thinking of Sioux City. Sioux Falls is in South Dakota."

"South Dakota? I thought you said he never leaves Montana."

"When he's in federal custody he does."

"He's in prison? Whatever for? He's hardly a flight risk."

"Says you. He responded to the news of his imminent deportation by attempting to slip into Canada. Eureka is only eight miles and change from the border, but his passport was flagged and our border guys detained him. Yes, we are *that* good. And at that point, we really had no choice."

"And there wasn't any place in Montana he could be held?"

"There aren't any federal detention facilities at all in Montana or Idaho, so the Federal Prison Camp in Yankton, South Dakota, is where he ended up until we can ship him out and the Germans can deal with him. It's only about eighty miles from the Sioux Falls airport. I'm sure it's a fascinating drive."

"You know how far Yankton is from Sioux Falls?"

Bill smiled. "I had to look it up. Google really does know everything."

"Does it know if I'm going to take this on?"

A broader smile. "Yes, Eric," he said, "it does."

I drove home, told Cathy all about my evening, then slept on it. The next morning, I got my partners to take on whatever cases couldn't wait ten days to be dealt with. (I knew them all well enough to know they'd be thrilled to spin this as an example of our firm's prominence, how delighted they would be to let the world know that even the DOJ, staffed by its own million and a half lawyers, turns to us for help when special expertise or discretion is called for.) I myself did what needed doing and was on an American Airlines flight with a single stopover in Chicago two days later. I landed in Sioux Falls, picked up my rental, found the nearest Starbucks with a drive-thru window, and was on my way south on Interstate 29 within an hour and a half of landing.

Yankton was easy enough to find and the Federal Prison Camp was right where Waze said it would be: on Douglas Avenue just east of the local Domino's Pizza. There was plenty of parking.

The place looked welcoming enough: a large brick building with an attractive arch over its front entrance, the place looked more like a church or an old-style high school than a prison housing five hundred men. There was no perimeter fencing. Nor were there any bars on the windows or guard towers. But that I knew to expect, of course, since escaping from a Federal Prison Camp would guarantee incarceration upon recapture at a dramatically less pleasant place. And so, recapture being more or less inevitable, no one *ever* escaped. Nor, I was sure, did anyone want to.

A large sign noted that visiting days at FPC Yankton were on Fridays, Saturdays, Sundays, and federal holidays, but that fortunately did not apply to lawyers. And even those wheels had been greased by the DOJ: sidestepping the usual procedures, I had been signed on—apparently overnight—as Judah Augenwehtig's attorney and granted full access to my client with no restrictions at all. So there really wasn't much red tape to wade through and, within an hour of strolling through the front gate, I was seated in an interview room awaiting my client's arrival.

For a long moment, I tried to run quickly through everything I knew about the case. There wasn't much, just really what Bill Witherspoon had told me and some background material I had had someone in my office ferret out about Frankfurt an der Oder and Eureka, Montana. (About Theresienstadt and Auschwitz, I already knew more than enough.) That same assistant, a lanky paralegal named Barry, had managed somehow to locate the three articles that appeared in the local press in the days following the discovery of Jürgen Nieland's murder and to have them translated into English, plus a longer article, which he also had translated, that had appeared about three months later in the

Süddeutsche Zeitung. So I had those documents as well, plus—of course—a copy of the German-American Extradition Treaty submitted by President Carter to the Senate in June 1978 and in effect since August 29 of the following year, a twenty-one page document in thick legalese that I had by now not merely perused but read through carefully several times. For good measure, I had a copy of Marion Kaplan's *Between Dignity and Despair: Jewish Life in Nazi Germany* in my briefcase as well. Now all this party needed to get started, I remember thinking, was the guest of honor.

And then, suddenly, there he was! I'm not sure what exactly I was expecting him to look like but I suppose I was taken off-guard, first, by his height: the man must have been six-foot-three. At least. Maybe more. And as tall as he was, that's also how thin he was. He was wearing the standard prison outfit of sneakers, green khaki pants, and a white t-shirt. He looked —and, yes, I realize how odd this is to say—he looked, well, healthy. And not at all on edge or ill at ease, which is what I've come to expect when I visit clients in prison. He certainly did not look not terminally ill, which is what Bill Witherspoon had told me unequivocally was how things were. Just to the contrary, in fact, was the case: he exuded an air of calm wellbeing that suggested that the Federal Prison Camp at Yankton, South Dakota, was *exactly* where he wished to be. I am well aware that not every seriously ill individual looks all that under the weather. (Not at first, at least.) But I have to say that I was surprised. And that was before either of us had said a word!

I introduced myself. He extended his hand to me and said his own name aloud as we shook hands. We got through the preliminaries quickly, then got down to business.

"So where do I stand?" he asked.

"The truth is that you are standing on relatively uncharted territory." I never lie to clients and saw no reason to start now.

"Do you think the Germans will decide that they've made their point, that now that they've secured an indictment they can just let it go with reference to me being so ancient?" He spoke an only slightly accented English, but his voice was robust and he seemed to have every single one of his marbles. This was not the doddering senescent with whom I had feared having to deal, but a strong-willed, articulate oldster who was asking his lawyer the same questions anyone in his shoes would want answered forthrightly and honestly.

To say the truth, I felt relieved and also slightly unnerved as I realized that the chances of him attempting to defend himself vigorously at trial were excellent. I assumed he could still speak German well. I was certain he remembered every single detail relating to the crime, its backstory, and its aftermath. It suddenly dawned on me that the whole youtube thing wasn't a semi-amusing instance of an old guy not understanding the power of social media to make a video clip go viral, but a calculated effort to goad the Germans into seeking his extradition. I'm not sure exactly how I knew, but it was suddenly crystal clear to me that he *wanted* his day in court. He was approaching his centenary, but not only was he *not* hoping to avoid extradition, he was counting on it and hoping then to use his advanced age to draw the attention of the world to his trial. And I also somehow knew that his aborted flight into Canada was hardly him attempting to flee our jurisdiction, but just a preliminary P.R. stunt undertaken to get some initial press before the big show could finally get underway.

All this I somehow knew just from watching his eyes and as I answered his questions.

"You could easily be found guilty," I felt obligated to say clearly. "To speak honestly, it's not going to be hard for the prosecution to make its case. You have the right to plead not guilty, of course, but they have your videotaped description of the crime featuring you front and center. And it's hard to imagine a more premeditated murder either—you traveled all the way to Frankfurt an der Oder to encounter the man you killed, and you had a crystal-clear motive."

He fell silent for a moment, then moved us off in a different direction. "And what punishment do the Germans mete out these days to murderers?"

This part of my homework I had undertaken to do myself. "There are two levels of murder in German law," I explained. "*Totschlag*—intentional killing—is regular, intentional murder and gets the murderer from five to fifteen years in prison." He smiled as we both calculated quickly how old he would be in fifteen years. "And then there's *Mord*—murder in its realest sense —for which the penalty could be life imprisonment." Another smile. "But they usually let such people out after seventeen or eighteen years."

"And what are my chances of being convicted of this more severe crime?"

"I don't think they'll go there. The German Criminal Code makes it clear that that the *Mord* charge is only brought when the murderer acts out of murderous intent—that is, killing for its own sake—or as part of some depraved sexual encounter, or out of greed, or insidiously or cruelly, or in a way that risks danger to the public, or in order to cover up a different crime. None of those really applies to you."

"I'm sure they'll think of something. I don't want them to get off easy by letting me get off easy, you know."

I knew. As things fell into place, I could suddenly see the larger picture. As Augenwehtig approached the end of his own life, he wanted to bring his parents' murderer out of the shadows in which he had moldered for decades and into the light where the whole world could see him for what he was...and know what horrific wrong he had perpetrated against Augenwehtig's family. And the only real way to do that—and, I had to admit, seizing this in advance was a stroke of brilliance—the only *real* way for Augenwehtig to do that was to force the Germans to arrest him for Jürgen Nieland's murder and put him on trial. Given his advanced age—and given the way his trial would appear to at least a certain class of German as some sort of payback for the trials of Oskar Gröning and the other ancient Nazis still being asked in *their* nineties to take responsibility for their crimes —he could be assured not merely of Germany-wide but world-wide coverage. And he truly had nothing to lose. If he was found not guilty, the scandal of his acquittal—the acquittal of a confessed murderer possessed of motive, opportunity, and the dictionary definition of *mens rea*—would guarantee that the case would be reviewed and discussed, at least by law students, for the rest of time.

And even if he was convicted, then what exactly were they going to do to him? If he lived long enough to face actual incarceration after exhausting the complex German appeals process, he could conceivably have gone to prison in Germany. But far more likely was that we would formally request that he be permitted to serve out his time in the United States, in which case he would likely end up back in a place like Yankton. Or perhaps even in Yankton itself. Would that be so bad? Most assisted living facilities, particularly the kind that cater to centenarians, cost a fortune. But life-long housing at a Federal Prison Camp is 100% free! He had no wife and no children. So why not wrap things up with five hundred or so new friends, almost all of whom surely have good stories to tell? It's true that we usually send convicted murderers to far more secure facilities than FCP Yankton, but given Augenwehtig's age and the details surrounding his murder of Jürgen Nieland—and particularly the fact that the latter was responsible personally not solely for the murder of Augenwehtig's parents, grandmother, and sisters, but *also* of his own wife's parents—given all that, it seemed highly unlikely that Judah Augenwehtig would end up at the Supermax in Colorado.

We finished our conversation quickly. I promised to stick with him, to get my partners to agree that I attend his trial in Germany, to make sure he would continue to have the full support of the Department of Justice and its resources throughout the coming ordeal. I promised to vet his German representation to guarantee it was top-notch. And I promised to stand by his side as he sought personally to serve as a living memorial to his parents, to his grandmother, to his sisters, and to the heroic German couple who risked everything—and paid the ultimate price—for harboring a family of innocents for whom they bore no legal responsibility. As I thought things through, Augenwehtig's plan made more and more sense to me. The Hermanns were shot in cold blood as punishment for having been decent, kind, and brave. No one ever has or ever will erect a monument to their memory. But not every monument is made of granite. There's also the kind fashioned of gesture and stance, of principled behavior, and of the willingness to do what it takes personally to memorialize an act of selflessness and charity that deserves to be remembered. And it was that specifically willingness that Judah Augenwehtig chose at age ninety-six to embody.

In the end, nothing came of it. He apparently looked way healthier than he really was. Three months after our time together at FPC Yankton, I was attending his graveside funeral at the Home of Peace Cemetery in Helena. There were, all together, fifteen people in attendance: myself, the rabbi conducting the service, and thirteen Eurekans who had taken the time to travel almost three hundred miles to Helena out of respect for their neighbor of almost seventy years. There were no representatives of the German government.

I myself spoke the eulogy, telling the story in the specific way I imagined the deceased had been hoping to live long enough to tell it in a German courtroom. And then we filled in the grave, the rabbi intoned the Memorial Prayer, the ghosts in attendance—and they were legion—vanished in the morning heat, and Judah Augenwehtig was finally able to rest in peace.

BOOKS BY THIS AUTHOR

The Truth About Marvin Kalish

The Shiur Qomah: Liturgy And Theurgy In Pre-Kabbalistic Jewish Mysticism

The Shiur Qomah: Texts And Recensions

Travels On The Private Zodiac

Light From Dead Stars

In Pursuit Of Wholeness

Travels On The Road Not Taken

The Sword Of Goliath

ספר העיקרים לבני זמנינו

Heads You Lose

Our Haven And Our Strength: The Book Of Psalms

Siddur Tzur Yisrael For Weekday Worship

Siddur Tzur Yisrael For Shabbat And Festivals

Siddur Zot Nechemati For The House Of Mourning

Riding The River Of Peace: A Book Of Mitzvot For Children

The Boy On The Door On The Ox

La Méguila D' Esther (With Rivon Krygier And Gérard Garouste)